# EXTRAVAGANT GESTURES

# *Extravagant* GESTURES

## CAROLE BAYER SAGER

A BELVEDERE BOOK
ARBOR HOUSE / NEW YORK

*Design by Richard Oriolo*

Manufactured in the United States of America
10 9 8 7 6 5 4 3 2 1

Library of Congress Cataloging in Publication Data

Sager, Carole Bayer.
Extravagant gestures.

"A Belvedere book."
I. Title.
PS3569.A323E95     1985     813'.54     85–7413
ISBN 0–87795–765–7

The characters in this novel are fictional. Their encounters, including
encounters with people whose names are known to you, are entirely
the creation of the author.

*For Burt,*
*for making my life so much more*

*I am very grateful
to the following people for
their support and encouragement throughout
various stages of the writing of this book,
John Dodds, Lynn Nesbit, Bob Gottlieb,
Rosalie Swedlin, Esther Margolis,
Robert Lorenz, and Lou Tracey.*

# EXTRAVAGANT GESTURES

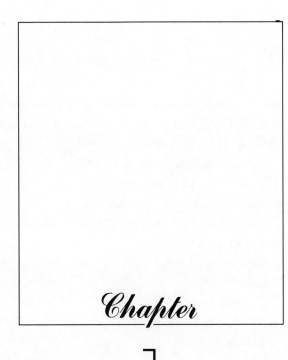

# Chapter

1

*P*hil Donahue was thrusting his phallic-shaped microphone into the face of the fiftyish-year-old polyester-sized woman, anxious to ask her question from the last row in the almost all-woman audience.

"Yes. You have a question. Speak up!" said Phil.

The little lady rose from her seat to the occasion. "I want to ask Ms. Fielding why I find myself acting more and more like my mother every day when I dislike her behavior so much?"

A few sighs of recognition could be heard in the audience. As the camera closed in on Katie Fielding's face, she looked as confident as the kid who knows she's one "i" away from winning the National Spelling Bee Competition.

"That's because we tend to attract what we resist. We become what we hate. The more you resist your mother, the more you will become just like her. It's that simple."

Phil and his oversized microphone continued to bounce about his harem of an audience.

Another question.

Bam!

Another answer.

Another question.

Another answer.

There didn't seem to be anything anyone could ask Katie Fielding on the subject of mothers that she didn't have a pre-packaged, drip-dried answer for. After having authored two best sellers (the first, now in its seventh printing, appropriately titled *Mother!* and the second, *More Mother . . . but Where's Father?,* currently riding the crest of best sellers), Katie Fielding was to the subject of mothers what Julia Child was to food. In a period of just four years, she had become The Mother Expert.

She had also become a familiar face to talk show watchers all over America; for whenever Merv or Phil or David was in need of a mother expert the call went out to Katie. The only one she still hadn't met was Carson. She'd done his show twice but both times with guest hosts. With the disintegration of his fifth marriage, Katie was now convinced that John was obviously unresolved on the whole subject of women and therefore unconsciously threatened by her appearance on his show. It was alright. Joan Rivers was just fine.

Katie was one of the few who could handle her with ease. Joan treated Katie with the respect reserved for someone who might see through her brash facade and expose the little girl from Larchmont still looking for mother's approval.

Another question.

"Ms. Fielding." The microphone was resting on the mouth of a preppy college student. "What does your mother think of your success?"

Without missing a beat . . . the answer.

"What my mother thinks is unimportant. The question to ask is what do I think. To the degree we care what our mothers think of us is the degree to which they still control our lives."

Phil Donahue was looking no less involved than he did yesterday when his ladies heatedly debated the nuclear freeze issue with Helen Caldecott as he broke to go to commercial. Ironically it happened to be a spot for Oil of Olay, where the viewer's asked to guess which of two women is mother to the other as they chat over dishes in their suburban kitchen. Was it Doris or Cindy? It sure looked like Doris. Wrong! Cindy was Doris's mother and although both women looked not a day past twenty-nine, Cindy was really fifty-two years old.

Katie whispered to Phil that they ought to shoot the man who produced that commercial. She also whispered something about hoping to have seen Marlo before she flew to Boston. Phil said Marlo was in China in search of a woman's movement but if that proved too difficult to find she'd settle for a few artifacts from the Ming dynasty for their new Fifth Avenue apartment.

Katie thought that sounded a little chauvinistic but decided to let it go. She figured being married to Marlo, he got enough confrontation at home.

A lady came over at the commercial with a big brush and

powdered Katie's nose. She could get to like these shows. On the TV monitors Katie came across as the definitive portrait of the eighties woman. Just as fashion reflects an exactness of its time, Katie too could only exist in the immediate now. Cool. Crisp. Pretty. High tech fashion. A mixture of Third Floor Bendel with Third Avenue flea markets. Nineteen eighties/Nineteen thirties. Tokyo meets Milan. Yamamoto meets Armani. Dark brown hair tousled around her face, cut short and layered but wispy on the neck, one Stephen Sprouse-colored blue streak going through the right side of her hair looked fabulously new wave and trendy. The same went for the zipper earring hanging from her left ear and the gold screw on her right.

She was her own woman. Admired and respected by females all across America and complete within herself. In a few hours she would board the shuttle flight to Boston to appear on their "Live at Five," and by evening she would be safely back ensconced in her own apartment in New York. She had worked through her fear of flying years ago, although she did refuse to fly DC-10's on the advice of a pilot friend. Her oversized leather pocketbook housed her Walkman and her Golden Voyage relaxation tapes, volumes one, two, three, and four, especially good for takeoffs and landings (in cases of extreme turbulance she wished she could play all four simultaneously!).

She said goodbye to Phil, kissed him on both cheeks (something she acquired and retained from her year of living abroad), and was escorted out of the studio to her waiting limousine. A few hard-core fans waited in the rain for autographs. One just wanted to touch her hoping some of her togetherness might rub off.

"I'm such a mess!" said the pimply fat woman waiting at the backstage door. Katie looked at her. What could she say? The woman was right.

"Was your mother a mess?" she asked.

"No," the fat woman said. "My mother was perfect!"

Click!

"Well, you don't have to be a 'mess' just to not be like your mother. Just tell yourself, 'I have a right to get myself together without being perfect and without being my mother.' " She flashed her extra warm smile and the fat lady felt like she had just undergone a religious healing.

She hopped into the waiting limousine and looked at her watch. Right on time. She reached into her bag and pulled out the day's schedule written in ink in her Filofax notebook that housed, quite simply, the contents of her entire life, that's all. Credit Cards, Addresses, Diary, Appointments, etc. She took out her gold Cartier pen and began drawing lines through those things which she had already done. She made a note to buy some refills for her pen. Whenever she got around to buying the refill, she would draw a line through it. The more lines she drew on any given day the better she felt. Accomplishment was key. At the end of the year she looked back on pages and pages of notes that had been lined out and felt a sense of pride. She would meet each January One with fresh white pages and a newly filled pen.

9 A.M. Good Morning New York—line. 10 A.M. Book signing Scribner's—line. 12 O'Clock, Lunch with Readers Digest—line. Buy Playtex tampons—line (personal reminders sometimes got squeezed in between appointments). 1:30, Phil Donahue show—line.

No easy profession this book touring business. This was not by way of a complaint. She was glad there were people who waited on line and that there were books waiting to be autographed. Still, she thought, it was no wonder those rock groups often wrecked their hotel rooms while on tour. A city a day can do that to you.

Phil was supposed to be the very last of the tour. She was originally scheduled to do his show tomorrow. But the bookings got messed up, and you don't mess around with Phil's show. You do it when they want you because Phil Donahue sold books. So she'd go up to Boston and come right back. Basically, the tour was officially over and she was relieved.

At Boston's airport she was met by her new driver. She thought he had said his name was Bill, but it might have been Gil or Will. She made a mental note to try and do better remembering drivers' names, but it was just that after seven cities in eight days, they all looked alike. A rather sexist thought but true nevertheless.

"Do you know how to get to where we have to go?" she asked him politely.

"I bet I can get you there in less than fifteen," he answered, looking straight ahead.

Actually it was excusable not to have remembered his name because they did all look alike. All she ever saw was the backs of their heads. Blond, gray, brown; all wore identical caps and jackets. It's hard enough remembering names that come attached to faces.

Katie, you are too hard on yourself, she thought. Why not? she answered.

To have survived her mother was a miracle. If only Phil knew that he had just spent the last hour and a half with a walking miracle.

"What time are you supposed to be at the station?" asked Bill or Gil.

She answered that she had to be On Air in half an hour.

"No probleemo," he said. "Just leave it to Limo Len. I'll have you there faster than if you were driving with Teddy Kennedy." He laughed. "How do you like our freezing city?"

"I've always liked Boston," she answered in a voice that really said I want to be alone.

"I bet you're sitting back there wonderin' why this town has so much traffic?"

No answer.

"A woman traffic commissioner. That's why. She totally screwed up the traffic in this city. You wanna know why? She thought she'd make certain streets just be for shoppers to walk around. Now is that like a woman or what? . . ."

No response was not enough to stop Limo Len. He kept right on.

". . . Walk around! It's two friggin' degrees here today and she's makin' streets for walkin' around."

She had deliberately told Pamela, the book tour lady, not to meet her at the airport because she'd prefer a few minutes to herself. If she wasn't looking for publishing chat from Pan, she certainly wasn't looking to be interviewed by Limo Len. If she wasn't interested in Pamela's version of what happened to Danielle Steele in Cincinnati, she definitely wasn't interested in Len's theories on Boston traffic. She knew what the solution was, but it seemed so rude to put the divider up when someone was just being friendly.

"So? What do you think of this wind we're having? Bet it could blow you cross town quicker than I could drive!"

That was it!

Window going up. Next stop peace and quiet. She told Len she needed a little time to prepare herself.

Here she was a woman other women looked to to tell them the truth living this . . . this lie. Lillian Hellman wouldn't lie. She would if she had my mother, she thought.

Her mother had left six messages so far. One in every city but Detroit. That must have been her way of telling her that she thought Detroit to be an unnecessary stop on the tour. Well, Katie hadn't called her back, and she wasn't going to. She just wished she'd stop leaving messages. Her life was turning into Hansel and Gretel with trails of message crumbs sprinkled from state to state.

So what if "they" found out, Katie thought. She would not die if they found out. It would not make her work any less valid. Just her whole life. That's all.

Why was her mother calling her, anyway? There were supposed to be no more calls. Why wouldn't she honor their agreement? She made the mistake of taking her "emergency" call exactly three weeks ago; the day her second book came out. Somehow her mother had already read all four hundred and fifteen pages of which she confessed to liking a total of "one." And that page, she said, was the one that read, "The End."

"Just because you did not see fit to get along with your own mother was no reason to have written a book destined to turn daughters all over America against their mothers as well. Aren't there better causes for you to champion?" she asked. "Why not try air pollution?"

She also said her lawyer would be calling to ask for a third of all royalties because if she wasn't the mother she was, there would have been no "Mother" books.

After that call, Katie refused once again to talk to her.

Yet if anyone asked Katie's mother what she thought of her daughter's books, she spoke in superlatives reserved for Chaucer or Hemingway. No one would ever suspect they were anything but the best of friends. She was not going to tell them that they had not seen each other in almost four years. She remained protective of her daughter. She was not going to expose the truth of their relationship, unless of course Katie continued to ignore her calls. Then she might be forced to take action.

Katie knew the possibility existed her mother could do anything. But her mother was manipulative, and she was not going to fall prey to her latest ploy. She'd gotten these same messages in the past, and urgent could mean anything except urgent.

The final interview of the afternoon went fine. There was no talk of her mother. Just the usual questions. It aired live in Boston at five o'clock, and a separate piece was taped and sent to New York for tomorrow's "Good Morning America" show. They were doing a week on "Authors on Tour" and were taping segments in advance and flying them in. They had caught up with Norman Mailer in Houston ("If this city has so much money, why aren't they buying my book!"), Philip Roth in San Diego, Fran Liebowitz in Los Angeles (poolside, hating every minute of it!), and Joseph Heller in Buffalo. Katie was their nonfiction author for the week.

As Limo Len sped merrily to the airport while listing all greats and near-greats he ever chauffeured (Ethel was the best . . . a good woman and a good tipper!), Katie saw the beginnings of the Phil Donahue show on the television in the back seat. She listened to herself giving advice to a frightened housewife who'd driven a hundred miles in the rain just to be part of today's audience. It was a good feeling to know she had an impact on the lives of other women. One other woman who happened to be watching "Donahue" this particular afternoon was Katie's mother. She examined her daughter as carefully as she could, reduced as she was to twenty-one inches diagonally, and thought to herself, "Well, I must have done something right!"

# Chapter

## 2

Lady Landamere wasn't always a lady. In fact when she met her second husband, she was a photographer's model living in London. A city she fled to after an unhappy affair with a powerful Washington attorney and after the untimely death of her first husband. While she wasn't always a lady, she was always a free and rare flower. Outspoken to excess, she was notoriously strong willed and anti-establishment in her views, two traits that proved disastrous to the fate of all three marriages. The first, a wealthy land developer from Texas, met Lady Landamere when she won the Miss Texas title in 1946. Her name then was Tracy Cambell. The second, a film producer who didn't share Lady Landamere's liberal philosophies, preferred divorce rather than the risk of being blacklisted. The third was Lord Edwin Landamere who without his title had the rather dubious distinction of being a contributing reporter to an almost defunct London magazine called *Style,* something the lord had very little of. But the invitations did come, though less frequently each year, freely. And once Lord Edwin succumbed to acute gout, Lady Landamere was left with the very best of the lord, his title.

Lady Landamere loved people and she loved to entertain. She thoroughly enjoyed her own irreverence to one and all. As her behavior got more excessive with her advancing years it seemed to be better tolerated and enjoyed by those around her. She considered these to be her golden years and believed that having reached the age of sixty, she was afforded certain privileges that those younger than she were not. (In actuality, this was the same thing she believed when she reached the age of fifty.) That is why she resented her son's and daughter-in-law's attempts to curtail her smoking and drinking in spite of the fact that she only last year survived a quadruple bypass operation by Dr. DeBakey in Houston. When the famous doctor came into her room five days later to tell her what a lucky woman she was to be alive, he found her sitting in bed smoking a Marlboro, with an oxygen mask tilted atop her head like a New Year's hat. It was then that Dr. DeBakey, in conjunction with Richard and Ellen Fields (her son and daughter-in-law), decided that "mother" should be moved upstairs to the tenth floor for psychiatric evaluation. Lady Landamere found the whole thing hysterically funny and decided it would be a fabulous experience and certainly one worth using if she ever got around to writing her autobiography. At last count she had over thirty journals that she had been keeping since the early 1950s. They ranged in subject matter from her most private recollections to ordinary shopping lists when she couldn't find a note pad. They had no form but that they were all written in ink. Lady Landamere hated pencils. "Life," she said, "was a series of impermanent events . . . so they might as well be remembered in ink." Anyway, she always had a journal nearby and on more than one occasion, threatened to "reveal the truth of it all one day."

What was wonderful about Lady Landamere, affectionately called Trace (rhymes with Grace) by her friends, was her ability to see life as a great feast. Her weakness was her inability to deny herself any part of what was being served. But as she herself said many times, "The only thing worse than death is boredom and moderation is boring. I will leave that to my accountants. Besides, what guarantee have I, if I were to stop my smoking and drinking, I would live any longer. I dare to say it would only seem like it."

And so, with a laugh and a carton of Marlboros Lady Landamere happily moved up to the tenth floor for "observation."

But now she was back in the Houston hospital again, having cut short her vacation in Cannes due to recurring chest pains. The cast of characters was the same. Richard, Ellen, the famous DeBakey and Sons (Lady Landamere said all surgeons were basically tailors). But this time there would be no tenth-floor observation. It was not her neurosis that was threatening to kill her.

Ten days later she found herself being discharged again with a long and ambiguous diagnosis which stated her mental health was in far less immediate jeopardy than her physical health. The team of attending physicians concurred that she had no more than six months left to live. If this prognosis came as a shock to Lady Landamere, she never once showed it. At least not to anyone present that day. Dr. Kenneth Stanton, her Houston internist, was the one who had the unwelcomed task of telling her the truth.

"Trace," he said, "I wish more than anything I didn't have to tell you this, but last year's surgery is not going to give you the years that we hoped it would. In fact it probably won't give you a full year more."

"Who knows about this besides you and me?"

"I've told Ellen and Richard, that's all."

"What about Katie? Did they call Katie?"

Dr. Stanton looked puzzled. "Who's Katie?" he asked.

"Katie," she said slowly, ". . . is my daughter."

"I never knew you had a daughter. I thought Richard was an only child."

"He practically is. None of us have seen Katie in years." She paused for a few beats and then said, "Did you ever see Carol Burnett's takeoff on *Love Story?*"

Dr. Stanton shook his head no.

"Well, she's lying in bed and her husband, I think it was Harvey Korman, just learned she's about to die and tells her to ask for anything she wants because he wants to fulfill her every wish before she pops off, so she asks for a hard-boiled egg and he looks at his watch and then suggests a soft-boiled egg instead."

She laughed her famous laugh. Loud and full bodied. "Oh, it was simply wonderful. So tell me, Dr. Stanton, is there time for a second opinion or do you recommend the soft-boiled egg?"

It was fact that Lady Landamere's doctors had the distinction of never lasting longer than any of her marriages and, like all her relationships, were always re-evaluated before they were renewed. This seemed like the perfect time to consider a new association.

"Dr. Stanton," she began, "do you know Dr. William Chase up at Massachusetts General?"

"Why, yes, I do . . ."

"Well, I don't. But I plan to. So be a darling and send my records up to him, won't you, and if you'd be kind enough to give him a ring and tell him I might be stopping by on my way to St. Martin, I'd be forever grateful. It's not that I don't believe you, Dr. Stanton, it's just that your prognosis interferes with a number of very important plans I have made for myself."

Dr. Stanton took Lady Landamere's hand and told her he appreciated the way she felt and went into the standard "Doctor's are not gods" routine rap. He wished her well and urged her to see him or whomever she so chose at least once a month to monitor her medication and then left the room. Trace lit up her fourth consecutive cigarette, circled the available stations on her television, and placed a call to New York. There was only one person she wanted to reach before checking out.

Four phone calls later, as the chauffeur who would be taking her to the airport was removing her Rigaud candles, her antique silver picture frames, and an unopened bottle of Dom Pérignon (1959) from her room, she had still not made a connection.


"Howard, I implore you to tell me the truth. I have left three messages for her with her current friend and she has still not called me back. I implore you to give me her phone number. May I remind you that this, Howard, is no time to show me you can keep a secret. You had many opportunities during the five years you and Katie were married and failed dismally. Now is not the time to start building character."

Lady Landamere was speaking from a red velvet chaise lounge in a very red bedroom with lots of gold trimmings and filled with beautiful antique French furniture. Scattered about the room were numerous magazines and newspaper clippings all waiting to be read.

The room was messy in the best sense of the word. Lived in. Alive. A Lhasa apso named Fred was lying half on her chest, with his head hanging over the edge of the chaise. She was wearing a black terry cloth jogging suit with big black furry slippers, each foot the approximate size of Fred. She was back home, at least for the moment, in her penthouse apartment in the Beverly Wilshire Hotel. She claimed to prefer hotel living to any of the homes she occupied while she was married to Jack and living in Beverly Hills. In her memoirs this period is referred to as "The Not Very Original Hollywood Years." She had been heard to say, "Originality and Hollywood are in themselves contradictions." Lady Landamere also said that if you have to live in California, it's best to do it in a hotel, that way you can always pretend you're only staying a few days. It's difficult to imagine she believed her own words for it was, after all, California she returned to after Lord Edwin died.

"Howard," she continued, "I'll bet you'd be interested in what the film critic from the *L. A. Times* is going to write about your darling Sandra's performance in next Sunday's Calendar section." (The Calendar section is a part of the *L. A. Times* that Trace believed was as inflated in its sense of self-importance as the people it wrote about.) "I happen to know because I happened to be seated to his left last night at a party the Allenbergs gave for the Kurt Platts. . . . Let's just call it an even trade."

There was a pause.

"Well, he said she was beguiling with a sensual quality that compensated for what appeared to him to be a small amount of talent. I believe he also said the picture was neither as beguiling nor as sensual as she was. So all things considered, Sandra fared rather well. Personally I always thought it was he who possessed the little talent or why would he still be writing those inane reviews?"

Another pause.

"Tell me that again, dear. Nine-eight-eight? Just a moment. Nine-eight-six? Oh. Nine-eight-eight, seven-eight-four-seven. Howard, not since Garbo has a number been kept as successfully secret as this. Thank you, dear. It's nice to know that you've never been above making a good deal. My best to 'beguiling sensual' Sandra."

She glanced over to Fred and in a stage whisper added, "The little harlot!" . . . "And to your amusing mother." To Fred again, "The original harlot!"

"Ta-ta!"

Trace was famous for her "Ta-ta's."

She put down the receiver and spoke aloud, presumably to Fred once again, who was now three-quarters off the chaise and hanging on by some miracle of gravity. "One of God's less fortunate, poor Howard. Always was."

# Chapter

## 3

*K*atie Fielding walked into her East Sixty-eighth Street apartment, and the phone was ringing. Neither she nor her apartment bore any resemblance to Trace or hers.

Trace was fair of skin. Katie was olive complexioned. Trace surrounded herself with as much color and gold as possible, Katie's apartment was soft, beige, and cloudlike. One of Katie's theories states that daughters who bear no resemblance to their mothers either physically and/or behaviorally have worked very hard to achieve this feat. For indeed, the apple does not fall far from the tree, so for the Katie Fieldings of this world, they have had to move that apple, inch by inch, year by year, in order to accomplish their goal.

She was putting a package down from the neighborhood health food store when the answering machine began recording the incoming message.

"Katie, are you there?"

Katie felt almost paralyzed with surprise. Had she wanted to pick up the phone her feet would probably not have gotten her across the kitchen floor. The voice continued. It was the voice she had studiously avoided for the past four years, and it was the voice she had done her best not to sound like for the past thirty years.

It continued. "Katie, this is your mother. I am currently in Los Angeles on my way to Massachusetts General . . . I do hope this thing is not about to beep me off. If so I am reachable in Los Angeles at two-seven-five-four-four-one-one. Area code two-one-three. I know my calling is contrary to our agreement, but I think it important that I see you. I have been told that I am dying. Of course, we're all in a process of dying, aren't we, but it's just sooner than I had intended and . . . and . . ."

She was beeped off.

"Oh, shit," she said. "I so hate those machines. If I was in favor of brevity, I would have sent a telegram."

She redialed. The telephone in one hand and her cigarette in the other. An ashtray resting on Fred's back.

Reconnected, she continued. "I want to deal with our difficulties now, so that you won't be wracked with guilt when I am gone. Also, it has not gone unnoticed by me that Thursday is your birthday so perhaps we can have a small celebration as well."

Katie was by now standing over the machine. She picked up the telephone.

"Hello! . . . Hello . . . This is Katie." She was trying to talk over Trace, which was no easy task. "Hello, Trace, this is Katie. I just walked in."

"Well, then let me start again. I am in Los Angeles now, and I will be flying to Massachusetts to see this Dr. William Chase at Massachusetts General this weekend and . . ."

"I heard you say that on the machine."

Trace paused and then said, "What is it you do? Do you stand there and screen your calls and if someone says the magic word, like 'dying,' the duck comes down and you pick up the phone? Did you hear me say I am reported to be dying?"

There was a moment's silence.

"Yes. I heard you say that on the machine. You said that's why you want to see me."

"I always 'want' to see you. This gives me 'reason' to see you. Let us say I will pick you up at your apartment at twelve-thirty on Thursday, and we will lunch wherever you choose. We'll call it a birthday lunch. I'm sure you wouldn't care for any of my old establishment eateries . . . Besides, they're probably dying, too. Oh, Katie, dear, exactly where are you living now? . . . Really! How lovely. I'm glad I won't be needing my pocket Mace spray this trip. Well, then, until Thursday . . . Oh, by the way, I happened to see you on the "Donahue" show yesterday. I think there must have been something terribly wrong with my set in the hospital because there was a ridiculous blue streak going through your hair! Ta-ta."

And she was gone.

Katie hung up the phone. She couldn't believe she was experiencing the same feeling hearing the infamous "Ta-ta" as she did all those years ago. Did anything ever change? Why didn't she know what she was feeling? Years ago that was excusable. Years ago she didn't even know "if" she was feeling. But now. Other than partial paralysis, what was she feeling?

Dying? That was impossible. Other people died. Not Trace. She was invincible. Maybe this was just another of her fantastic inventions. But for what reason?

"Feel your feelings," she had shouted to the woman in the third row just three hours ago, and here she was exhibiting the emotional response of a scrambled egg. Feeling what?

Trace would know what she was feeling. Trace felt everything in excess. Like lava through Mount Vesuvius feelings flowed through Trace. Volcanic eruptions of emotions that were all larger than life.

Trace felt with enough volume for mother and daughter both. With a mother so overpowering it once seemed as though there was no room for them to co-exist in this world. One former therapist once asked Katie if it was necessary for Trace to die before Katie could begin to live. It was all textbook perfect. The subject Katie had mastered in self-defense. Mother. The symbiosis. The letting go. The self-nourishment. And here it was again. The past stuff. And this time there was no avoiding it.

So confidently she looked into the cameras and told the television audience that life continues to mirror what we still need to learn. So confidently she shook hands with Dr. Joyce Brothers at Phil's studio as they passed in the hallway. Now her hands were shaking and she was all alone. She still needed to deal with what even four years of distance could not erase.

When *Mother!* was first published, reviews were staggeringly good. "Written with the depth and sensitivity of a wise old soul," said Nancy Friday. ". . . Required reading for every woman attempting to be conscious and alive today," said Gloria Steinem.

Two books and numerous accolades later Katie Fielding was feeling as much a mess as the fat pimply lady she left at the backstage door.

She began to cry. The house phone rang and the doorman announced that Rebecca Holmes was on her way upstairs. It would be questionable if this would be considered being "saved by the bell!"

"Hap-py birth-day to you, hap-py birth-day to you, hap-py birth-day, dear Katie, hap-py birth-day to you."

Rebecca Holmes never looked more fabulous than she did standing in the doorway dressed in something very soft and pink and cashmere with a wide-shouldered self-jacket, tight ankle length pants and pink suede boots to complete the outfit. She looked like the woman you'd most want to meet if you happened in on a party at Jay Gatsby's. She was holding a big gift-wrapped box, and Katie could only hope that a similar outfit was inside. Katie just adored Rebecca's sense of style.

Katie knew exactly why Rebecca was her mother's favorite. Friends since childhood, Katie went through the years hearing, "If only you could do this like Rebecca . . . if only you could do that like Rebecca." Amazingly their friendship survived. But past the anger Katie felt toward her mother's lack of sensitivity by putting her in direct competition with her best friend was her total agreement with her mother's point of view. Rebecca always had her act together. Even as a kid. It came as no big surprise that today Rebecca Holmes was the country's number one female box office attraction. She always had "it." That charismatic thing. That thing that said, I'm different and I'm glad. In fact, that's exactly what Rebecca and Trace shared in common, and today was the first time Katie ever put that combination together.

Today the two women found themselves on equal footing. Both at the top of their chosen professions. But the difference was simple. Rebecca Holmes was always Rebecca Holmes and was always destined for greatness. Katie Fielding may have been destined for a lifetime of insecurity and oblivion if she hadn't fought long and hard against a mother who dwarfed her even as she claimed she was only trying to make her better.

Anyway, Katie loved Rebecca. She trusted her friendship although it was hardly a fifty-fifty split. They hugged at the door. "How come you always look so incredible?" Katie asked. "Does it come with being a star? I think stars age differently than we regular mortals."

"That's probably true," Rebecca answered. "We have our plastic surgeons and our press agents to thank. Anyway, you know what I think about life after thirty. Maintenance and repair. That's all it is, my dear friend. Maintenance and repair. But let us not get depressing on your birthday. Open your present."

"I hope it's what you're wearing. You look so great!"

"Good, because it is. It's exactly what I'm wearing except in white. I think you've been looking too somber lately. Too monochromatically gray."

Katie opened the box with delight. "I'd try it on but I'd probably get depressed when it didn't look as good on me as it does on you." She tried it on anyway.

Rebecca said something about noticing that Katie was not in the best of spirits on the day before her thirty-fifth. "You know," she said, "I'm really not nearly as beautiful as you and I never was. I just had a better time creating who I wanted to be. My imagination always had more flights of fancy."

It was true. Rebecca Holmes had taken what God had given her and what might by some be considered a less than generous allotment of physical gifts and turned each limitation masterfully to her advantage. Her hair, which she might have given up on as too curly, through her ingenuity became a style women the world over asked their hairdressers to imitate. Her eyes, which Fred Gibbler, her high school boyfriend, used to say were in the back of her head (because Rebecca's eyes saw everything), were now referred to as "intense and sexy." They were a brilliant blue and although not large, like laser beams they pierced you with their power and instantly commanded your attention. And finally, lips that all but Mick Jagger would consider too big, became, in fact, the most famous lips in the world.

It was amazing what the mind could create if you liked yourself enough to invest the energy. Rebecca always did.

And Katie didn't. She was looking at herself in the mirror and trying to like the reflection she saw staring back at her. She wondered if she was imagining that her face was suddenly looking more like her mother's.

"My mother called me today," she said to Rebecca.

"She called you! And you waited till now to tell me. What did she want?"

Katie looked at Rebecca and said, "She wants to see me. She said she's dying . . . and she said she wants to talk to me."

"Dying?" Rebecca was stunned. Here was a subject that she avoided even more than the paparazzi.

"We'll have to rearrange our luncheon topics with this news bulletin," she said, "but do promise me that we'll still have some time to devote to my life crises too . . . like Mark and my movie."

That was Rebecca.

They gathered their coats and once downstairs popped into Rebecca's waiting limousine for what was to be a five-block hop. Rebecca's limousine was outfitted as though Rebecca had checked in for a three-week stay. It housed all of her favorite videos (mostly her own films), cassettes, Perrier, juices, plus makeup mirror and table (originally designed for Elizabeth Taylor when she played in *The Little Foxes*. If she was running late she'd do her makeup in the car). It had a speaker telephone and a white mink rug. Just your basic taxi. Anyway its interior was lavender and silly and perfect, especially on an eighteen-degree day.

Lunch was about as good as lunch could be, considering. The trouble with having lunch is that you have to eat, and eating was something neither Rebecca nor Katie ever figured out how to do properly. Both were either dieting or losing weight throughout their entire life. In fact, it wouldn't be inappropriate to conclude food was the bond that connected their friendship through the years.

Though never referred to, both remembered that summer in Switzerland where Rebecca shared her "most secret discovery" with her sixteen-year-old best friend. After pigging out on roast beef sandwiches with russian dressing and coleslaw on rye followed by double pints of Rocky Road ice cream, Rebecca discovered you could throw up and then repeat the very same meal again, throw up again . . . and not gain a single pound.

Neither woman ever really came clean with the other as to if and when they ever really overcame what was to each of them a very humiliating secret. But through the years they watched each other wrestle with the horrors of compulsive eating, fat farms, spas, fad diets, etc. Between them they read every conceivable book written on the subject of dieting. And in spite of or because of their mutual obsession they each managed to keep their weight within a seven-pound very reasonable sliding scale for years.

Once, in the early years of Rebecca's film career, she found she was having a particularly hard time with the pasta in Milan, and the producer threatened to close down the shooting if she didn't lose ten pounds fast. Rebecca's love of the camera was probably the only thing she loved more than her love of linguine, so it was resolved. She fasted and filming continued. For Rebecca, her career, more than any man, has always proved the motivation in her remaining slim. And for Katie, the same remained true. How could she pass herself off as an expert on mothers and weigh in at one hundred fifty-five pounds (a weight she once saw, looking below her double chins to the numbers on the bathroom scale). For women, in America today, the appearance of togetherness definitely included thinness. Therefore, Katie Fielding remained thin.

What they enjoyed discussing together was how hard it was to maintain their thinness. Every phone conversation included "Are you thin or are you fat?" Both women somehow knowing that neither was ever going to be fat again, though they might think fat forever. They were glad they had each other to obsess with. What a step forward for their own self-esteem and for women the world over when Jane Fonda admitted that she used to binge and purge . . . eat and throw up. Why that would be like Gloria Steinem admitting that she liked to be beaten by tattooed men while watching porno films nightly.

Anyway they always laughed about where to go for lunch because they always knew exactly what the other was going to eat. There was something almost perverse in listening to the waiter give his lengthy dissertation of the specialties of the house only to order the house salad with the dressing, ON THE SIDE, or the fruit salad or, on a big day, the mushroom omelet or the broiled fish, NO BUTTER. Sometimes, throwing caution to the wind, a glass of wine would be permitted (seventy calories for a light buzz), but more than likely a Perrier or glass of Poland water (the current favorite) was the preferred beverage. Clearly, a walk through a museum would be less of a strain and more nourishing to the soul than the torture of lunch with the pastry cart never more than inches away from view. Though lunch with Rebecca was alright because at least they could substitute drama for food. In fact lunches and dinners were never the problem if the company was exciting enough. Katie always knew when a relationship was in trouble when she found herself desiring all the food on his plate as well as her own. In fact his plate and her weight were good barometers of the condition of her love life, until Peter.

She'd been with Peter (on and off) for almost four years now, and although they were long past the romantic illusions of the first two months of love, her weight had still remained constant, in the 110-pound area. This was a fact that she was proud of, sort of. What she was proud of was that she didn't throw up anymore. That was the good news. She was no longer harming her digestive system. But her self-esteem still remained tarnished by the habit she had replaced it with.

She would fill up a paper cup with the food she planned to eat and then only chew it, enough to get the taste and the oral gratification, and then discard the chewed (unswallowed) food into a second paper cup. Obviously she did not indulge her habit at dinner parties or with friends, but she looked forward to her time alone in the apartment when Peter wasn't around, when she could savor some of her favorite paper cup specials.

There was, she discovered, "good" chew food and "bad" chew food. Bagels were good, ice cream impossible. Doughnuts were pretty good, cookies not too good. Granola was good. Nuts and seeds were good. Chocolate and carob were not good. It is worth noting that chocolate is never good and that the least a person like Katie, who pictured herself a nutritionally conscious person, could do was to try and keep her chew foods within the limits of good nutrition.

Occasionally she would even dare to do it (chew and spit out) in front of Peter. It was almost as though she wanted to see how far she could go before he'd notice. Every time she got away with it, it simple reinforced her belief that she wasn't really worth noticing.

For her upcoming thirty-fifth birthday, she promised herself there'd be no more spitting into paper cups. She was about to share her secret with Rebecca when Rebecca asked if she'd like to go to a health spa with her to lose a few pounds and try to learn, once and for all, to eat properly. She'd heard of a place in Mexico which was supposed to be fabulous and low key, and Rebecca thought her schedule would allow her to get away in a couple of weeks. Katie said she thought she could pull it off. She said observing all those women might help her with the new book she was beginning. Rebecca was pleased. She never asked Katie what she was planning to write about. Katie decided there would be time to talk to Rebecca about the paper cups in Mexico. So they both drank their brewed decaffeinated with Sweet 'N Low, NO SUGAR, and moved to the next topic, and of course that topic was Rebecca.

Rebecca put the *n* in narcissism but for some reason it was okay. Mainly because Katie was almost as fascinated by Rebecca as Rebecca was. Rebecca was a great character and, Katie, being a writer and having grown up with Trace, had a true appreciation for great characters.

One of Katie's more interesting observations the year and a half she spent in group therapy was it was alright to monopolize the group's time if you were the most entertaining character in the group. If you were John Doe and worked in the city bank as a cashier and the most interesting thing that happened to you all week was your sister asked to borrow a hundred dollars for the third time in one month and you happened to speak in a monotone as well, chances are the group would have little patience for your tale of woe. If, however, you're Rebecca Holmes and shooting has just halted on your current picture because you've had a fight with your director who also happens to be your current lover, it is amazing how much more time the group will permit you.

As they sat finishing their coffee, Katie listened to Rebecca's complaints and couldn't help noticing the absurdity of her situation.

"It just seems like it shouldn't have to be so difficult. Your drama, my drama. I mean, at what point do we just say, 'This is the hand I got, so deal. Count me in'?"

Rebecca agreed that it was time they started enjoying what they had. Then she added that what she had was a problem.

Two women and a man who were having lunch at tables nearby stopped to tell Rebecca what huge fans they were of hers. This made the fifth interruption since lunch began.

"If they only knew how rough it all is," Rebecca sighed as she played with her American Express card.

"Rough will be seeing my mother tomorrow," Katie said, steering the conversation back to herself for the moment. It was kind of like they took turns.

Rebecca said she never understood why it was all so rough for Katie. She said she always had tremendous admiration for Trace. Even when they were teenagers she said she looked to Trace instead of her own mother for approval. Katie said she was sure it would have been much easier to enjoy her if she wasn't her mother.

Katie knew that Rebecca had kept contact with Trace. Maybe, secretly, she even liked that. Rebecca respected Katie's wishes not to try and reunite them, but the news of Lady Landamere's illness did not surprise Rebecca. She had begged her to stop smoking. Just a month ago she called her to tell her of a program she heard about

where the smoker chews this nicotine gum and loses his or her desire
for a cigarette. She said she never got to give Trace the details
because Trace interrupted her by going into a long tirade about how
singularly unattractive it is for a lady to chew gum. "Far worse than
smoking!" she said. Besides, she'd heard the gum withdrawal was
worse than the cigarettes. So she thanked her and bid her "Ta-ta."

But dying. Rebecca thought of her as being almost as invincible
as Katie did. Trying to find something positive to say, she noted that
maybe it took as dramatic a situation as this for them to make their
peace. Rebecca also noted that for a birthday lunch this was not
turning out to be at all light and gay. "If I wanted this, I could have
had lunch with Mark."

Before they were about to begin their third cup of coffee and the
latest Mark story, Katie enticed Rebecca to head for the limo,
dangling Bendel's as the carrot to get her to the car. Katie reminded
her of the T-shirt she had given her which read, "When the going
gets tough, the tough go shopping." Other than a few scripts a
month, the trades, and the Arts and Leisure sections from both
coasts, T-shirts were just about all the reading Rebecca had time for.

Just one thing worth making note of. Going anywhere with
Rebecca was a big responsibility. Katie always felt the need to
protect her from all the people who wanted to get at her. You see,
it was kind of like a big circle. Because so many people intruded
on her when she was out in public, she made herself less and less
accessible to her fans, which made her few public outings even more
a cause célèbre, which in turn kept her even more secluded. It was
kind of like the difference between seeing Barbara Mandrell in a
store or Barbra Streisand. One is more accessible, more approacha-
ble, and therefore less exciting. Certain stars created their own aura.
Like Sophia! She hadn't made a film in years and still. . . .

Anyway shopping was usually a sure way of curing whatever ailed either woman. But not today. Today was supposed to be a celebration of Katie's birthday and all she could think about was her mother's illness. Her mother's dying. Even a spree through Bendel's third floor couldn't cure that.

## Chapter

4

$\mathcal{I}$f you were to ask Lady Landamere and Katie each to give her version as to what caused their imposed separation, you would hear two very different stories.

Lady Landamere is quicker to tell you her version of what actually happened than Katie. In fact there was one year when Katie refused to discuss anything that had to do with her mother other than matters that needed to be dealt with for tax purposes, etc. The only thing they both agreed upon was that there was no single incident that caused their current estrangement. There was that final straw that broke the camels back, but both women admit to a very checkered past together.

Katie saw it all at its best as simple neglect and at its worst a case of total rejection. This is the way she perceived it as far back as she could remember. Unfortunately, one of the reasons her therapy seemed to have left certain gaping holes in its wake was because Katie was unable to remember all that much. Particularly the early years. Today she believed the reason for that was her own built-in protection system against what was too painful. She'd talked to Peter about it, and they both agreed that when she could no longer take the emotional pain of her mother's rejection she just went unconscious. Peter, who had years of study in this very field, said that the textbooks referred to it as "splitting off." Anyway, Katie said she was aware early on that she was an unwelcomed addition to Trace's busy life.

Her memories of her nannies were sometimes more vivid than of her mother.

She didn't remember the first one who helped raise her in the big mansion outside of Dallas until she was three. She didn't really remember her at all, but the second one, who moved with her from Dallas to join Trace and her new daddy for their brand new life in California, she remembered far better. Zella!

Zella stayed with the family for five years and when she left Katie was eight and a half. By then, Richard was three years old and already on his way to securing the position he still holds today as professional sibling.

Her recollections of her half-brother were almost as hazy as those of her stepfather. Jack Fields may have been a powerful figure in Hollywood, but for Katie it was his frequent absences that held the most power. He was always off somewhere making a movie, and she remembered that her baby brother often got to travel with Trace and her new daddy because he was still a baby and not in school, while Katie had to stay home with Zella.

Zella was scary because she had a habit of falling asleep while sitting up, when she was supposed to be baby sitting. Always a child with an active imagination, Katie, who was supposed to be asleep, would sit up in her bed and watch Zella. She watched her transform herself into a human pendulum, rocking back and forth, back and forth, every minute, plunging herself into a deeper sleep. Little Katie would watch as big Zella gained momentum, rocking furiously from side to side, on a backless chair, until she would be seconds away from falling off the chair onto the marble floor. At that point Katie would scream, "Wake up, Zella. You're gonna kill yourself and I'll be here all alone."

But Katie also remembered that awake Zella was not exactly a whole lot of fun. There were not many activities they could find to participate in together (Zella did not know how to play Checkers, Sorry, Poker, or Clue). Zella only knew the Ouija board. Zella used to place Katie's ten little fingers on top of the circular plastic sphere that sat in the middle of the fortune-telling board and ask it over and over again, "Ouija board, Ouija board, is Zella gonna get a new pair of shoes?" Every time they'd sit down at the board she'd ask the same question.

Katie used to feel very sorry for Zella and her old brown leather shoes, and she also used to get very uncomfortable watching her nanny behave in this unorthodox manner, so in order to end the game she would end up sliding the little sphere over to the big Yes on the upper left-hand corner of the board. Zella would then smile her big smile and, satisfied with her fortune, tell Katie it was her turn to ask a question. Katie, who had by now figured out the game, would ask, "Ouija board, Ouija board, am I going to get a delicious chocolate fudge surprise?" She would wait half a minute, and when nothing happened, she would slide the little sphere, with Zella's ten big fingers resting on its other side, right up to the big Yes and that would be that. Although fudge was a "no-no" in the Fields's home, Zella would be forced to give Katie her favorite cookies.

In fact, Zella and the Ouija board was Katie's first indoctrination into the world of the occult, metaphysics, and the beginnings of some bizarre hookup between religion and superstition. Zella said her prayers nightly, as religiously as she played the numbers every morning. Just fifty cents a day, but she had a cousin who lived in New York who once won fourteen hundred dollars playing her phone number, and Zella just knew her turn was coming, if she just kept praying.

So Katie remembered Zella and she remembered her mother's long absences. She was in Paris. She was in New York. She was in London. Where she wasn't was with Katie.

When Trace would return from one of her sojourns, Katie remembered her always bringing back a beautiful white pinafore or party dress for her to wear, which invariably was at least one size too small. This meant that Katie remembered always feeling at least one size too fat. She also remembered Trace bathing her after each trip because she'd complain, on returning home, that Katie looked dirty.

It wasn't the bath that Katie hated. The warm water felt good, and Trace rubbing her back with a soft soapy cloth was probably one of the more intimate acts they shared together. The problems arose when Trace would scrub Katie's elbows and knees so relentlessly trying to get the dirt off. She would scrub so hard that Katie would start to cry. But the really painful part was that there was no dirt. That was Katie's natural pigmentation. Olive. Like her father. Trace would eventually give up and say something like, "Maybe we can bleach you when you're a little older. Isn't it unfortunate that we can't manage more control over our genetic inheritance. Certainly you were not lucky with your skin. Such a shame because mine is beautiful." And it was.

That's not the only thing I wasn't lucky with, Katie would think to herself. I wasn't lucky with my mother. I would have liked Donna Reed or even Lucille Ball. But as Katie was to write years later in her first book, "Children learn how to survive early on and they do not . . . under penalty of death/abandonment . . . ever voice such feelings. They secretly wish them, and then feel guilty about them, but they do not speak them aloud."

You see, Trace called things as she saw them and sometimes, that kind of truth could be cruel. Especially when speaking to a little girl. Sometimes she'd realize that she hurt her daughter's feelings and she'd give her a little pinch on the cheek and tell her not to worry, "Beauty is only skin deep."

Katie blamed Trace for her lack of self-worth. When she was ten and eleven and twelve and thirteen and fourteen, they would shop for her clothes. Something, believe it or not, Katie once hated with a passion. That was because her mother used to humiliate her. In each department store, Trace would enlist the aid of one of the salesladies to help her with "her problem." As a general rule it is not good for overall self-esteem to grow up as "somebody's problem." It is a little like having a hump.

"What can we do with her?" Trace would ask each new confidant she made while shopping throughout the store.

Katie remembered a series of saleswomen all shaking their heads worriedly. The entire experience was most unpleasant. If only for the sheer reality of finding out the size twelves didn't fit. She thoroughly hated the saleslady at Saks who suggested, after trying in vain to find a party dress that would just get on her (forget about style!), that they try Lane Bryant's Chubby Department. And what was worse was they did. Lane Bryant's Chubby Department, where they greet you at the elevator with little sugar cookies to insure your continued patronage. Lane Bryant's Chubby Department, where they invite you upon leaving the store to join their friendly Chubby Club, where little tubettes from all over the country gather to compare baby fat in their size twelve and a half party dresses, which are stained in a matter of seconds with chocolate fudge dripping from their fat little fingers. Oh, the pain of being a preteen with "baby fat" and a "pretty face."

She never forgot Trace once telling her "walk behind me, Fatty" on one of their shopping excursions.

She also blamed Trace for the diet doctor with the multicolored pills when she was fifteen. And for the divorce from Jack when she was sixteen, which meant the boarding school at sixteen and a half; and for Lady Landamere's excessive drinking, which Katie got to witness during her vacations from school.

And the psychiatrist the school recommended she see. That's a lot of blame.

She knew all the answers from her therapy, and she knew as well that forgiveness was hers alone to give but she withheld it, tenaciously, as though her very identity depended on it.

Through the years she and her mother tried to get along but Trace would just have to say one wrong thing, and it would trigger all of Katie's old anger. Anger that lay dormant for twenty-five years. So when it started to finally come out, it came in an unending flow.

It was during the six weeks in 1980 that Katie stayed at Rebecca's house in Beverly Hills that she took a course called The Technology of Change. It changed her life.

Basically the doctor who gave this course said that if someone you know is "toxic" (polluting the air you breathe), he has to be eliminated from your life. He said your survival depended on it. Three young guys in the back of the lecture room were wearing buttons that read "Toxicity Kills!" The doctor said that whether it was a friend, a lover, an employer, a brother, a sister, or even a parent or child, if they were toxic they were endangering your life. He gave a very lengthy criteria by which one could determine who in their lives were toxic, and when Katie completed her homework assignment, there was Trace at the top of her list. What to do?

She went to Trace and asked her if she would come and see this Dr. Lawrence with her, since, he said, people who were open to changing their behavior were not truly toxic. They showed they could change. She asked her mother if they could sit down with Dr. Lawrence and try to find a way to eliminate some of the toxicity from their relationship.

Lady Landamere found the whole thing one of the most ridiculous theories she'd heard in her entire life. She said she wasn't the least bit surprised that this guy found an audience in California. "Next you'll be wanting me to go to Moonie meetings. Absolutely not. We are who we are and we love each other in spite of and because of it."

Well, her refusal to explore their problems only reinforced Katie's definition of who really was toxic. Dr. Lawrence had said that the truly toxic would display resistance to change of any kind. He said they would refuse to talk over any existing problems. So far Trace was behaving exactly as he said the toxic person would behave, true to every definition. This, as you can see, left Katie with no choice. She was forced to tell her mother that until they could sit down and dig into their relationship and redefine it, there could be no relationship at all.

It was also true that through the years Katie could not stand to watch her mother's self-destructiveness. Her smoking. The disregard for her health. It made Katie totally uncomfortable when she was around her. Probably the real fear was that if that's how self-destructive her mother was, why would she be any different. When she was around her mother, she would find herself falling into her identity. She became the canary and Trace the cat; and all too soon she would disappear.

And so she decided, and it was decreed, on December eighth, nineteen hundred and eighty, all contact between mother and daughter would cease and desist. Lady Landamere was to have said at the time, "I am absolutely certain that you have now gone quite crazy. How lucky for both of us that you were not in Jonestown, for you surely would have drank the Kool-Aid."

Katie answered that, to the contrary, she was "becoming sane. A very frightening thought to the toxic individual."

For Katie any chance for a reconciliation officially ended five months later when Lord Edwin died in London, leaving behind him along with his dubious title, the controlling interest in what was becoming a large ice cream factory in Milan. It made a type of dessert called gelato, and Lady Landamere had absolutely no interest in overseeing this questionable business. Her advisors told her that franchised, this could produce a lucrative income for her. They needed her decision on what she wanted to do with what was now her controlling shares of the company. Lord Edwin had no children, and Lady Landamere made her decision without consulting her own.

She decided that the last thing Katie needed, what with her chronic weight problem, was to inherit an ice cream factory. Besides, Katie was a writer. Therefore, why in the world would she be interested in Rum Raisin Gelato. So she kept a twenty-five percent interest for herself and gave the controlling shares of the company to Richard. Just like that.

Within one year Richard had overseen the franchising of sixty gelato cream parlors throughout London, Paris, Italy, and the United States. Gelato had surpassed frozen custard or frozen yogurt as the new dessert. The company grossed fifty million dollars in 1984, and of this Katie was not to see one dime or one lousy pint of Rum Raisin Gelato.

Toxic! Toxic! Toxic!


Lady Landamere had a very different story. First of all, she is quick to point out, "My daughter, like most writers, has a very active imagination. Now she has seen fit to invent a past that suits her remembrance of how things were and that has nothing at all to do with how they really were."

To this Katie answers, "I cannot invent the fact that my mother was and is still crazy." But this is Lady Landamere's side of things.

Lady Landamere begins by saying, "If her father had lived it would have all been different." And that is probably true.

There was no one like Austin Marcus. Oh, perhaps if a comparison had to be made, he might be spoken of similarly to P. T. Barnum. Born in Texas in 1909, he worked in the oil fields for his uncle until he was nineteen. When his uncle died in the late 1920s, he left his unimpressive seventy-two acre ranch to Austin to develop if he so chose or to sell and use the money as he saw fit. Austin did neither. Instead, he traded the ranch for a hundred-and-fifty-acre piece of land thirty miles south of Houston that was considered by most to be an area that would never be much more than worthless. Three years later, Austin found a sudden interest developing in his property. The government offered to buy it and so did Getty Oil.

They offered him so much more than its supposed worth that Austin knew it was time to begin some serious drilling. The rest is history.

Ten years, and some twenty million dollars later, Austin Marcus had become one of the wealthiest land developers in America and one of Texas's most eligible bachelors. It's anyone's guess how long he might have remained in his enviable position had he not been asked to judge the Miss Texas Pageant in Houston in March of 1946.

Trace Cambell was the most beautiful girl Austin Marcus had ever seen. She was statuesque, long legged, and blond, with a special quality that could light up all of downtown Dallas in a blackout.

It was one of those courtships girls dream about, and women read about in magazines while waiting at supermarket checkouts all over the country. He sent dozens of roses weekly. Then he found out that Trace hated roses. ("Particularly red, they're so unoriginal.") So he sent orchids and lilies. And he sent champagne and caviar and diamond baubles, but in truth, he needn't have sent anything at all, because Trace was madly in love with Austin from the first evening they spent together. She had just learned from her mama that "the longer you play hard to get, the more men think you're worth the getting." This was the same woman who said, "Why buy the cow when you can get the milk for free?" Trace's mother was a fountain of such feminine advice. Had she lived her life in modern times she probably would have been Helen Gurley Brown.

It was one of the biggest weddings Texas had seen in years. Five hundred and forty guests. Austin, known for his extravagant gestures, spared no expense to make this the wedding of the decade. Although he was fifteen years Trace's senior, they were every bit the beautiful couple. They were the pair atop the wedding cake, and they lived their life like the enchanted couple they were born to be.

Austin wanted a baby with the same immediacy that he wanted Trace and there is nobody who can tell you of a time when Austin failed in getting whatever he desired. So it was expected that Trace and Austin Marcus were delighted to announce, exactly nine and one-half months following their June wedding, the birth of their first child, Katherine Marabella Marcus. Trace hated the Marabella part, but she knew how much Austin wanted to honor the memory of his mother so she acquiesced figuring a middle name had about as much importance as one wanted to give it. She had already decided to give this one none.

Little Katie instantly became the light of her father's life. The lilies and orchids that used to arrive for Trace were nothing compared with the stuffed teddy bears, gold bassinets, and dolls that cried real tears that paraded steadily through the pink and white nursery suite that occupied the whole third floor of the mansion on State Street.

For almost a year Trace was used to being the center of attention of her husband's life and suddenly things had changed. A change that did not please the new bride one bit. She also complained to Mrs. Finley, the first nanny, that she wasn't being allowed to develop her own connection to her new daughter because Austin was always there first. This whole business of motherhood was not as much fun as she imagined it would be, but she didn't dare tell anyone that.

Those were not nice thoughts to have, but she was at her happiest when she and Austin would go away alone, together. Then her life was most like she imagined it would be. Austin loved to take Trace with him when he traveled so basically there was little to fret about. They had many happy times.

They were in New Orleans when it occurred. It was a little before midnight when Trace announced to her husband that she was famished. Austin loved Trace's excessive appetite just as he loved all her excesses and room service at their hotel had closed at eleven. Although Trace protested, Austin insisted on popping out to the all-night bakery in the French Quarter to fetch his bride some beignets and coffee. He kissed her on her forehead as she lay in bed reading Colette, in a pink satin peignoir (she chose her books, like her clothing, by locale). As it turned out, there were to be no more kisses and no more beignets.

By three A.M. Trace had alerted the police that Austin was missing and within an hour and a half, the chief of police was at her hotel, reporting the tragic details to her.

The taxi Austin had hailed was hit by an inebriated driver in an old pickup truck, causing it to crash through a guardrail and into the Mississippi River.

Of course, he left everything to Trace and Katie.

And that was the next shock. What he had was very little. All of the millions were lost in bad real estate deals. The bank held title to most of his land. Always an optimist, he had never wanted to burden his beautiful bride with all the intricacies of his business dealings and being a gambler at heart, he believed it was just a matter of another toss of the coin to turn his momentary adversity around again.

Trace had very few coins left to toss. What she still had was the mansion and enough money to keep up appearances for a year or two. So it was up to Trace to make the most of her assets in the shortest amount of time.

So you see, it would have all been very different had Austin lived. Lady Landamere always started her version of what happened with that statement.

Then the stories changed. As far as Katie's weight, God knows she tried everything. And yes, it was true that she would have preferred a daughter who was less fat, one who could wear pretty clothes like she could never afford to wear when she was growing up. She just couldn't understand what was wrong with Katie. What she never admitted was that she viewed Katie's problem as a reflection of her role as a mother.

What she did say about the whole weight issue was she hated to see her daughter missing out on the fun of being thin.

She said she hated to watch Katie return from camp with that awful rash between her thighs because they rubbed together in the heat. She said she hated to see Katie not going to the beach with her friends because she was ashamed to let them see her in a bathing suit. She said she hated it because Katie hated it. She said she never would have gone to the lengths she did to try and control the problem if Katie weren't so humiliated by it. Katie never admitted hating being fat just as Trace never discussed that in former years she herself used to take diet pills to control her then perfect size ten figure.

As to her frequent absences, she would say, she was only away trying to find a better life for her little daughter. The next part of her tale altered depending upon whom she was relating it to.

Today she wasn't relating it to anyone. At least not this morning. She was rushing to pick up Fred at Bowser Boutique in time to make her one o'clock flight from LAX to Kennedy. Lady Landamere liked to have at least three-quarters of an hour before a flight, unlike her daughter who, she said, never seemed to leave more than five minutes to spare before she boarded each plane in total chaos.

Lady Landamere wound up getting to the airport with time to spare. Fred, who was now semi-asleep in a traveling kennel, was placed directly under her first class seat. One of the stewardess's aboard the Pan Am 747 remembered Lady Landamere from a flight earlier in the year. Actually, anyone on that previous Flight No. 7 would have remembered her. They had just begun selling the upstairs lounge seats as additional first class seating. Trace was supposed to be seated in Smoking and by some error she was seated in

Non-Smoking and no one wanted to switch seats with her, and the upstairs was completely booked.

Lady Landamere had to go into coach to smoke her cigarettes. She was so annoyed at Pan Am's carelessness that, like a female Robin Hood, every time she walked into the back of the plane to light up one of her cigarettes she brought "gifts" from the first class cabin to the coach passengers. Plates of caviar. Bottles of brandies. After-dinner mints.

Somewhere over Pittsburgh, tired of her constant parade through the plane, she settled herself in the first class lavatory with her Marlboros and a book she was reading on the life of Sir Laurence Olivier. She probably would have stayed in there indefinitely. The light was good. No one was bothering her, and she was busily smoking away despite the red light that spelled out "No Smoking." She was actually comfortable for the first time since the plane left Los Angeles, when her cigarette fell out of the ashtray onto the floor and Lady Landamere couldn't find it. And she couldn't seem to open the door. The last thing she wanted to do was to panic, but the door was definitely jammed and the little lavatory was getting quite smokey. One of the stewardess's heard her calling for help at the same time as two of the passengers noticed there was a trail of smoke coming out from under the door. Quite a commotion ensued culminating with the door being forced open by one of the male flight attendants with a great big wrench.

Lady Landamere gathered herself together, apologized for the concern she may have caused, and on exiting the lavatory advised all the Pan Am employees around her to keep their aircraft in better working order or on her next flight she would do her smoking in TWA's bathrooms. No one even reprimanded her. She had a unique way of making wrong right.

The stewardess who had recognized her said, "Hello, I see you're still smoking."

Lady Landamere replied, "Better me than the airplane, don't you agree?"

And that was the end of their conversation.

Soon after takeoff Lady Landamere ordered a cup of coffee, black, no sugar, and fed half of her roasted almonds to Fred, who was now a little less sleepy. She looked down and told him, "These are much too salty for either one of us so I shall split them with you and get you some water and me a glass of wine." She peeked in his little kennel and said, "Sorry about your accommodations, Fred, but I was not about to buy you your own seat."

The gentleman sitting on Lady Landamere's left was trying to decide whether she would have had this same conversation with her dog were he not seated next to her to overhear it.

"Does he ever answer you?" he asked.

"Of course not. He just serves as a perfect reason for a handsome young man such as yourself to want to chat with me."

That made sense. He was a terribly attractive man, somewhere in his mid-forties. Lady Landamere found out within the first three minutes of conversation, he was a television producer, he lived in Bel Air, and he was single. She immediately popped right into one of her favorite roles, that of Dolly Levi. She offered to find him the perfect woman. She then went on to tell him about Katie.

"Actually you quite suit my daughter. I wonder if she's still living with Peter?" adding that she herself would not exactly call that living.

The television producer was surprised that Trace wouldn't know whom her daughter was living with. Trace replied that there was much about her and her daughter he would find surprising and that if he should not be fortunate enough to enjoy Katie's company through the social ritual known as "dating," he could read Katie's books or he could learn more about them both when her own memoirs were published.

Curious, he asked, "And when might that be?"

"Either before or after my death," she answered.

"I don't understand," he said. "Have you not decided when you want to publish your memoirs?"

"No, rather I have not decided when to die. I like to think we all have some choice in these things."

With that the "Fasten Seatbelt" sign lit up. The captain announced that they would be experiencing some moderate turbulence due to a storm system three miles south of Chicago. A baby started crying. Lady Landamere's coffee spilled on the television producer's script and she said, "Oh, well, if this turbulence gets any worse your script might be found with the flight recorder." It all seemed reminiscent to her of that foolish little movie *Airport*.

"Of course, if our plane were to go down now," she continued, "the coffee wouldn't make much difference and we hardly would have exercised any free will about when we chose to die, would we? Except perhaps existentially speaking."

She watched as the television producer reached into his briefcase for a small pill bottle. She saw him take a yellow tablet out of the bottle and swallow it with a big gulp of his wine.

"Is the Valium for the turbulence or for me?"

He swallowed his pill and put his headphones on and either watched or pretended to watch the end of the movie in flight. As for Lady Landamere she looked down at Fred's cardboard kennel. She opened the lid. She gave him a little pat on his head and told him, "Much too weak for Katie. He'd never have survived 'Live Television.'"

They never spoke again until the plane landed safely in New York's Kennedy Airport. Fred, looking rested and wearing his winter coat, followed Lady Landamere out of the first class cabin. She smiled at her anonymous producer, only to bid him her famous, "Ta-ta!"

## Chapter

5

*R*ichard and Ellen knew that Trace was in New York. They had called her in California and were told she was reachable at the Sherry-Netherland.

They were nervous. Not a new feeling to either one of them. Ellen grew up nervous, like some people grow up smart or pretty, and Richard in some areas didn't grow up, period.

When it came to business Richard, however, could give anyone a run for his money. A graduate of the Harvard Business School, he did his alma mater proud. He did n't need a pocket calculator or an IBM computer; he was a computer, and a calculating one at that. Richard knew figures and he knew how to make money. He always had a knack for making money.

When he was nine, he set up a lemonade concession between the tennis court and the front door at the house in Bel Air and anyone coming on or off the court, thirsty or not, was forced to purchase a cup of Richard's Home-made Lemonade. He had Zella prepare an extra gallon on Sundays, when Jack and Trace would have their weekly tennis parties. He posted a big sign that said "All Proceeds to Charity," but he hadn't the slightest intention of parting with a dime of his profits. On one hot Sunday afternoon he spotted Zella drinking a tall glass of her own lemonade and insisted she pay the fifty cents like everyone else. Trace found the money stashed in Richard's room and put it all in a gray flannel bag and accompanied Richard to the main office of the Red Cross where she made him donate every last quarter. Richard wanted to kill Trace for that, but the following Sunday it was back to business, except now the sign over his stand read, "Half of All Proceeds to Charity."

When he was twelve he charged Billy Crawford (no relation to Joan), who lived in the mansion across the street, one dollar to spy on his sixteen-year-old sister while she was getting undressed. Billy didn't want to pay the whole dollar because he said she was fat, but a deal was deal.

The following week, Billy offered Richard the opportunity, for the same dollar, to spy on his seventeen-year-old sister, who, he said, the guys all "die over." Richard said he didn't feel like "dying," and he could look at his own sister, for free.

He met Ellen soon after he moved to Houston after graduating Harvard. He says he moved to Houston because it showed the most upward mobility of all the "new cities" and he wanted to be in the place that had the greatest chance for economic development. He quickly went into land development. In some ways he preferred the more mythical stories he grew up hearing about Austin Marcus than the life he witnessed, belonging to his famous father. Richard didn't want to make movies. He didn't see pictures in his head. He saw numbers and figures.

Ellen had a nice figure. He noticed that when he first met her at a social gathering hosted by a mutual friend. Growing up around "ballbusters" like Trace and Katie, there was something real wholesome and appealing about this quiet girl from Dallas who told him over and over he was the smartest man she'd ever met. She was twenty-three at the time, and in Dallas if you're still unmarried at twenty-three, you are moving rapidly into a dangerous age category. So Ellen most definitely wanted to get married, even more than she wanted to get married to Richard, and she very much wanted to marry Richard. He had potential and he already had a nice condo in the city. She took Richard home to meet her parents. They were impressed, though they never said by what, and Richard took Ellen to London to meet Trace. Trace was not impressed, but there was nothing to be done about it. They were obviously a fait accompli.

They were well suited. Richard was thin, except for his little pot belly. Ellen was thin, too, but it didn't help her all that much. She had one of those faces that once you saw, you immediately forgot. It wasn't that she didn't leave a lasting impression. It was as though she never made one in the first place. She had plain brown hair, and it was thick and shiny. Many said it was her best feature. That in itself was unfortunate. She was about five feet four or five feet five inches tall. Even if described in perfect detail, you'd still never find her in a crowd. None of the above could have made her too happy, but no one knew what made her so nervous.

Trace had once told Richard, in her opinion Ellen suffered from being "ordinary." Somewhere during this very same conversation it occurred to her she was "barking up the wrong tree" for it was at that very instant she realized her son suffered from the same aforementioned malady. What was worse, Trace knew of no cure. She talked it over with herself and decided there might be some wisdom in the old, slightly revised saying: "Two fairly ordinary souls were better than one." And so she decided on June fifteenth, nineteen hundred and seventy-nine (a June wedding being as predictable as the bride and groom) Trace would make a beautifully ordinary wedding for her son and daughter-in-law to-be.

And it was just that. She extended invitations to as many of Jack's family as she could remember and whoever cared to, came. As a whole they were a pretty boring group so those that attended fit in rather well. Trace was certain Richard took after Jack's side of the family. Only Jack had elevated himself above his genes. "The one that got away from the fold," he used to say when asked about his youth, growing up in Chicago.

Richard and Ellen had all their friends in attendance. It is amazingly true how "water seeks its own level" since the mind could not imagine a more homogeneously bland group of young adults.

There was never much hope for a great sister and brother relationship between Katie and Richard. Aside from the very real sibling rivalry that exists in any family, the truth was the presence of each made the other too uncomfortable. The differences between them were too extreme.

Richard worked hard all week from nine to six (he was always proud of the extra hour). He had already developed part of a new shopping mall, B.G. (Before Gelato). They belonged to the appropriately named Middleberry Country Club, right in the middle of

town. Richard didn't smoke or drink (Ellen drank "just the eeni-
est bit" of wine), and when Joshua was born, Richard handed out
cans of Wilson tennis balls. They made a point of having sex
approximately once a month, usually after "Dynasty." This enabled Richard to fantasize about Linda Evans. Ellen didn't dare
*admit* to any fantasizing. She might have an orgasm, become less
boring, and then she might leave Richard, and it would all be too
much of a mess.

Now they were united in their obsession about Trace and their
fear of her reunion with Katie. Nowhere does it say boring means
dumb. Always proficient in mathematics, he and Ellen both knew
the simple numerical axiom: With Katie in the pie they got less.

"Ellen! Where are you?" Richard called from their big bedroom
at the end of the hall.

Richard was trying to decide which of three gray ties he liked
better with the gray pinstripe suit he was wearing for his luncheon
meeting with the president of First Central National of Houston.
He was planning to close a five-hundred-thousand-dollar deal
today, and he was looking for the appropriate tie for such an
occasion. "Ellen, I need you to look and tell me which of these ties
looks better?"

The bottom line was they all looked identical, but Ellen would
never say that. She was squinting her eyes and staring, trying to
decide. Joshua, who had just turned five but was regretfully no less
likable now than he was at four, was also in the room, throwing
Q-tips at his father and getting no response.

"Ellen, I don't want you to leave this house today until you talk
to Trace." This was Richard at his most assertive.

"Richard," she answered, spacing her words evenly, with an
extremely annoying monotone effect to her voice, "it just so happens that I wasn't going anywhere today, anyway. Mary Jane is up

in Dallas and Janice and Hillary have their nouvelle cuisine cooking class today, and . . ."

It was more than he ever wanted to know. He interrupted her in self-defense. "If you can't reach her leave a message. Tell her to call us tonight. Anytime."

He had picked tie number two, or maybe it was number one, and he appeared pleased.

Harris, the chauffeur and sometimes bartender, came in to tell Richard he was back from putting gas in the family car. (A 1983 Rolls Royce, with a license plate that read JOSHUA. Ellen told Richard she was worried that those kinds of gestures would spoil their son. Richard answered, "What should I do, drive a Pinto, or do you want me to put some other kid's name on our license plate?")

This clever bantering of theirs could continue for hours. It loses something in the repetition.

"I sure hope she doesn't call at two A.M. like the last time," Ellen said nervously.

"Me, too. But if she does, we'll just have to cope. This is important stuff, Mollybeeb."

Ever since Joshua was born, Richard took to calling his wife, "Mollybeeb," and she has never, to this day, asked why.

Joshua was back in the bedroom. He was eating a Strawberry Daiquiri Gelato cone. (Ellen had some concern that it might teach him to like the taste of liquor.) He ran to his daddy and pushed the remainder of his cone right square in the center of his daddy's gray tie.

"Bull's eye!" said Joshua laughing wildly.

"That's not a nice thing to do to Daddy's tie," said Ellen. The truth was that underneath it all she was rather proud of her little boy's aggressiveness. She could have never done a thing like that at five years old. In fact she could never do it, period.

"That's not a nice thing to do to Daddy's tie," repeated Richard. Then he took the remainder of the gelato cone and squished it smack in the middle of Joshua's face, landing it right in the center of his nose where it dripped furiously down his face and onto his clothing. Joshua ran from the bedroom crying hysterically.

To an outsider's eye the possibility existed that Joshua might be showing the beginnings of some real artistic talent. There was no doubt the tie definitely looked better with the pink gelato on it. It was less boring.

Richard changed ties and left for his meeting. Joshua changed T-shirts and left in a huff for the playground. Ellen never changed. If she did, no one would have noticed. She did switch books. She put down *The Ten Minute Gardener,* which Richard had given her for Christmas, and picked up the book her girlfriend had given her, *The Cinderella Complex.* She was only up to chapter two since she felt guilty reading it in front of Richard. He believed all those women's books were the same. He said most of them were written by unhappy, ugly "dykes." Ellen wondered if he was including his sister in his theory.

Anyway, between the two books and the needlepoint pillow she was trying to finish by Richard's birthday (it was one she personally designed that read "RICH, RICHER, RICHARD" in big blue letters), Richard found her sitting in the same chair he had left her in when he returned home at seven-fifteen in the evening.

Obediently she was right next to the phone, and Trace had still not called.

## Chapter

### 6

$\mathscr{R}$ebecca Holmes was speaking with the manager behind the
desk at the Sherry-Netherland. In her attempt to go unrecognized
there was not one person who didn't stop to stare at her. She was
in her Garboesque disguise. She was draped in so much black mink
fur, including a ten foot scarf and matching hood, that although you
might see her and ask, "What becomes a Legend most?" you would
never know which Legend she was since she was barely visible,

hidden by tons upon tons of fur. Big black sunglasses covered her famous blue eyes and big black boots and stockings covered her not so famous, but attractive legs. One thing was clear. For someone trying to look anonymous she most certainly looked like a star, which served to make people curious as to who she was, thereby defeating her own purpose.

She had refused to do those Blackglama print ads for the last six years. It wasn't that she didn't like the list of people who'd already done them; she just liked not having done it more. Though when last approached, she had said if Blackglama would meet her requests, she would join the ever growing list of Legends endorsing their sumptuous fur.

Payment was the same for everyone; from Sophia to Elizabeth to Liza (part of being a Legend is that you can usually be identified by only one name). Each was given a full-length ranch mink coat for the right of reproducing her photograph as part of the Black-glama campaign.

Rebecca liked all of her business deals to be at very least "precedential" so she had said she would agree to being photographed but the coat had to be sable. To the floor. It wasn't the one-hundred-thousand-dollar difference that the advertisers voiced concern over. Reportedly, it was the favored-nation clause Blackglama used with all their Legends. How could they break precedent now? Rebecca was reported to have replied, "So I won't be a Legend this year. One of these days they'll either run out of Legends or they'll change their campaign. How many of us do they think there are?" She said in her opinion they had already started to cheat when they asked Martina Navratilova. She figured the whole thing meant much more to the furriers' association then it did to her so she could afford to wait. It wasn't as though she was freezing out in the cold as she stood at the increasingly warm front desk, looking like an extra from *Doctor Zhivago*.

All of her fur was causing her to break into a slight sweat when she saw Trace and Fred come sweeping into the small well-appointed lobby.

"What a delightfully perfect coincidence," said Lady Landamere as she floated past the manager and the deskmen to embrace Rebecca. "How absolutely perfect."

Rebecca was equally happy to see Trace. She was always surprised by how much real affection she had for her best friend's mother. She used to wish her own mother had some of Trace's flair and savvy.

Lady Landamere insisted they have a quick drink in the Sherry bar, while the hotel registered her and brought her luggage up to her suite.

"My dear Rebecca," Trace said, "you look simply wonderful."

Rebecca always loved to hear she looked wonderful, but she seemed surprised and said, "How would you know that? You're not supposed to be able to recognize me. I'm incognito."

"And very successful indeed," answered Lady Landamere. "But you'd be surprised how much I can see with my X-ray vision. Just the hug was enough to tell me you've taken off six or seven pounds since I've seen you last. Marvelous costume, my sweet. Great style. Very creative in a Garboesque kind of way."

Rebecca was glad Lady Landamere appreciated her sense of fashion. She knew what a great eye Lady Landamere possessed. Both women paid enormous attention to details. She remembered Trace telling her years ago, "True greatness lies in the details."

Trace handed Fred over to Rebecca and said, "Be a darling and just sneak Fred under all that fur of yours. Even if anyone were to notice him, which I assure you they won't, he'll look like a part of your coat."

An expected buzz went through the cocktail lounge as the two women were seated at a small round table in the back of the room. Rebecca explained to Trace that she was supposed to be at the theater, but she had gotten nervous at the last minute about the crowds. And then she said she heard they didn't seat anyone for the first twenty minutes of act one, so she told her friend to pick her up at nine o'clock and she would decide then whether it made sense to try and see act two. She wanted to know if Trace thought that would look funny or if the cast would find out she came in late, and she was concerned about which was worse, "coming in in the middle or not showing up at all?" Rebecca was the queen of the run-on sentence. It was part of her style. She asked Trace what she thought she should do. Trace said she certainly shouldn't waste her time vacillating about such trivia. "Don't sweat the small stuff. Save it for what's really important. That's my new philosophy."

Rebecca was drinking a Perrier with lime when the waiter returned and placed a menu in front of her and a pen in her hand and asked for her autograph. He said she was his very favorite. Unfortunately for the young fan, Fred once had a very nasty experience with a bartender at one of Lady Landamere's infrequent dinner parties. It seems the elegant bartender had a sadistic bent and enjoyed dropping ice cubes on Fred's little head whenever no one was looking. Since that fateful night, whenever Fred spots a male hand attached to a tuxedoed sleeve (particularly one holding a drink), Fred, the mildest of mannered dogs by nature, loses all his innate sensibility and becomes a full-fledged "killer."

It was over in less than a second, but the waiter did let out a scream and his index finger was dripping blood. Lady Landamere quickly tied her napkin around the wounded finger and said calmly, "We won't mention that an employee of this establishment foolishly intruded upon Miss Holmes's privacy, and I'm sure you won't mention the overprotective behavior of her loyal watch dog."

"Here," Rebecca said, returning the autographed menu to the waiter.

"Sorry," she said. "He's had all his shots." She ordered another Perrier since hers had overturned during the "Great Attack."

The waiter, holding the napkin tightly around his bloody finger, kept apologizing to Rebecca and Trace for his terrible behavior and hurried off to bring his movie queen another Perrier.

"Stardom does have certain rewards, don't you think?" Trace said. They both laughed.

Trace lit up another Marlboro and suggested Rebecca order a double martini and stop keeping such tight rein on herself.

"They'll probably discover in a year or two that Perrier causes cancer. I tell you, my friend, it will be a great mistake if you wait until you become my age to wish you had let go more in your life. You've certainly taken chances in your career but you live the rest of your life like some . . . old lady."

"What rest of my life? The rest of my life hardly exists," she answered.

Speaking of life reminded Rebecca for the first time of what Katie had told her. "I saw Katie yesterday," she continued, "and she told me you were coming in and that she had spoken to you . . . and . . ."

Lady Landamere interrupted her, "Yes. I'm sure she did. I imagine you're still her best friend so I assume you still tell each other everything."

"Yeah. I guess so," Rebecca said.

"That's because you're both too self-obsessed to cultivate any new friends, if you get my drift. Relationships, friendships notwithstanding, take a great deal of effort and giving. In the end, most people quite honestly turn out not to be worth it." She paused. "But a few are."

Rebecca listened and then said, in what appeared to be one single thought, "You know I think it would get back to the cast if they heard I walked in at the intermission. I really think I'm probably better off not going. You know, Trace, you don't look like you're so sick?"

"How sick am I supposed to be?" Trace asked with what appeared to be a playful smile.

"Oh, very sick," Rebecca answered.

"Well, that remains to be seen," Lady Landamere answered. "Right now I want to see my daughter and settle a few of our past disagreements and you can help me, beautiful superstar."

"How?" Rebecca asked.

"Well, tomorrow Katie and I will lunch as planned. Hopefully all will go smoothly. That is my intention." She lit another cigarette. "In the evening I must leave for Boston through Tuesday evening, but on the following Friday, that's a week from tomorrow, I would like you to throw a little dinner party in my honor. Say, ten people. I can't think of anyone better than you to draw all the necessary R.S.V.P.'s"

"Sure, Trace," Rebecca responded. "I'd love to. Will anyone I know be there?"

"Oh, most definitely. I'll write out the guest list and the phone numbers and you can have whoever make the necessary calls. I'll just leave it at the desk for you, my precious."

"Leave it under the name of Miss Joyce," she whispered. "That's how I'm registered."

"Not terribly original but I'm sure it serves your purpose," Lady

Landamere noted. "You always had an appreciation of intrigue, didn't you?"

"Absolutely. And knowing you, you must have something more than a little dinner party in mind. Any hints?" Rebecca asked.

"Suffice to say you'll love it!" Trace answered. "Lot's of high drama. Shall we say *Dinner at Eight* or *Guess Who's Coming to Dinner?*"

Trace was pleased. She prepared a cracker with a little guacamole on it and slipped it to Fred who blended so perfectly with Rebecca's coat that she almost fed the cracker to Rebecca's black leather button thinking it was Fred's mouth. Fred popped his little pink tongue out of another black button hole to alert Lady Landamere to the fact that she had missed her mark. With the error now corrected he partook of a little guacamole.

A bellman came in to announce to Rebecca that her friend was waiting outside in a limousine. Lady Landamere remarked that the timing was perfect and not to worry about missing tonight's play because the greater theater would take place next Friday.

"By the way," she asked, "who is the friend in the limousine? Anyone amusing?"

"Unfortunately, only to himself," Rebecca answered, and with that she was off. Seconds later she was back. "For God's sake, Trace, your maternal instincts seem to be a bit rusty. You forgot to take your spoiled dog."

"Nonsense. Why should I deprive him of an evening with Rebecca Holmes. He's with me all the time. Kisses and ta-ta."

## Chapter

### 7

Katie was supposed to have been at the theater tonight, too. She and Peter had tickets to see Sondheim's new musical but she knew his shows required concentration, particularly this new one, and her mind was on Trace. Peter understood. That was the thing about Peter. He was very understanding. Of course it was his business to be very understanding, but still. . . . He had asked Katie if she wanted him to sleep over, and she had said she thought she'd rather be alone. And that was the way she was feeling, very much alone as she got ready for bed.

Tomorrow's lunch was long overdue. She glanced over at the back of January's *Vogue,* and saw the Virginia Slims ad with its famous slogan, "You've Come a Long Way Baby." The beautiful blond in the photo seemed to be staring up at her. Katie smiled and, looking at the ad, thought to herself, Yes, I really have. I did better than she did. She's still smoking!

That was something Trace might have said. She reminded herself of her mother, and she said out loud, "I haven't even seen her and I'm acting like her."

Did she just talk to herself out loud? Oh no! Trace talked out loud to herself, not Katie.

Trace talked and then she talked some more. She was always talking. Whenever Katie tried to tell her a story, she talked over it. Katie wondered if a lot of writers wrote because their mothers or fathers weren't interested in what they had to say.

Trace talked all the time. She said mean things and funny things and nice things and angry things. She talked to Katie and/or Jack or Richard. And when she was alone she talked to herself. Half of the time that she was talking to her family, Zella included, she was really talking to herself anyway. At a certain point in time everyone would stop listening. Trace's famous voice would become a background drone. Katie was particularly good at being able to tune her out.

It didn't seem to matter to Trace whether anyone listened or not. She continued to talk to herself because she quite simply liked to hear herself talk. When no one was in the house she talked to Hocus. Hocus was the Fred of the 1950s.

Katie remembered how Hocus used to have this unique habit of

scratching his ears a lot and rubbing them on the carpet at a furious tempo (a condition commonly known in veterinary circles as
fleas) and how Jack would laughingly say, "Trace is 'talking'
Hocus crazy again." Katie believed that Trace's love of dogs was
born out of her instinctive knowledge that, more than people,
dogs made the best listeners. They also made her appear less crazy
to the world around her and despite what she said, Trace did care
what people thought.

Katie's thoughts were decades away from Hocus when she
walked into the kitchen to get a glass of water. She was preparing
for bed. She always got a glass of water before she went to bed. It
sat on her night table to the left of her bed, even if she didn't drink
it. It was just one of those habits that sneakily cross over the
imaginary border and suddenly become rituals. When Peter slept
over she'd get two glasses of water. He happened to share the same
ritual.

Her friend Eileen Sussman (the famous one) had done a great
three-parter on sleep for *New York* magazine. The second part was
Katie's favorite. It was called "Sleeping Pills and Other Ills (Or Are
You Sure You Set the Alarm!)." Besides being a very well-written
piece, it made Katie feel better to learn how many other late night
neurotics were out there tossing and turning on their sleep machines
or plugging up their ears before they "called it a night."

She filled up the water glass and was leaving the kitchen when
she felt herself being taken over like in all those B horror movies
by a powerful alien force inhabiting her body and moving her
toward the refrigerator. The hand that seconds ago was attached to
her arm and belonged to her was now independently opening the
freezer door.

It was time to summon all her forces. Okay, Katie, she thought.

You can close that door now. That's your hand! You can take control of it.

But I'm so hungry. Just one bite!

Who said that? Who was she now? Who was that little child talking to that mean disciplinarian?

How delightful, she thought. Here she was becoming Sybil right before her very eyes, just in time for her thirty-fifth birthday.

"Leave the kitchen," urged the Voice of Reason.

"But the ice cream," said the Hungry Little Girl.

Ice cream! How did ice cream get in the house? Oh, yes. The Cookie Monster. Peter and his cookie ice cream. Why wasn't he there when she needed him, she thought. Trace talked. Katie thought.

Don't eat the ice cream. Dairy is bad. It clogs the arteries!

Katie believed that after enough time people who ate a lot of beef and dairy began resembling cows. Luckily, this was not a theory she incorporated in either of her books.

She tasted the ice cream. And when that failed to do the trick, she thought, What else can I eat? She was clearly veering out of control.

The war was on. Katie told herself that one little snack was not worth doing battle over. Besides there was always the old compromise solution. She could always find something that would fit into her paper cup. Something that would make for good chew food.

She fixed her hungry eyes (eyes that had looked at a plate of dinner only two hours ago) on a piece of frozen carrot cake purchased from the Natural Gourmet (no sugar, no salt, no white flour, No Taste!) and she thought to herself, Whoever said "You can't have your cake and eat it too" obviously hadn't discovered "The Chew Food Diet."

It's just that Katie hadn't been playing that game too much lately, and she always liked herself better when she wasn't engaging in what she personally knew to be pretty compulsive behavior. She looked at the kitchen clock. It was just five minutes before her official Birthday. Thirty-five.

Thirty-five.

"It's my birthday. What's a little paper cup full of carrot cake going to do anyway, on this, the very birthday researchers the world over refer to as the Year of the Female Mid-life Crisis.

Katie was now in deep negotiation with herself. She knew how overly dramatic she was being. She could have some real addictions. She could be a cocaine user (it never even took her appetite away!). She could easily be addicted to amphetamines (made her much too "speedy!") or a heroin addict ("Please! I'd rather die").

How did she get to be so hard on herself? What was so wrong with two little paper cups and a plastic spoon? Chew it. You get the taste. Spit it out and throw away the evidence. You don't gain a pound or wash a dish. She wasn't crazy. She was damn clever.

Well, good, so much for that. So much time spent on garbage. Eat it! Don't eat it. Just let's get on with it! She could have written The Great American Novel (well at least a diet book) just in the time in her life spent obsessing about food. Who really cared?

I think too much, she thought.

Peter's right. No wonder he's not here tonight. Katie was not about to leave herself alone. He probably was relieved when she said she'd rather be alone. He probably didn't feel like being probed like a rack of lamb. Thinking and analyzing. There were the doers and the thinkers. He was probably out doing something.

And there were the eaters. The doers, the thinkers, and the eaters, she thought as she continued to think about eating. How boring! Peter was a doer. He was probably out getting laid. Some pretty dumb blond with big tits whose vocabulary consists of two words, "Let's dance."

No! Basically Katie trusted Peter. Just occasionally she used her time to indulge in the ever-popular sport known as self-torture.

Enough! Halt! She called for a truce. Out of the kitchen and safe at last in the bedroom, she realized it was safer to obsess about food then really face up to what she felt about seeing Trace. And if Trace was really dying, playing with paper cups helped to diffuse Katie's overwhelming feelings of aloneness and sadness.

Finally in bed, it was now time for a little Dalmane to assure a good night's sleep.

"Drug addict," she said to herself accusingly.

So far, thirty-five was not shaping up as the "kindest" of ages.


She was awakened by the doorbell. If she didn't know she was awake she might have thought that she was in the middle of some Felliniesque dream because at the door stood a Dolly Parton look-alike next to a Ronald Reagan look-alike, who was standing beside a Rebecca Holmes look-alike, all singing a trio of birthday messages from Peter. He later said he tried desperately for a Democrat, preferably Teddy Kennedy or Paul Newman, but "Ronnie" was all they had available. Looking at this tired old actor, Katie could understand why he wasn't overbooked. Anyway, it was a great way to wake up.

After bidding her chorus of celebrities adieu, it was time for juice and coffee. As she perused the *New York Times,* Katie was having a difficult time deciding where to have lunch.

She wanted to choose a place that was "up," one that was "nonthreatening" and above all, one that was "neutral." No past memory. That meant no Russian Tea Room. Katie flashed on the time Lady Landamere discreetly put her cigarette out in the center of Katie's blini and sour cream, because she wanted to help her lose weight. It also meant no Maxwell's Plum. Warner LeRoy was not amused when Trace tried to exit one night carrying with her one of his most beautiful lamps.

"I told him it was just because Sixty-fourth and First was such a dark and dreary block," she said with her famous laugh.

The No Past Memory List was growing longer than Katie cared to remember. No Côte Basque (the episode in the men's room), no Le Cirque, no Tavern-on-the-Green. Maybe lunch was not the best idea. Desperate, she picked up a copy of the current *New York* magazine. She turned to the Restaurant Directory and looked up "Above 60th Street, East Side." She spotted the Carlyle Hotel.

Hmm, she thought. Too stiff . . . The Plaza.

She kept reading. The Oak Room. The Oak Bar. The Palm Court.

The Palm Court! Perfect. She had never even been there. Kind of like a New Yorker never having seen the Statue of Liberty.

She walked to the telephone. She caught her reflection in the mirrored living room wall and thought she looked excellent. She was wearing black leather pants and boots and a great oversized Krizia cashmere sweater with a big red heart in the center. She called and made a reservation. She used her mother's name. She was quick to admit that in New York society circles Lady Landamere's name still carried weight. She went to the hall closet and put on her silver fox jacket (this year's Christmas gift from Peter), checked herself out once again in the hall mirror, liked what she saw, and closed the front door behind her.

There was such a fine line between anxiety and excitement. She preferred to think she was excited. Rebecca had called and told her about her chance meeting with Trace last night and filled her in on a little of what to expect. She also said she'd be busy all day at a shooting with Richard Avedon for *Vogue* (her second cover) and offered Katie her limo to use for the day. What a good friend.

As she got out of the big black stretch in front of the Plaza Hotel the inevitable could be postponed no longer. There she was. Right in the center of the lobby. In the middle of the Palm Court.

The woman who began it all. The original Eve. Mother.

She looked different. Katie approached her with a smile and said, "Hello, Trace."

Trace was smiling, too. Katie wasn't sure if she detected a tear in Lady Landamere's eye. She liked to think that she did.

Trace got up and gave her daughter a nervous hug and a kiss on the cheek. Katie wasn't sure whose nervousness she was feeling. Trace's or her own.

"Happy birthday," she said. "Here!" She handed Katie a large and heavy gift-wrapped box that had been sitting at her side. Katie didn't see the three little holes in the bottom of the box.

"Should I open it now?" Katie asked.

Trace nodded. "Of course. Open it."

Katie had just begun unwrapping the box, when the top popped open on its own, and there was dogdom's answer to Prince Charles. Fred was looking less than amused, what with this foolishness he was forced to endure. He also had to suffer the indignity and poor taste of wearing gold sparkled "happy birth-day" letters around his neck.

Katie had to laugh.

"I thought you two should meet," Trace said. "Fred's been with me for as many years as you have not. Your real present is in the car," she said very happily.

"Mother, they don't allow dogs in restaurants. It's unsanitary," Katie said.

"Darling, if you could only see the condition of some of the kitchen help. Just put his top on and place him on the floor and stop worrying. It's Fred who has something to complain about. The floor is not his idea of heaven. I just wanted the whole family to meet and get along."

Katie was trying with all her heart not to be judgmental, but there was no doubt Trace was still quite crazy.

She looked different. Not as big? No, that wasn't it. Katie couldn't figure out for sure what was different. Her face looked good. Still no face lift. She still had all the same lines that Katie feared were hers someday to inherit. So what was it?

She looked softer. She looked less overpowering. Katie wondered if what she was observing was real or the illusion created by the elapsed time and her being more in charge of herself.

"You look really good, Trace," Katie said. "Much better than I thought you'd look."

"Well," she said, "with your imagination I'm sure you saw me being carried in on a stretcher. Perhaps I'd have a few sips of white wine intravenously. Settle our differences. And die somewhere between the chocolate soufflé and the check."

Katie smiled and said, "You know, I've always thought you were very funny. It's just that I used to have such a hard time laughing at your jokes. Even when my friends all laughed."

"Maybe you were afraid they were going to be about you," said Trace. "They often were."

Katie was surprised by her mother's truthfulness.

"You know, I'm pretty funny, too," Katie said. "But I was never able to be that way around you."

The waiter stood at attention and asked in his most congenial tone if they were ready to order. Both women looked at their menus. Katie noticed her mother was now using glasses to read her menu. She didn't consider this very unusual, but being a writer she liked to feel that she noticed the details.

"How long have you been wearing glasses?" Katie asked.

"Fifteen years, dear. I'm happy to see you're as observant as ever." And then to the waiter, "Do you have steak tartare?"

"Yes, ma'am. We do and it's quite good. I recommend it." The young waiter stood proudly at attention.

Katie made a face as if to disapprove of her mother's selection. Lady Landamere glanced up at Katie and said, "Don't look at me that way. Your little brother Fred is starving."

The waiter looked slightly confused since he saw no evidence of anyone's little brother.

"Will someone else be joining you, ma'am?" He addressed himself to Lady Landamere and the empty chair in his wonderfully British accent.

Lady Landamere, always delighted to engage in a bit of playful chatter, answered, "Well, we never know who might be joining us, do we? We are at The Plaza and we are quite visible, aren't we?"

The waiter was losing just the barest trace of his studied English manners. It was Friday and he was tired. Katie stepped in. She had saved many waiters in distress in her life. "I think I know what I'll have," she said. "I'll have . . ."

Lady Landamere interrupted her. Katie made a note to herself that in this area her mother was still running true to form.

"Let me see if I can guess what you're going to order," Trace said.

"My daughter will probably have the spinach salad, no bacon, dressing on the side. Isn't that right, dear one?"

Katie laughed. She was trying to decide between the spinach salad and the chef's salad. "Almost," she said. "But I think I'd prefer the chef's salad. That is, if you can prepare it very finely chopped."

"Yes, ma'am," answered the waiter, regaining his composure and preparing his retreat to the kitchen.

Katie was not finished ordering. "But I'd like that with no ham, no bacon, and no cheese."

Lady Landamere was smiling. The waiter was failing dismally in his attempt to appear unruffled. "But, ma'am," he said in his perfectly pitched voice which was now threatening to become an octave too high, "that simply leaves lettuce, chicken and a few egg wedges."

"Oh. I'm very glad you told me that. No egg, please," said Katie, smiling widely. In fact she had learned to enjoy many of her mother's games more than she even realized.

"Marvelous! Simply marvelous!" said Lady Landamere. "It's Nicholson's great scene from *Five Easy Pieces.*"

"Dressing?" asked the waiter, obviously not a film buff or a Nicholson fan.

"Oil and vinegar. On the side please," Katie said.

"To drink?" asked the waiter.

By the conclusion of the ordering the waiter had reduced himself to single syllable dialogue. It was safer.

"Wine?"

"White."

"Ice?"

"No."

"Fine." And he was gone.

There was a quick sliver of silence between his departure and

Katie's next question. The waiter had enabled Katie to postpone the reason for this lunch. She cut right to it. "Why Massachusetts General?" she asked.

"Well, you know how I feel about Houston after more than three days with Richard, Ellen, or any of Dr. DeBakey's clan," Trace replied.

"No, I really don't. You forget, Trace, how long it's been. The only time I ever spent with Ellen was two hours in nineteen seventy-nine, the day before she and Richard got married."

"Well," said Lady Landamere, "that's fifteen minutes over my limit unless, of course, I'm in need of a good nap." She laughed. "Don't you remember how we could never get Richard to nap when he was growing up? Well now he's up to two naps a day and building toward three."

Lady Landamere had rolled up a bit of steak tartare and passed it over to Katie.

"Give this to Fred, won't you, dear."

She passed Fred the steak tartare but continued her questioning. "Why are you going to Massachusetts General? I mean . . . what are you dying of?" Katie was aware she and her mother were continuing to postpone the inevitable.

Trace lit up another cigarette and looked at Katie squarely.

Katie thought Trace's eyes looked tired. She was looking for the sparkle. She was looking for the same sparkle Trace still had in her conversation. In all their years together, she never remembered seeing her brown eyes so clearly or so directly fixed on hers. Any remembrance of Trace in conversation circled around movement. Trace created her own whirlwind of activity. Cigarettes and lipsticks and swizzle sticks and pointed fingernails; all props and all parts of Trace's conversation.

Katie on the other hand was always complimented on her calm.

Her poise. Her "Easternness" (not Bostonian, Indian).

"I'm sure you recall," Trace said, "all of the many trips taken, while you were growing up. I know very well you do, because I've already been found guilty and convicted for them in some of our less than pleasant past encounters."

Katie tried to interrupt her.

"No, no, let me finish," Lady Landamere continued. "If you remember, my bedroom was always a mess. I was never ready for any of those trips. Whenever they came up, I was not prepared. I wasn't sure what clothes to take or how many suitcases to pack, what plane or whatever. Anything could happen, and I think I was afraid with each trip I might never return home so I'd just wind up taking everything I had with me."

Katie interrupted and this time continued, "If you took 'everything' you had with you, then why didn't you take me?" She felt herself feeling unhappy.

"Katie," said Lady Landamere, "I do so wish you wouldn't go to that place now. 'Everything' is not 'everyone' and the fact remains that you were with me many times. You possess a very selective memory. It happens that you simply loved Indianapolis (Only God knows why!), and you adored going abroad."

"Abroad," Katie said sarcastically. "I never saw anyone except that English nanny with the blue rinse in her hair, and . . ."

Lady Landamere interrupted before she could finish.

"You will let me finish. Please. I was talking about something very important. This could be my finest soliloquy. How many times in one's life does a person learn they're about to die?"

She paused. That seemed to have done the trick. Katie was silent.

"Where was I?" She lit another cigarette.

Katie pointed to the ashtray. "You already have one still lit. You were saying you weren't prepared," Katie answered.

"That's right. I wasn't prepared. I never seemed to have enough time to get everything all together. I always thought there was more time then there was." She paused again.

"And I'm not prepared now. I thought there'd be more time. I'm going to see Dr. Chase at Massachusetts General because I want him to tell me what Dr. Stanton in Houston didn't tell me. I want him to tell me there'll be more time. If, however, he should concur with his Texas colleague then I want to spend the remaining time making sure that for the, shall we say, final journey . . . I'm prepared. There. Do you understand that?"

Katie was visibly touched. "Yes," she said, "I think I do. But you still haven't told me what it is you're dying of. Is it your heart?"

Lady Landamere looked at Katie and said, "I guess you could say I'm dying of too much life. I seem to have O.D.'d on life."

Katie was staring at her mother. She had never thought of her as being courageous. But she did now. She wondered if she would ever have felt the compassion she was feeling now if all of this were not happening this way.

Trace added as a final note, "And once I have cleaned up all my unfinished business, of which you are more than a small part, then we shall have one wonderful Bon Voyage Party, because as Arthur said in that delicious movie with Gielgud, 'Isn't fun the best thing money can buy?' "

They had finished their coffee. The waiter was looking less pallid, having survived Lady Landamere's outrage when she found that they no longer had house accounts at the Palm Court. She had given him her American Express card. He returned it without incident. The ladies were standing, about to leave, when the poor fellow made the foolish mistake of reaching down and helping Lady Landamere with her cumbersome box sitting on the empty chair.

It wasn't that Fred was hungry. He had more than enough steak tartare for one sitting. The waiter, once again, simply had the extreme bad luck to be clothed in a formal tuxedo and there were those three holes in the bottom of the box and, well you know Fred, and you can imagine the bloody rest!

## Chapter

8

*R*ebecca Holmes returned from her shooting session with Richard Avedon exhausted. She was there for seven hours. Most of the hours were spent being beautified. Makeup, hair, etc. Rebecca was wondering if the photo sessions were getting longer because she was getting older and needed more "work," or if they just seemed that way.

She remembered when the explosion happened. It was in 1970.

The cover of *Newsweek* (*Time* thought The War on Organized Crime was more important but . . . ). All those magazine articles, and, finally, the cover of *Vogue*. Although she would never admit this if asked, but that *Vogue* cover meant more to her in a way than *Newsweek*. When your childhood and adolescence was spent being different and the boys you dreamed about were dreaming about the "pretty" girls, then the cover of *Vogue* can become more important than *Newsweek*. Your face can be on the cover of *Newsweek* if you've done something very smart or very important, or even very catastrophic. But *Vogue*. It didn't matter what you did, you had to look great. And she did.

She looked at herself in the mirrored lobby. It was hard to believe this was the same Rebecca Holmes who suffered the barbs of those asshole boys in her senior year of high school. Objectively speaking, she had to admit she looked damn good. She was thinking it was a shame to let this terrific makeup job go to waste as she waited at the elevator while Wanda, her secretary, checked the desk for messages.

There was a message from Katie and one from her agent. There was one from her publicist, one from her lawyer, and one from her business manager. A few unpleasant thoughts passed through her mind as she continued to thumb through the list. There was one from Jason, her hairdresser, and one from Mark Hammond. She had wanted to talk to Katie about him at lunch, but they'd run out of time . . . (Mark might say that was because of where she positioned him in her list of priorities).

She thought for a moment about all the people who were dependent on her for their incomes. How their lives would substantially change were she to change hers. She thought about how they all yes her all of the time, and she wondered if soon there'd be no one around her except the people she employed. Would she one day become like those tragic stories the Community likes to tell about Dietrich or Garland or Monroe? What an unpleasant thought! Happily she was able to dismiss it like a passing cloud that just happened by only temporarily blocking the sun (a little something she learned in her yoga lessons).

As promised, Lady Landamere had left an envelope for her at the desk. Curious, she opened it in the elevator. Her famous mouth broke into her equally famous smile as she read the enclosed letter.

Dear Superstar,

Hope you "let go" last night. Fred and I are on our way to Massachusetts. I will call you when I am settled so we can further our arrangements. Here is my list for your party. Let's make it black tie.

Here was the list. Rebecca read it twice.

Me (if we don't put ourselves first, who will!)
Rebecca
Mark Hammond (I know all about him!)
Katie
Peter Carriston
Richard and Ellen Fields* (Call anytime, she's always home)
Baveral Flower (Weisler, Flower, and Kent)
Please leave seating at the table for two more guests both of whom I shall be inviting personally.
*preferably without Joshua
I am forever grateful.

It was signed Trace. Her name scribbled in big generous letters.

Also enclosed in the manila envelope wrapped in tissue paper was the most exquisite silver and ivory bracelet Rebecca had ever seen.

It was from the thirties, Rebecca's favorite period. (Many Hollywood stars share a love of the Art Deco thirties. Maybe it's because life always looked so much richer and more elegant than their own in those Fred Astaire-Ginger Rogers musicals. Or maybe they just copy each other.)

Rebecca shook her head in disbelief. I'd never give away a bracelet this beautiful, she thought. Rebecca wasn't known for her extravagance.

A separate note was attached to the bracelet.

Like you, My Love. I don't miss a trick. I saw those X-ray eyes of yours examining my bracelet even through my coat so I wanted you to have it.

Rebecca gave the note to Wanda and asked her to start calling the names on the list. She counted them to herself.

That would be ten or ten and a half persons. Depending on whether or not Ellen brought Joshua.

Stepping off the elevator on the top floor, she wished she had some great date picking her up and some fabulous place to go to looking as good as she did. It was a shame to waste it. (She still liked doing covers because they always employed the best makeup artists, and Rebecca was never above learning a new way to use those contour brushes. She did have one rule though. No matter what, she always did her own lips. They all understood.)

Opening the door to her penthouse suite, she thought about Mark.

Mark Hammond was born with an ego as big as his original name. Mark Hamonofensky. He was good looking in a California sort of way, which was funny since he grew up pale and not overly hearty in New York City. The extent of his physical exercise consisted of running to the O.T.B. office in time to get a bet in for the daily double. He worked hard making the transition from successful clothing manufacturer to successful motion picture director. He said if you could make a good jacket, you could make a good picture.

Until he met Rebecca he only made good jackets and good-looking pleated pants and dresses with medium-sized shoulder pads. Then he began to make great-looking jackets and great pleated pants and great dresses with big shoulder pads. He made them for her, and she wore them in her movies. And it goes on like that. And a lot of people said a lot of expected things. Except it was not like that.

Yes, they fell in love, and yes, he made the transition from clothing manufacturer to director/producer in the same time frame as their relationship, but this is where tongues jump to the wrong conclusions.

The truth was they enhanced each other. They both not only looked better, they were better because of the other. They were a lot alike. Maybe too much alike. They mirrored each other so that when their egos collided, which they often did, the roar could be heard in galaxies even Spielberg or Lucas have not yet found.

The last time they were together was just over two months ago. It did not go well. They decided in the interest of taking care of themselves, something many said was their only interest in life, they would be better off apart. They had been together for three years, and they both felt a little cheated by what they thought they were supposed to be getting and what they didn't get. They were also each more than a little tired of feeling that way. They were also just a little tired of each other. When you live your life at a dramatic pitch anything less than intense emotion can be construed as boring; e.g., real life.

One night Rebecca told him, "The trouble is we both need a wife."

His answer was, "The trouble is we both already have one. We're married to our careers."

So they split up.

Rebecca wasn't sure how she felt about Lady Landamere's requesting Mark's presence at dinner. Well, that's not exactly true. She was glad she was going to see him. She asked Wanda to try and reach him first and when she found him she said she'd like to speak to him. It bothered her that he seemed to do well without her.

She entered her bedroom and fell on the bed completely exhausted. She took a deep breath. She was even more tired than she thought. She had given herself generously to that camera. She changed her mind and was no longer sorry she didn't have a date or some place to go. She practically had to drag herself into the bathroom to begin the long and tedious process of taking off her makeup.

She studied herself in the mirror. All of her makeup was off. Her skin glowed in appreciation of the respect with which it was treated. She felt her body begin to relax as her mind plugged in to the steady rhythmic vibrating sound her Water Pik made as it pulsated and throbbed against her very famous mouth.

In actuality, it really wasn't all that bad being alone.

# Chapter

## 9

Peter Carriston and Mark Hammond had more in common than either realized. They were both unmarried. They were both involved with very powerful women. They were both ambitious, and each thought the other to be self-centered.

They met only twice and both times because Katie and Rebecca engineered the evenings. Had they ever spent any time together alone, they might have gotten to like one another quite a bit, but for the most part, men take a meeting or attend a luncheon, but they don't, like women, make plans to just have lunch.

Peter trusted his first impressions. It was part of his job. He was a psychologist though his private practice was now reduced to seeing his eight women patients two days a week since the staggering success of his self-help book, *The Principles of Loving.* It did not hurt the sales of his book, or his waiting list of female patients-to-be, when he showed up on the "Donahue" show, looking not at all unlike Robert Redford. They all wanted to get into treatment with him and some wanted to get into anything else he might have in mind.

Katie and Peter met while doing a "David Susskind Forum" for Group W Cable in San Francisco. The subject was "Love and the American Family." Katie, of course, was the obligatory mother expert and Peter was the pop psychologist, whose book underlined his sincere though less than original belief that ultimately love is the only answer. Also on the panel were one battered wife, one gay feminist, one teenage runaway, one anti-abortionist, and a partridge in a pear tree.

Katie thought Peter was "great looking." He thought she was "fascinating." Later they argued about whether it was better to be great looking or to be fascinating.

"You can be fascinatingly ugly," Katie told him at dinner that same night. Obviously Peter found her fascinating in the "pretty" sense of the word, or he would not have asked her to dinner during the station break that afternoon. They were both semivegetarians so they ate in a very chic, very meatless restaurant called Greens, where they continued their conversation surrounded by lots of potted plants, soft lighting, and a lot of broccoli and cauliflower spears disguised as chicken.

Peter answered her. "Yes, but to be fascinating is to hold someone's undivided attention," he said. "You can be good-looking and not hold anyone's attention. . . . Like these chairs," he added. "They're very good-looking, but so what!"

Why were they both so interested in attention. Most first dates are about holding hands. Theirs was about holding attention. Peter noticed that. Katie noticed that he really did look like Robert Redford with a little darker hair.

Katie flew back to New York the next morning, but not before purchasing *The Principles of Loving* to read on the plane. Peter had to stay another day to meet with his editor. A number of self-help books by young psychologists come out of West Coast publishing houses, a holdover from the Berkeley/Esalen days.

They made a date to have dinner four nights later in New York, which happened to be home for both of them. Either this was a match made in heaven or it had enough of the trappings for both their fantasies to continue.

Two bright, creative, attractive, seemingly adult people. Both were authors writing about human nature; and both were attracted to each other. Even a cynic would agree this was a good beginning. One of them was bound to screw it up. All you had to do was examine their track records to know that neither one carried a great history in relationships.

Katie referred to her five-year marriage to Howard Beanerling as a period of learning. When asked what she learned, she said she learned what true happiness was. When questioned further, she said, true happiness was not being married to Howard. After five years of trying, she decided that most marriages worked better in concept than theory. The notion of two becoming one seemed to add up to less instead of more. Like clothing when sent to a bad cleaner, she'd seen too many of her friends shrink behind their men in an attempt not to overpower them. Desperate not to be accused of being aggressive or even worse, emasculating, women traded their careers for children and their power for protection until eventually their great protectors screwed up. And then along with the anger and disillusion came laundry lists of broken marriages.

Peter thought about the women he had been involved with until now. There was Sylvie, the French fashion model who was always spraying her face with Evian water and leaving used cucumbers around the apartment after she'd applied them to her eyes every morning. She was responsible for his becoming a vegetarian. Half the time she was pampering her face he thought she was preparing his meals. She was into everything green. Green juices, green vegetables, and money. They lived together for two years. The first year he just looked at her and thought how beautiful she was. The second year he looked at her and thought how being beautiful just wasn't enough.

Then there was Jasmine Walters. Jasmine was a publicist. She was very smart and very thin. She lived on gossip, which isn't fattening but which also is not very nourishing. Peter was to have said after their breakup that Jasmine suffered from Black Cord Fever. She needed to hear from her "sources" in the morning before she could even have her coffee. When after a year and a half they mutually decided their relationship was not working, she actually sent out a press release reporting their breakup.

Jasmine and Sylvie accounted for almost four years of disappointment.

And then came Mary Lou Langhorn from Kalmuth, Mississippi. Mary Lou was different. Well, there really was something to what's been said about those Southern belles. They were brought up knowing how to turn on their men. They were raised on *Gone with the Wind* and bigotry. But Mary Lou knew how to treat a man. It was the way Mary Lou treated everyone else that first aroused Peter's suspicions. When Maggie, Peter's cleaning lady of five contented years, quit one Tuesday morning in a huff saying that Mary Lou had obviously never heard of Abraham Lincoln, Peter began to lose his desire for Mary Lou's Mint Julips and in short order thereafter for Mary Lou.

So now, at forty-two years of age, it was clear that women were a never ending series of disappointments for Peter. That is, except for his mother.

As he lay in bed in his hotel room overlooking San Francisco Bay reading Katie's book, he found the first major difference between them. Reading between the lines told him that Katie was a lady who had a lot of anger for her mother. He couldn't relate to that at all. His mother was perfect. It was his girlfriends who all left something to be desired. Katie later told him what he desired was his mother. She said his mother had managed to ruin it for all the real women in his world. Unfortunately his mother could not be brought back to life as evidence, and the only thing worse than fighting a living saint is fighting a dead one. If his mother was perfect in life, she become practically canonized in her holiness when even her name was held to the light.

Peter lived on Central Park West and Katie just across the Park and it didn't take long before they fell in love. (In fact it probably didn't take long enough.) But it didn't take long before Katie thought of Peter all the time. She fantasized about what a great couple they would be and even with all her liberated thinking, she fantasized about what it would be like to be married to him. In spite of all her past knowledge, and in spite of all her knowledge of women's false dependency needs, she truly believed she could be with Peter forever.

Katie did not fall in love by herself. Peter believed he had finally met the right one! Katie was everything he ever promised himself.

As their courtship progressed they alternated king-size beds; his and hers. Peter was not used to two king-size anythings in one family. Most women Peter went with in the past didn't even have their own apartments; and of the few who did, at the very most they had queen-size beds, which were not quite comfortable enough for him to sleep in because he was, after all, used to his own royal bed, so he made it a rule never to stay overnight.

For Peter, Katie was a whole new ballgame. She was trying to be as cautious as he so they began by each giving the other a drawer apiece in their respective apartments, for their personals. By month four each had been upped to two drawers; by month six, each had an almost equal share of the other's closet space. In the eighth month there were serious discussions about giving up one apartment or the other. A lot of East Side vs. West Side. Discussions that were once fun were now a bit too serious.

By the tenth month those discussions were less frequent and after a year they hardly ever took place. Two apartments were once again a necessity. Especially on the nights they fought. After a year and a half, "I think I'd better go home" became as commonplace as "Where's the clicker for the Sony?" There was so much he didn't understand about her. If she was a writer about women, how come she couldn't tell him what it was she wanted from him.

And there was so much she didn't understand about him. If he was a psychologist who believed love was the way, why did she often feel she wasn't getting enough of his. What she claimed to want was intimacy. And it seemed that as the relationship progressed the intimacy level decreased; and their sex life which began in March with the roar of a lion was now, in December, quieter than a lamb.

Peter knew all about the correlation between long-term relationships and diminishing sex drives. Not only in his own life but in his patients.

It seemed as though most of his women patients loved to talk to him about the subject of sex. Maybe they suspected that he enjoyed that particular topic, because he did. He particularly liked to hear their sexual fantasies. Not only because they were erotic. They made him feel less guilty about his own fantasies after they described theirs. It made him feel better still when he learned how many so-called normal couples were not just exercising their imaginations but were actually acting out their sexual fantasies.

Peter also knew that one of the most viable alternatives to intimacy, which about ninety-nine percent of almost all relationships are trying to avoid, was the porno film. With the advent of home video, porno movies were now as simple a choice as Home Box Office or the Z channel. Gone were the seedy little theaters filled with perverted-looking men wearing big black raincoats. Now hard-core porno could be purchased and watched in the privacy of your own home right after Carson. Or during Carson if you didn't care for his guests.

Peter knew all about the psychological reasons for man's need for erotic stimuli, but he also just enjoyed it. Like he enjoyed a good Knick's game or a good dinner. It was one of life's sensual pleasures.

So one night, about a year and a half ago, in an effort to give their lovemaking a cosmetic lift, Peter brought home an X-rated movie. Katie had expressed interest in seeing one so they made love while watching *Behind the Green Door* starring Marilyn Chambers, who Katie definitely thought was a hot number, and Peter obviously did, too, because when they finished making love they made love again. That was one more time than usual. That was also the first twinge of discomfort Katie felt about the combination of lovemaking and porno films.

"How come we never did it two times with just the two of us in bed together?" she had asked Peter bluntly.

"But the two of us were in bed together. Who else was there?" That's what he answered, but he knew exactly what she meant.

In the week that followed they watched different parts of the same film a couple more times. Sexual frequency was definitely on the rise. Katie said she'd prefer seeing a different film rather than continuously watching the same one. She said she felt like she was getting too involved with Marilyn Chambers. She told Peter she'd seen more of Marilyn in the past two weeks than anyone else she knew.

In the two months that followed Peter brought home about five more films. Another Marilyn Chambers film, *Insatiable,* and some other pretty famous ones. That's what she was told.

It did not take long for mild discomfort to turn to anger by the fifth week when Katie noticed Peter kept gravitating back to the two Marilyn Chambers flicks in favor of such porn classics as *Inside Seka, Hot and Wet,* or *High School Memories.* That made her angry. As if her expectations of herself weren't unreal enough, now she had to compete with a goddamn porn queen and all that make-believe panting and screaming. She couldn't believe women got that carried away. She thought she liked sex but next to Ms. Chambers. . . . What was worse was Katie thought Marilyn was hot, too, so now along with her feelings of anger and jealousy she had to contend with something else. Now she could wonder whether she was a dyke. (She later had this discussion with Rebecca who told her everything she felt was very natural.)

But the main thing that was making her angry was that all the films did was to exaggerate to Katie how fucked up she and Peter were where intimacy was concerned. She said if his mother hadn't been such a saint, he wouldn't need pornographic films to get off.

All of her romantic fantasies that she lived on for years could never support the acceptance of porno films. Would Romeo and Juliet have watched *Behind the Green Door?* Their love was their passion. Would Anthony and Cleopatra have watched the *Story of O? . . .* Well, perhaps; those Romans did manage to bring the whole empire down with them with their infamous orgies.

In all their efforts to better understand each other and to communicate their feelings, it would always come down to Katie's saying it all had to do with their mothers. For Peter this was the most frustrating of all the statements she could make, because he truly could not understand what she was talking about.

His mother adored him. All the years he was growing up, he never came home to an empty house. His mother cooked, baked, and sewed. She took pride in his every accomplishment and she told him more times than he could remember that he was the world's best son. Katie pointed out that this in turn made her the world's best mother.

Katie tried to convince him that this was the way his mother controlled him. That this was the way she manipulated him.

And he would try and listen lovingly and understand. But their experiences were so different. Katie said Trace never understood anything she was trying to say. Evelyn Carriston understood everything; even what Peter did not say. It was increasingly clear to him that Katie had a distorted view of mothers, which he thought was really a shame, because other than that she was absolutely perfect!

*Chapter*

10

Richard Fields pulled his Rolls into the driveway at seven-fifteen. He had spent the day at his main office at the Fields Gelato factory three miles outside of Houston. The original gelato plant was in Milan, but when it became clear that Richard and Ellen were never going to be jet setters, they moved the major portion of the operation to Houston. They still kept a small factory in Milan that was run by Lord Edwin's second cousin, Cecil. Richard trusted

Cecil to oversee the European parlors, and Cecil was not about to do anything to put his job in jeopardy. He very much liked his two trips a year to the United States to meet with Richard. Being without title or, for that matter, being without the wherewithal to live off the fat of the land, he was forced to seek employment and grateful that he could find it in a nice cushy job like this one. Yes, it was possible that old Cecil, unwatched, might be skimming a little bit off the top but as Lady Landamere pointed out, "Fortunately, Cecil was from a long line of Edwins, all of whom thought small!" But most of all Cecil was one of the only people who ever voiced his deep respect and admiration for Richard and for that reason alone his job seemed insured forever.

Richard walked in the front door just in time to be greeted by Joshua dressed in his brand new Indian costume. Undaunted by the fact that Indians do not carry guns he pulled his silver .45 out of his holster, pointed the gun at his father, and fired off six loud shots in succession.

"Bang. Bang. Bang. Bang. Bang, and bang," he screamed with glee as he continued to circle the downstairs like an authentic Apache warrior. Richard retreated into the kitchen to look for Ellen and put down the gallon of Chocolate Soufflé Gelato he had brought home from the factory. Joshua must have taken a shortcut because when Richard entered the kitchen, he was there to head him off at the pass.

More shots.

"Bang. Bang. Bang. You're dead." Joshua shot his father again. The slightly curious part was that there was no laughter coming from Joshua. He seemed fairly serious. Perhaps it was a blessing that Richard had no psychological awareness and therefore saw nothing in Joshua's hostile behavior to concern him.

"Look what Daddy brought you, Joshie," he said. Whenever

Richard was having difficulty with Joshua he called him "Joshie."

"What?" asked Joshua, only mildly curious.

"Chocolate Soufflé Gelato. A brand new flavor. Here. Take a taste."

He handed the box to Joshua, who put it up on the kitchen table. He then took his gun out of his holster and shot the gelato three times.

"Bang. Bang. Bang. I hate gelato."

It was at this point that Ellen walked in the kitchen.

Joshua was trying to open the freezer door. "I want Häagen-Dazs. I hate gelato," he said.

Richard was getting a headache.

"Richard, sweetheart, don't let Joshie stand in front of the freezer door. Move him away before he catches a death of a cold."

Richard stood there looking stunned. Fortunately, he went through most of his life unconsciously so he didn't feel very hurt. For the most part he didn't feel much of anything. Just a little surprised. Ellen went to the freezer and took out a quart of Häagen-Dasz and proceeded to fill a dessert dish for Joshua. Richard looked as though he had been wounded through the heart.

"Don't worry, Rich," Ellen told him reassuredly, "Joshua knows not to tell anyone how he hates gelato."

She didn't want him to get into a bad mood because she'd been waiting all day to tell him the big news. It wasn't often she had any big news to tell him. "Guess who called today?" she said.

"Who?" he asked.

"Guess," she said again.

"Who," he answered again.

This game was not going too well.

"Rebecca Holmes. Guess what she wanted," Ellen continued to try to stimulate his interest and get him to play with her. It wasn't often Ellen had anything that Richard particularly wanted to play with so she was trying to milk the moment. "She wants us to come up to New York Friday night for a small formal dinner party she is having," she said.

Richard was definitely more interested.

"I wonder if Jacqueline Bisset will be there." He was kind of thinking out loud. "I remember Trace once said they were good friends."

He looked at Ellen, who looked nothing like Jacqueline Bisset or Jacqueline Smith or Jacqueline Kennedy or Jacqueline Kane. Jacqueline Kane was not as famous as the other Jacquelines unless you were an avid reader of *Penthouse* magazine. Then you would know she was the Pet of the Year (1982). Richard only read *Penthouse* in the bathroom and usually hid it between the covers of *Sports Illustrated*. He was looking at Ellen trying to remember what it was about her looks he had liked in the first place.

"The dinner party is for Trace," she said. "It's in her honor. That's why we were invited, Rich—ard." She had a way of lengthening his name to the point where he wished he was only given a one syllable name at birth instead. "And Katie will be there, too." She waited for his response.

When the synapses in his brain appeared to make no connection, he said, "Well, that doesn't mean that Jacqueline Bisset won't be there." He wasn't about to have his bubble busted so quickly. He was still thinking. "I don't think Linda Evans will be there though. I've noticed that movie people don't usually mix with television people."

Ellen was thinking about what to wear. Rebecca always wore the most terrific clothes.

Joshua came running through the den with a bow and arrow

slung over his chest and a bright red feathered headdress wrapped around his forehead.

"Rebecca suggested we leave Joshua home, but I told her we had no one to leave him with. I called Margaritta and offered her straight cash and she still said no. She said she was off the crutches now but she was still needing the cane."

"Well, he didn't deliberately trip her, for God's sake," Richard said. "He saw that banana trick in one of those old Marxs Brothers movies, that's all."

"Well, no one wants to stay with him," Ellen continued. "So I guess he'll have to come to New York with us."

"Well, I think that will be alright," Richard said. "Trace would probably love to see him, anyway. After all he is her only grandchild."

Ellen was still thinking. "Do you think I should wear the gown I wore to Janet's anniversary party last week?" she asked.

"Which one was that?" Richard asked disinterestedly. It had been a hard day, and he was pouring himself his second glass of Perrier.

"You know the turquoise one with the little beads on the bodice and the open back."

No response.

"You know, Rich—ard, the one with the big puffy sleeves that looks kind of like Marie Antoinette."

Marie Antoinette. He was hoping for Jacqueline Bisset, and he was getting Marie Antoinette. Life was hard. He didn't have the heart to tell her that, one, he didn't remember and, two, even if he did it wouldn't matter. He suggested instead, partly out of guilt and partly just to put an end to the conversation, that she buy herself something new. This pleased her enormously. She walked over to him and gave him a big kiss on his cheek.

Joshua, who was standing at the door, got jealous. He didn't like it when they kissed. Fortunately for the little fellow, it didn't happen with much frequency. He put down his bow and arrow and picked up his Colt .45. "Bang! Bang! Daddy's dead!"

Not dead. Just dead tired. But basically tonight wasn't much different from every other night of the week. Daddy may have made ice cream, but he wasn't getting his just desserts.

Chapter

11

$\mathcal{B}$ack home Katie thought of calling Dr. Stanton to hear in his own words exactly what his prognosis was but decided instead that she would wait to hear the report from Dr. Chase at Massachusetts General. It was an unfamiliar role to be in, feeling like her mother's mother, but it felt like what she wanted to do. She certainly preferred getting her information first hand from either doctor than from Richard, Ellen, or Trace. Between the three there wasn't one who could be counted on for a nondistorted picture of what was going on, and more than anything Katie wanted to know what was really going on.

She didn't much feel like meeting Rebecca but she had been so insistent. She said it was extremely important. "O.K. Where?" Katie said, giving in.

"Do you know where Simon and Schuster is?" Rebecca asked her.

Of course, she knew where Simon and Schuster was, they were once her publishers. But why would Rebecca, who hasn't read a book since *Miss Piggle Wiggle's Magic,* know where Simon and Schuster was. Rebecca, who thought *The Sun Also Rises* was a movie first and then a book, and that *Cat on a Hot Tin Roof* was personally created by Tennessee Williams for Elizabeth Taylor.

"Yes, I know where Simon and Schuster is. They used to be my publisher. Remember?"

Rebecca answered that, of course, she remembered and asked Katie to meet her in Dick something-or-other's office. You know the one who's married to Joni Evans.

Joni Evans! Dick (something-or-other who happened to be Snyder and who also happened to be the publisher of Simon and Schuster). Where was Rebecca pulling these names from?

"Why?" Katie asked.

"It's a surprise. Can you be there in thirty minutes?"

"Yes, if you promise me I can be out of there in forty minutes. Spending the afternoon with my ex-publishers is not my idea of fun."

Former publishers were similar to most ex-marriages. When it was over, it was over. Anyway, Katie always felt they spent a few too many dollars on *The Body Principal,* at the expense of

*Mothers!* Of course they tried to convince her this was not the case but. . . .

Anyway, everyone was all smiles when Katie walked in to meet Rebecca at the aforementioned time. Hugs and smiles. Not terribly real hugs and smiles, but a lot of well-capped, newly bonded teeth.

"Katie," Rebecca said looking at her watch. "I'm so glad you're here. I told Joni and Dick that until I had your approval I was not going to go one single step further."

"A step further where?" Katie asked with a seventy/forty combination of suspicion and naiveté.

"With my book! Show her," Rebecca said to the young editor, who had just entered the office holding the proofs of the four-color book cover. The young man folded back the tissue paper to reveal the cover.

"You've just got to be kidding!" That's what came out of Katie's mouth when she looked at the gigantic pair of red lips smiling at her from across the room taking up three-quarters of the oversized coffee table book cover.

Rebecca's famous red lips. And what was it entitled, this . . . this . . . book? In big fire-engine red script letters drawn with what was supposed to be a red lipstick was the title *WOULD THESE LIPS LIE?—Rebecca Holmes Personal Guide to Beauty!*

Unbelievable. Was there no lane that she was going to leave for somebody else, especially her best friend?

"I wanted to surprise you. I thought maybe we could go out and promote our books together. Anyway, what do you think?"

"Oh, don't ask me that Rebecca question, at least not here." She had now mastered the same fake smile that everyone else in the room was wearing. "Aside from the fact that you have used a title of mine that I told you I might use for my eventual autobiography . . . I suggest you don't ask me that question."

Rebecca remained undaunted. "Well, we were wondering, Katie, if you'd do us a favor and write some terrific endorsement about the book for the back cover so we can add yours to the other quotes I have. . . . But we need it by tomorrow."

"Well, I can't read the book tonight, Rebecca. I have theater tickets tonight, and I'm not going to miss this show again."

"What show?" Rebecca and Joni asked in unison.

"Sondheim's show and . . ."

Rebecca said that she saw the first half last night and that it was very creative and ambitious.

Katie asked if it was so creative and ambitious why she only saw the first half. She answered because she was more creative and more ambitious than even Stephen Sondheim and had a ten o'clock meeting that she couldn't cancel. She then told Katie that Trace wrote a beautiful quote for her book before she left for Massachusetts, and she wrote it without having even read it yet.

Katie continued to smile.

Her mother had written a quote for the back of Rebecca's beauty book. Unbelievable.

"They think it's going to be a big hit book. Right, Joni? Right, Dick?"

The Steve and Edyie of the book world both reinforced their new writer's hopes.

"And your saying something would be very good for it because all those women who think you're this great feminist will buy it, too, because you will tell them that it's alright to be a feminist and still want to be beautiful."

Joni handed her the bound prepublished copy to peruse.

Katie answered that if Rebecca wanted to talk some more about the book, they could do it on the way home because she really had to go. One thing she had learned in dealing with uncomfortable situations was to get the hell out before they crossed from uncomfortable to unbearable.

Going uptown Katie told Rebecca she was pissed off. Not because she had written a book. She said she hoped her book would be a big success. She was pissed off because Rebecca was so goddamn competitive. She always wanted what Katie had.

"You're the goddamn movie star," Katie said. "Couldn't you let me be the one who writes books? You don't see me auditioning for "The Love Boat."

"Well, I should hope not," Rebecca said. "If you want to do television, there are much better shows to do than that. 'Hill Street Blues' seems to be a pretty respected one."

It was useless. Rebecca's lips weren't only the most famous lips in the world. They were the hungriest, too. Put her in a scene and she ate the scenery. Katie wondered just how hungry her oldest friend, who taught her the secrets of two pints of ice cream with roast beef sandwiches, really was. How much did she need to achieve?

"I want to know why you are so competitive with me," she asked her.

"I thrive on competition. It makes me do better. You should know all about that. Look at you and Trace. Look what that competition produced. Two books. I only got one from you. You're twice as competitive as I. Please don't be angry, Katie. I think you'll like the book. Oh, and I hope you won't mind, but I borrowed your secret hair formula and your trick with putting the eyeliner pencils in the refrigerator before you sharpen them, and your five-minute makeup for getting out of the house for emergencies."

Katie looked appalled.

"Really, Katie, don't look so shocked. Did you honestly think I was going to divulge my beauty secrets which took me thirty-four years to acquire for fourteen-ninety-eight? It would take millions for me to part with them."

"Maybe that's what I can write on the sleeve of the book then," Katie answered. "And by the way, while you've borrowed all of that from me, what is the reader getting that is yours, may I ask?"

"Well, Katie, it's kind of like Rolls Royce. They're getting my name."

The car was at the Sherry-Netherland. Rebecca popped out. "Ciao!" she said.

"Rebecca, you must believe that even Ta-ta! is better than ciao! Ciao sounds like you got buried somewhere in Rome in a Tony Curtis/Virna Lisi movie in the 1960s. I'd say, Have a nice evening, but you know it is not my style to lie."

"Not to me perhaps," Rebecca said from outside the car. "Just to women all across America."

There was no sense in fighting for the last word.

# Chapter

## 12

From the visitor's chair next to her bed at Massachusetts General Lady Landamere was able to admit that there were more than a few things she would do differently were she able to do it all again. It wasn't just her deteriorating health that produced this feeling. She'd been thinking about it ever since Katie first cut off communications. And Trace, always one to put her thoughts into action, had already begun doing something to change things. That's why Baveral

Flower of the famed Weisler, Flower, and Kent was going to be at dinner. She was thinking about how magnificent old Baveral had been in the past six months. His assistance had been invaluable. She was sitting in her visitor's chair smiling at the thought of how well her plans were all coming together. That's why she was looking anything but unhappy when Dr. William Chase walked in the door.

"Stunning. Positively stunning," Lady Landamere said in a more than approving voice. She was examining her new doctor with an eye of experience. Since she was seated on the room's only chair he sat down on the bed. She feigned an exaggerated Texas drawl, one similar to the one that sent Austin Marcus reeling that first night and said, "I do hope your handsome good looks are not going to overwhelm my poor and fragile heart, kind sir."

Dr. Chase laughed. A hearty laugh. Fuller in texture than the characteristic doctor's laugh. He knew about her before Dr. Stanton called him and sent her records on to him. He liked her immediately. He found himself hoping Kenneth Stanton might be wrong. He also knew the chances for that were doubtful.

"Tell me, are you married, Dr. Chase? I do hope you excuse my directness, but I believe a lady in my circumstances hasn't time for lengthy formalities."

"No. I'm not married, Lady Landamere. I am a widower," he answered. "My wife passed away last year."

"I'm very sorry to hear that." She paused. "I hope you weren't treating her. I'm sorry. That was a very bad joke." She paused again. "What a wonderful father you would make for Fred and Wan Ling," she said melancholically.

"And who are Fred and Wan Ling?" Dr. Chase inquired.

"The children. And I am their mother. And that would make you my fourth and, considering my present medical status we could safely say, my final husband."

He laughed again. "Are your children here in Boston with you?" he asked.

"My children are scattered all about the states at the moment. Katie's in New York, Richard's in Houston, and Fred is here with me in Massachusetts. Travel is always so difficult on the little boy. Wan Ling was supposed to travel with Fred, but she caught a terrible cold at the last minute. Fred had it first, and being a doctor you know how damaging flying can be to your ears."

Dr. Chase seemed a little confused. A feeling Lady Landamere managed to elicit in anyone who engaged in more than three minutes of conversation with her.

"I thought all your children were grown, Lady Landamere," he inquired.

Trace laughed. "Oh, Dr. Chase, I'm just being naughty and having some fun with you. Fred is a Lhasa apso and he is five years old. But it is true that currently he is in his own room at the Ritz Carlton because they would not let him stay with me here at the hospital. I wish they would have though because he still has a nasty cough." She laughed again.

Dr. Chase, beginning to feel more relaxed, explained what tomorrow's procedure would entail. The tests themselves were not going to be painful or uncomfortable. They did have one surgical procedure used by their heart team at Mass General that was not yet in operation in Houston, and there was an outside chance that Lady Landamere might qualify for it. He also told her she'd only be required to stay in the hospital two days unless, of course, the tests revealed something that required immediate attention.

Lady Landamere said she thought when someone was supposed to be dying in the very foreseeable future then everything would require immediate attention.

Dr. Chase displayed a true appreciation of Trace's unusual

humor. You could see it in his eyes. When he laughed he appeared much younger than his sixty-three years. It wasn't that he didn't see the insecurities her behavior attempted to cover, he just enjoyed her. No doubt she was like a runaway car in five o'clock traffic but at least she was a Rolls and not a Pinto.

If the floor nurse hadn't walked in the room to take Lady Landamere's blood pressure, there's no telling how long their dialogue might have continued, but her white stiff uniform and equally white stiff face reminded Dr. Chase of where he was, and the stark reality of why he was there.

"I think I ought to examine you now, Lady Landamere, and see if I can't get some idea of what's going on. So if you wouldn't mind trading places with me . . ." He stopped speaking for a moment to clear his throat. He was trying to get back to business.

Trace offered him the glass of apple juice the nurse had just left on the hospital tray table. He drank it and continued, trying to regain his doctor's identity. "And so, Lady Landamere, if you would please get into your bed then I'll . . ."

Lady Landamere interrupted him. "Oh, do call me Trace . . . William, dear." Trace was now openly flirting. For a moment she couldn't have been more than twenty-five years old. She batted her eyes at him exaggeratedly. "Whatever you're going to do sounds positively divine."

It was a shame Katie couldn't have been there. She would have seen that twinkle she couldn't find the other day at lunch.

## Chapter

## 13

Baveral Flower had told his secretaries he was not to be disturbed. He was in the middle of reviewing the final draft of a multimillion dollar off-shore oil contract for Exxon, one of his biggest corporate clients, when Lady Landamere called on his private number. There was nothing in their relationship to assume that he would have given her his private phone number except that Lady

Landamere asked for it and old Baveral always had a hard time refusing Trace anything.

"Yes, Trace. What can I do for you, my love." Baveral removed his Ben Franklin glasses and leaned back in his big old leather chair. It was the first time in hours he'd taken a deep breath.

"I'm up in Massachusetts, Bav," Trace said. "There's not much one can do lying here hooked up to all sorts of testing gizmo's besides the telephone." Trace was smoking. She stopped long enough to take a puff and long enough for Baveral to wish he hadn't heard her.

"I wanted to know if Rebecca Holmes had gotten in touch with you yet?" Trace asked.

Baveral had to think for a moment. His memory wasn't as sharp as it was a year ago, which wasn't as sharp as the year before that. It wasn't getting old that frightened him. It was watching himself lose the edge on all the things he once took for granted. For the most part he was glad God had granted him years, seventy-six to be exact, and glad too that he still possessed enough of all his faculties to wheel and deal with the best of them.

"Yes, Trace. Rebecca did call," he answered. "Dinner party this Friday night. Yes. Sounds fine, Trace. Just fine."

Baveral had a habit of repeating the name of the person he was speaking with a few more times than necessary in conversation. Perhaps this came from all the years of returning phone calls with the "name call" list placed directly in front of him.

"Well, darling," Trace continued. "I'd like the evening to have a purpose if you know what I mean."

He didn't.

"I want to take care of everything at dinner. I mean 'everything,' Bav. The whole family will be there. It seems like the perfect time to let everyone know my wishes and bequeaths, now while I'm still alive. It's far more civilized, don't you think, dear?"

Baveral nodded yes. He forgot he was on the phone.

"Baveral, are you listening to me?"

"Yes. Yes, Trace." He caught himself napping. "I know what you mean."

"Well, make sure you bring all my documents and bring the agreements concerning Fred and Wan Ling as well. I think we should pull out all the stops."

"Bombs away," he said.

Trace took another puff of her cigarette.

"I do wish you wouldn't smoke so much, Trace, dear. It worries me deeply, you know."

"Bav, you're crazy. I'm not smoking. I'm breathing air. It's an exercise my new doctor has asked me to perform. Air breathing is said to reduce stress and strengthen the heart muscle. Listen." She made an exaggerated sound into the phone receiver. It sounded like someone either taking a monstrous puff of a gigantic cigarette or perhaps it did sound like air breathing, if there was such a thing. She smiled. She liked her new invention. She did it again.

"You know, Bav, it's not a bad idea for you to give it a try. Dr. Chase, that's my new doctor, said that there's a book about to be released about the benefits of air breathing for men and women over sixty."

Baveral was listening with skepticism and interest. Never a smoker he attempted to inhale some air, which felt a bit awkward. He swallowed the air, which resulted in his letting go a big burp.

"What was that, Baveral?" Lady Landamere asked.

"Interference on the line," he answered quickly. "When are you leaving the hospital, Trace, dear?"

"I'm leaving this Thursday," she answered.

"You know, I have to be in Massachusetts Wednesday and Thursday for a deposition. Why don't you let me drive you down to New York . . ."

Lady Landamere interrupted him. "Drive? Whatever is the matter with you, Baveral." Her voice registered her surprise. "Have you never heard of the airplane? Drive with you, you old buzzer. You'd kill us both and ruin my entire dinner party. Absolutely not. Now you've got me worrying about you in that old roadster of yours. You'd better fly down with me." She lit another cigarette. "And fly up, too."

Baveral laughed.

"If you travel too fast you miss the journey," he said matter of factly. "I like to drive, Trace, dear. No phone calls. No disturbances. Such a peaceful time," he said.

"Well, I'll be having more than my share of 'peaceful time' right now. Personally I do not have all that time so I suggest you fly down with me."

"Alright," Baveral gave in. "But, by the way, Trace, dear, I've long traded in the old roadster. I drive a new Bentley. 1969. Lots of legroom for big Bav's spindly old legs. What time shall I pick you up?" he asked her.

"I think eleven will be good," Trace answered appreciatively. "I'll phone you up tomorrow and let you know."

Baveral liked the way Trace's speech reflected her years spent living in different parts of the globe.

"Well then," she concluded, "all appears settled for now."

Baveral Flower felt a tinge of regret that the conversation was ending. He looked down at his desk and saw the contract he was working on, with twelve more pages to complete. That would take him another half an hour, maximum. Then he would drive home, in the Bentley, to the big sprawling estate out on Long Island, where he would dine alone, served as always in the finest of fashion by Mrs.

Pierce, who cared for him for the past twenty-odd years.

Lilly Pierce used to be half of a couple who with her husband served the Flowers devotedly, but Edward Pierce passed on one year before Daisy Flower lost her bout with pneumonia. So, for the past seven years Mrs. Pierce continued to look after Baveral here on earth and both she and Baveral were comforted by the thought that Ed Pierce was taking care of Daisy in the big "upstairs in the sky." What neither Baveral nor Lilly Pierce ever knew was that Ed Pierce took care of Daisy plenty good in the big upstairs guestroom while they were both right here on earth.

"So, Bav, until tomorrow," Trace was winding it up.

Baveral Flower was glad she was going to call again tomorrow.

Trace ended with, "Keep up that air breathing I told you about. You'll notice improvement almost immediately. Ta-ta."

There it was. And she was gone.

# Chapter 14

They were having dinner at Auntie Yuan's. It was Peter's favorite Chinese restaurant, and Katie liked it as well because they had good vegetables.

They had been seeing less of each other since their latest breakup, but Katie needed a friend to talk to, and when it came down to it, she really did consider Peter her friend. Besides, if it weren't this it would be something else because neither one was ready to let go.

(Last week Peter needed Katie's advice on whether he should let the William Morris Agency represent him for lecture tours.)

"I know the thing with Rebecca and her book shouldn't bother me," she was saying, "not with everything that's going on with Trace, but it's so competitive of her. And then she actually told me that it was nothing compared to me and Trace." She paused long enough to reach across the table and take a taste of the dumpling sitting, half eaten, on Peter's plate.

"Why are you eating mine," he asked, "when there's a whole plate of them right in front of you?"

"Because I just want to taste it. That's why . . . and if I eat it from your plate it's like I didn't really eat it."

"That's not true. You want to eat it from my plate because, one, you want me to feed you, and, two, at the same time you want me to police you and tell you not to eat it. Dumplings are fattening."

Katie disregarded his comment, which was right on the mark.

"Well . . . Don't avoid the question. Do you think I'm competitive?" she asked him.

Peter asked her why it had suddenly become a dirty word. "Competition is healthy," he said. "We built our country on it."

"You mean you think I am," she said. She took another bite of his dwindling dumpling.

"Yes, I think you're competitive. And so is Rebecca. It often helps to have someone to compete against in order to be competitive."

"Explain it to me. What are we competing for?" she asked him.

"What is this, your night to play dumb? You're the writer of *More Mother . . . But Where's Daddy?*" You know the answers."

"Not *Daddy!*" she corrected him. "*Father.*"

"If you could graduate to Father, you might be less competitive. I think it's all about Daddy," he said.

Katie didn't really want to know the answer. She asked him how come he knew so much about daddies and so little about mommies "Why aren't daddies sacred? How come you don't mind dissecting daddies?"

Peter looked annoyed and said, "I'd really like to know why you asked me to meet you for dinner? Just to eat my dumpling and attack my mother?"

The waiter appeared, bringing their chicken dish and asking if they wanted anything else. Peter asked him to please remove the dumplings. He said they were taking up too much of their dinner and he was starting to feel competitive with them.

Katie laughed. Peter laughed, too. Peter told her he liked it much better when they laughed.

Over the remainder of the chicken, Katie talked about Trace and the hospital and she said maybe she wouldn't have reacted the way she did to Rebecca's beauty book if Trace weren't back in her life and in the hospital and sick and . . .

Peter said he thought she would have reacted that way no matter what because Trace has always been very much in her life.

"Well, I'm not competitive with you," she said, not one hundred percent sure that was the truth.

"Not as long as I'm Daddy. But you weren't all that thrilled when the *Washington Post* wanted to do a profile on me and not us.

"That's not true. I was totally thrilled . . ." She thought. "It's just that they were supposed to do a piece on me and . . ."

"And you think I took your space. You know, Katie, there's enough love for everyone to go around."

"Love!" Now she was raising her voice. "Who the hell is talking about 'Love.' It's like you have one answer to the whole of life's . . . everything."

Peter smiled at her.

She glared at him. "You're doing it. You're using your love shit on me. I'm talking about Rebecca wanting to get in my lane. She wants to do everything I do. Why did she need to write a book? And . . . she says she's my best friend."

Peter kept smiling.

Katie warned him. "If you don't stop smiling, I am going to tell you again how your mother has totally fucked up your understanding of not only me but every woman you have ever met."

They weren't having a bad time, and they weren't having a particularly good time. But it had a certain comfort in its discomfort, and it could still go either way. There was a smile and a tear underneath the surface of the whole dinner, and it all depended on how they both wanted to view it.

Now on dessert, Katie reached over to taste Peter's Green Tea Ice Cream.

He told her, "It tastes the same as it did last week, and the same as it will next week."

She put her spoon down and sipped her coffee. She looked hurt and felt about seven years old.

"Here," he said, taking his dish and putting it directly in front of her. "I don't care if you eat the ice cream or not, I just hate it when someone eats from my plate."

"Why?" she asked. "Why don't you see it as loving? We're all just in this one big universal Green Tea Ice Cream World together, aren't we?"

She pushed the ice cream to the center of the table.

The waiter arrived with more tea. "Will that be all, sir?"

"Yes. I'd like a check, please," Peter said. "And perhaps we could have a doggie bag for the rest of the ice cream."

Before the waiter could look confused, Katie told him her friend was just kidding. But she did ask him for a fortune cookie.

Waiting for the cookies, Peter told Katie that in spite of her problems she was looking very beautiful. Katie, who only recently learned to say "Thank you," instead of "No I don't," appreciated Peter's show of affection.

The waiter was back within seconds with two fortune cookies. Katie was first to take hers. Peter took the one that was left over.

"What does yours say?" Katie asked Peter.

Peter read aloud. "It says, 'You will be successful at whatever you do!' What does yours say?"

"It says, 'You will be more successful!' "

And they both laughed.

She leaned over and kissed him and apologized for being such a lunatic tonight, and he said he understood. It was rough, he said, what she was dealing with. And it was. And he did understand.

# Chapter

# 15

TWA's Flight 44, nonstop, L10-11, Houston to New York, was readying itself for takeoff. Every seat in first class was filled. In seat 4A sat Richard Fields. He was reading *Forbes Four Hundred*. It was his favorite of all their issues; across the aisle in seat 4C sat Ellen Fields. Next to her in seat 4B was supposed to sit Joshua Fields, but at the moment he was missing.

Ellen and Richard knew he was on the plane. The door had

already closed when he was last seen running down the right aisle of the coach section of the aircraft pretending to be a 747. The passengers all thought he was adorable. Not one single person on board had ever seen a five-year-old child dressed in an authentic aviator's costume before, including goggles and a leather hat. He looked like a baby Howard Hughes.

"Richard," Ellen said worriedly, "I wish you would go and look in the bathroom. We're taking off and he's missing. We have to strap him in."

Richard was annoyed. He was up to the three hundred and fifty-first richest man in America and was still hoping he might find his name amongst the forty-nine remaining multimillionaires, and he didn't like being disturbed.

He told Ellen, "Ring for the stewardess and let her look in the bathroom. That's why we fly first class. So she can look in the bathroom."

Ellen put down her copy of *Vogue,* surprised to know that was the reason they flew first class, and rang for the stewardess.

A very pretty young woman with a bright smile appeared in no time flat. "Hi, there!" she said happily. Even her smile had a Texan accent. "How can I help you, Mrs. Fields?"

"I can't find Joshua. Our little boy. Could you see if he's in the bathroom for us, please?"

Ellen couldn't quite understand why she was asking the stewardess to look for her son. It wasn't like asking her for a drink or a pillow, but that's what Richard wanted so. . . .

"Of course, I will," said the pretty young stewardess. Her smile seemed to have expanded by at least a quarter of an inch. "He's just the cutest little boy. Why, we'll be right back."

That was at least three minutes ago. Another pretty stewardess was in the front of the plane demonstrating the safety equipment aboard the aircraft before taking off, something Richard absolutely refused to ever watch. A phobic flier at best, he buried his head in his magazine, a big believer in Camus's Ostrich Theory (if I don't see it, it doesn't exist!) and tried to concentrate on reading his economic bible. He was now at the four-hundred-and-eighty-sixth name and hopes of making this year's list were growing dim.

Ellen was about to get up and search for Joshua herself, when she looked up and saw The Smile approaching.

Her voice was so cheerful she was almost singing. "We've found your son and he couldn't be in better hands." She knelt down in order to tell Ellen something in secret.

"Our flight engineer, Captain Flynt," she was whispering but she was still smiling, "thought he was just so adorable, he snuck him into the cockpit to let him see the inside and to let Captain Matthews, our pilot, take a peek at him."

"Thank you," Ellen said. She was relieved. She leaned over and told Richard, word for word what SueAnn had told her.

Richard, remarked that names like Captain Matthews, Captain Flynt, and SueAnn did not instill confidence. He said they sounded like the crew of a disaster movie.

He was close.

Suddenly. "Bang!" One loud shot rang out from the cockpit.

"Oh, my God! We're going down," screamed an old lady seated behind Richard in first class.

"We can't be going down, we haven't gone up yet," said the ever-rational Richard.

Before anyone could panic Captain Matthews was on the loud speaker telling the passengers not to worry. The sound they heard was nothing for anyone to be concerned about. He then asked the stewardesses to take their seats and announced they would be taking off momentarily.

Simultaneously the cockpit door flew open and there stood Joshua with another very pretty stewardess with red hair and a not-so-big smile, being led quite effortlessly to his seat, his toy gun still smoking. He had a nice calm smile on his face. Not unlike the smile seen on the face of a mass murderer in a UPI news photo the moment he's being apprehended and led away.

The cheerful stewardess, with smile still intact, suggested to Mrs. Fields that Joshua might be better off with his seat belt fastened throughout the trip ahead.

And the flight was still young.

Chapter

16

$\mathcal{M}$r. James Catering was said to be the finest catering service on either side of the Atlantic. Well, at least everyone in L.A. said it was the best in New York. Not that Rebecca actually knew anyone who had personally used Mr. James's service. Why would anyone from California want to throw a dinner party in their hotel suite. People from California complain that they always eat at home, so when in New York, they're thrilled to get out and see people. Besides, usually when visiting another city, it is customary to dine out.

But Rebecca had decided on having dinner in her suite because, one, she felt that eleven guests were too many for a decent table in a restaurant and, two, she thought privacy would be a good idea for a group such as this. There was no telling what Trace might do, and it was best to protect herself whenever she could from the all-invasive *Enquirer*.

Mr. James and his all black staff were dressed to the nines. The three waitresses in their black uniforms and starched white aprons and the bartender in his white tie and tails all looked like something out of Broadway's *Ain't Misbehavin'*. One expected them to break into a chorus of some finger-snappin' jump tune and tap their feet straight to the dinner table. Mr. James, an elegant looking man, was complaining about the lack of space in these hotel kitchens. The Sherry-Netherland was also complaining. This was the first time they were allowing an outside caterer to serve a formal dinner in their hotel. They had their own catering department, and they were not above collecting the additional money to be made on room service, especially when it included caviar and champagne. They acquiesced without much ado though, for it was, after all, Rebecca Holmes.

The rooms looked exquisite; the dining table simply magnificent. It was amazing what bringing just a few things from home could do to warm up an impersonal hotel suite. Rebecca had brought with her two suitcases of accessories, including seven antique silver picture frames containing some of her favorite photos of herself with assorted celebrities, two boxes of Rigaud candles, two Lalique vases, and she had added an abundance of flowers to the suite. Trace had taught her long ago that fresh flowers were essential to the beauty of a room. Looking out from the three-sided glass dining room on the twentieth floor all the eye could see were three splendidly clear views of Central Park, alive and twinkly. It made Rebecca wish she was living in New York again. The small dusty rose candles placed judiciously in pairs throughout the suite gave the room its sensual scent and the various easy arrangements of soft white and pink flowers, its look of perfect elegance.

It was seven-forty. Rebecca's makeup and hair were complete. In fact Jason was just leaving. She was about to slip into her dinner clothes when Trace phoned up from her suite to ask Mr. James to please add one more place setting to the dining room table. From the commotion in the kitchen one would have thought she had asked for something far more catastrophic. Rebecca picked up the phone to intervene.

"But the table was perfect," said Mr. James, sounding as hysterical as he was famous for getting. "Now it will throw everything off balance."

"Rebecca, dear," Trace said, "tell him this isn't Ringling Brother's high wire act he's dealing with. It's a dinner party. Just a little family gathering."

Trace looked excellent. She was stuffing a few extra cigarettes inside her exquisite 1931 Cartier box and was just minutes away from exiting her suite.

Rebecca told Mr. James to do whatever he could to accommodate Lady Landamere and hurried off the phone to finish getting dressed. She decided to wear the Fabrice. She could have worn something of Mark's, but she decided that would have been too extravagant a gesture. She looked at herself standing in front of the full-length mirror in her bedroom. A vision in all white and silver. Padded shoulders, bugle beads. Very thirties. Very beautiful. It should be beautiful, she thought. She still didn't like paying over four thousand dollars for a dress. She didn't mind the hundred thousand for the Hockney. That was an investment. But a dress. She didn't even mind the thousands for the jewelry. Another investment. What she did mind was she bought it all for herself. It probably would have comforted her to know that most "Lady Legends" bought their own jewels and their own Hockneys.

Ten blocks away, Peter and Katie were getting into a waiting taxi. Peter was giving Katie a last minute pep talk about the evening, and Katie, surprisingly, seemed to be in agreement with everything he was saying. Yes, she agreed, it was altogether possible that her mother had changed, and yes, it was more than possible that they might finally enjoy each other in the remaining time they had left together.

In the taxi, Katie told Peter how different Trace had seemed to her at lunch. Softer. Peter suggested that maybe it was Katie who was doing some of the softening and for the first time in their "mother conversations" Katie admitted that might be true as well. Katie also said that she even was looking forward to seeing Richard. She said she hoped that she might find some new level of relating to her half-brother. As the cab approached the Sherry-Netherland, Katie felt hopeful about her role in this family reunion and told Peter she was glad he was going to be a part of it. She leaned over and kissed him on his cheek. He was hopeful too he said as the meter clicked off at two-fifty. Peter had reason to be happy. He always believed that if Katie could work things out with her mother, each relationship would reap the benefits of the other. In a mood of generosity he gave the driver five dollars and told him to keep the change. A big smile appeared for the first time on the face of Juan Carlos Satorelli (as his name appeared on his license in the front of the cab), and he wished the couple good luck with tonight's dinner and with the mother and the brother. Katie told Peter that was the second reason she preferred limousines. Nothing was private in a taxi cab. Juan Carlos could be a source for Liz Smith. The first reason was because they were cleaner and more luxurious. Out of the taxi cab, Peter said he'd buy one for her tonight but the limo store closed at five-thirty. They laughed, walked into the lobby, and waited to be announced. Suffice to say she was more than a little apprehensive as to what Peter would think of Trace and Richard.

Rebecca could hear voices in the next room. Some of Trace's guests had begun arriving. She thought if she were home in California the staff would have to ring and tell her. Her bedroom in Beverly Hills was at least a football field away from the dining room. Perhaps she did prefer California living after all. She checked herself one final time in the bathroom mirror, adding just a little bit of the routine extra lip gloss. She took a deep breath and walked into the living room. There was no doubt in her mind that she was a good friend, because to waste all this on a private little family gathering was extremely generous. It wasn't even her family.

Her family was quite another story. The alcoholic father and the brassy pushy mother. To say she had transcended her roots would be more than an understatement.

"Hi," said Rebecca, extending her hand to Ellen Fields, who was nervously standing in front of Richard, holding Joshua tightly in front of her.

She looked at Ellen and could not remember if she ever had met her. She decided it was best not to say, "Good to see you again."

So Ellen, nervously, said it instead. "Good to see you again."

Well, that answered the question of whether they had met before.

"You know Richard," said Ellen. "And this is our little boy, Joshua." Ellen stood with a polite though slightly terrorized expression on her face.

"Hello, Richard," Rebecca said acknowledging Katie's half-brother by extending her perfectly manicured hand. "It's been a long time. Good to see you again."

Richard thought Rebecca looked absolutely sensational and thought perhaps he detected more than just a "hello" in her "hello."

He was wrong.

What Rebecca did think was that Richard looked better than the last time she met him. She thought it was probably that he was thinner.

Richard greeted Rebecca in a voice Ellen never remembered hearing before. He sounded like he was imitating Cary Grant. Badly.

"Hi, Joshua," said Rebecca. She bent down and shook his little tuxedoed hand. Rebecca believed in treating little children like regular people.

Joshua thought she was very, very pretty. So pretty that he didn't say a word.

"Joshua's so quiet!" Rebecca said. "And well mannered. Maybe I'd have a kid if I thought he'd be so well behaved."

With that Trace and Dr. Chase walked in. And Baveral Flower could be seen approaching, walking down the long corridor.

"Don't you just love dinner parties. They can be such fun if they're cast properly," Lady Landamere said as she came sweeping into the room wearing a bright red Bill Blass dinner gown and lots of big chunky jewelry. She gave a little wink to Rebecca and kissed her on both cheeks without messing up her makeup even one bit. To Rebecca this was a good test to determine who your real friends were. Those who didn't really like you always used an occasion such as this to either mess your hair or make sure they left lipstick marks on your cheeks.

Lady Landamere made the necessary introductions. Upon seeing Joshua, she said, "Win some, lose some!"

Joshua on seeing Trace said, "When are you going to die?"

Opening lines are often important indicators of how people really feel about each other.

Dr. Chase was slightly ill at ease. He wasn't sure why he accepted Lady Landamere's invitation to dinner except that she was the most persuasive woman he'd ever met. To help him over his shyness in new situations he ordered a vodka martini from the bartender.

Katie came in with Peter and Mark. Rebecca was very happy to see them although she pointed out they were late.

Katie looked wonderful. All black and rhinestoned. She, too, was wearing a wide-shouldered number designed by her friend Norma Kamali. She remarked to Rebecca that she thought it was interesting that once women took the padding out of their bras, they added it to their shoulders. Peter said that was their way of showing they were contacting their masculine sides. He certainly had contacted his looking like R. R! and Mark quietly looked intense. He always wore an intense look. He wore it like you wear a great coat or hat. With style and comfort. He looked kind of like Pacino through the eyes of Astaire. They all told each other how well they looked and they were correct.

"Well, we *are* the handsome young psychologist, aren't we?" That was Trace's official greeting to Peter. "Usually those book jacket pictures bear no resemblance whatsoever to their authors, but in your case, my dear, it fails to do you justice. Why, Katie, he's simply divine."

It would be difficult not to show appreciation for such an effusive greeting, so Peter thanked Trace smiling warmly.

Katie smiled saying, "You can see where I get my way with words."

Peter was trying to take in the entire picture. Here he was face to face with Katie's monstrous mother, who appeared anything but monstrous. She was handsome. She was chic. She was elegant. Her demeanor seemed to reflect years of confidence. But monstrous would not be an adjective Peter would choose to describe her.

It was clear that Lady Landamere was interested in Peter. Leading him by his arm, she walked him over to the dining room windows where she had a chance to ply him with Mr. James's salmon mousse, along with a battery of questions. Once satisfied that he was not a colleague of that "crazy man" in California who calls himself a doctor, she led him back into the living room and returned him to her other guests.

What followed was a lot of chat, a lot of caviar, and a lot of watching and waiting. Rebecca was watching Mark, who was watching Rebecca. Peter was watching Katie, and Katie was watching Peter and Richard and Trace, and Richard was watching the door hoping that the two guests yet to arrive might still turn out to be Jacqueline Bisset and Linda Evans. Ellen was watching everyone, and as to be expected, no one was watching Ellen. Everyone was waiting for dinner.

Katie complimented Trace on how well she was looking, and Trace introduced Katie and Peter to Dr. Chase. Katie said something charming to the effect that if Dr. Chase was taking care of her mother then she knew she was in excellent hands. Dr. Chase remarked that it was obvious Katie had inherited her mother's charm.

Katie must have meant what she said to Peter in the taxi because she was making a point of being extra warm and friendly to Richard and Ellen. She even engaged her nephew in some conversation and, though a bit forced, commented that Joshua seemed like a very cute little boy and she hoped in the future she'd get to know him better.

Katie asked Richard how he liked being the Gelato King, all the time studying him trying to find out who this man was who shared the same mother as she. She kept looking for telltale signs to prove they were brother and sister. They were hard to come by. Richard seemed so cut off from his feelings. It's not that he wasn't smart. Anyone who could build an empire from one little ice cream cone had to be smart. He just seemed unrelated. To her and to himself.

If there was a level of anxiety permeating the room, everyone was doing his best to conceal it.

Rebecca was doing a lot of whispering to Mark. There was really nothing that couldn't have been said aloud, but being a superstar required a lot of whispering, which after a while became habitual. Rebecca took Trace aside to ask her when the others would be arriving. It was eight-forty and dinner had been called for eight.

"How silly of me not to tell you we should all be seated. Fred and Wan Ling won't be coming up until dessert." She explained they hadn't the patience to sit through an entire dinner.

"Mrs. Pierce was kind enough to offer her services. She'll be bringing them up from my suite in a bit. She was putting little bows in their hair when I left them."

Even Rebecca couldn't help but notice Trace's eccentricity. Dogs, bows, and dinner parties. Everyone I know is crazy, she thought. She whispered something to one of the waitresses and within minutes they announced that dinner was being served.

It was a perfect picture if your eye didn't happen to notice the two empty seats on either side of Joshua. Lady Landamere was seated at the head of the table with Baveral on her right and Dr. Chase on her left.

Joshua hadn't taken any notice of Mr. James until he saw him supervising the entrance of ten perfectly garnished Cornish hens. Well, actually nine perfect ones. The tenth looked a bit maimed.

Joshua on seeing Mr. James for the first time began pointing and screaming, "Doody face! Doody face!"

Ellen apologized to everyone explaining that Joshua had never seen a black person before.

Rebecca suggested to Richard that it might be a good idea to let Joshua out more often.

When the platter got to Joshua, Mr. James served him the one slightly mangled hen that had earlier dropped on the kitchen floor. Joshua looked down at his place and screamed, "Doody hands! Doody hands!"

"He's thoroughly delightful," said Trace.

Then she looked at Mr. James and said, "You have the good fortune of going home tonight and never seeing him again. He's my grandchild."

Willie (he dropped the Dr. Chase after his first martini and William even before the second glass of wine) made some reassuring remark to the effect that given time Joshua would grow out of it. He did not say exactly what "it" was.

Peter thought to himself that the kid was simply the tangible result of his parents' repressed behavior. Peter noticed that Richard was staring at him.

Finally Richard said, "So you're the shrink! In Houston we have less need for your profession. I have my own theory that people get crazier and crazier as they get closer to the edges of our country. That's why New Yorkers and Californians are so nuts! It's geographic."

Peter said that was a theory he had never heard before but he'd certainly give it some thought.

Katie made a point of controlling whatever judgmental thoughts she was thinking in her all-out effort to establish better relations with her brother.

Ellen said that Janet Rolsten (as though everyone knew exactly who Janet Rolsten was) certainly was "nuts" and she lives in Houston and was born in Shrevesport, so she wasn't sure about Richard's theory being one hundred percent accurate.

Ellen was more interested in what film Mark was currently working on. She had seen his last two films and thought they were "fabulous." She asked him what kind of man Warren Beatty really was, and he suggested she ask Rebecca. Rebecca smiled a smile that said she didn't appreciate his answer. Ellen, ever the admiring fan, continued. "What are you working on now?" she asked.

He told her most recently he was directing Rebecca's picture, but they fought bitterly and shooting closed down after three and a half weeks, and that ended the film and their conversation. Trace picked it up telling Mark, "Rebecca fights bitterly with all her directors. It shouldn't stop you, dear, it should just fuel you. In fact that's what it does for her. She was probably just hitting her stride when you closed down."

Ellen, looking for safer ground, said the duck was delicious.

Trace said it was Cornish hen, but an honest mistake, since it was a little fatty.

Joshua said he hated corn.

Rebecca said they probably should have eaten out.

Mr. James agreed.

Baveral left the table to go and get his folders and almost on cue, Trace asked Rebecca to bring out the carousel.

"Oh, boy," said Joshua. "Merry-go-Round!"

Rebecca, who was much better at delegating responsibility than actually carrying it out herself, summoned one of Mr. James's staff, who brought out the Kodak projector. At the same time the bartender set up a portable screen at the far end of the dining room.

Lady Landamere explained that she had arranged for a short slide show that she hoped would help to enlighten and entertain all of those present. She suggested everyone proceed with dinner and if no one objected, she said, she would begin showing her slides.

"Trace," Rebecca said, "no one has slide shows anymore. People have video recorders or films. Slides are obsolete."

Joshua on seeing the screen got over his disappointment. Now he only wanted popcorn and was hoping with every fiber of his fifty-three pounds that the movie would be *E.T.*

Instead the first slide was the old logo of the MGM lion roaring. Except it wasn't a lion. It was Trace imitating a lion. Then the screen went to a credit that read "Lady Landamere presents *Slides of the Family.*"

"You've got to be kidding," Rebecca's voice was heard in the darkened room. "I can't think of anything more boring."

Mark put his arm around her and told her to be quiet and watch the screen. He kissed her cheek.

The first slide was of Katie. So was the second and the third and the fourth and fifth. Katie at one. Katie at one and a half. Katie at two, etc.

Trace began her narrative commentary from her seat at the table. She had the slide clicker in one hand and her cigarette in the other. "These are some baby pictures I found of Katie. To me she looks terribly happy there, don't you agree?"

Out loud, Katie said, "I hope this is not going to get embarrassing." She was feeling just the beginnings of that old discomfort/ anger at the possibility of humiliation. Peter squeezed her hand lovingly.

Trace's voice-over continued and so did the slides.

"Now, this was Katie a little older, and as you can see she was becoming fat . . . so maybe she was not that happy. But that was a long time ago."

A slide of Katie and Trace smiling at a swimming pool next appears on the screen. Both mother and daughter are in bathing suits.

Trace is posing like she is still Miss Texas, and Katie is covering as much of herself as is humanly possible with Trace's big hat.

Next we see a slide of Katie holding her *Mother!* book up at a bookstore.

"Katie, as you probably know, had an extremely critical mother, who it turns out helped her become a writer. . . . A good one. But she doesn't believe that she is all that good. I've been told all that insecurity comes from what she was supposed to get from me when she was a child and didn't. . . ."

There is an effective pause as the film freezes on another slide of Katie at three years old.

"Nice sequential editing job, Trace," Mark said in the darkened room.

"Well, Katie, all I can say to you as your mother is no one can give what they don't have. If I had it, you would have gotten it."

Katie asked Peter if he didn't see these slides as a rather controlling mechanism, and he told her to let it play out before she condemns it.

Next we see Richard. Richard at three with his baseball bat. Richard at four with his catcher's mitt. Richard at five with his cash register selling peanuts to Trace and his daddy.

"Why don't you have any pictures of me at one and two?" Richard asked.

Trace disregarded her son's question.

"I wasn't able to find any pictures of Richard and Katie together because they were always running away from each other."

Next a slide of Richard at his office at Fields Gelato. He does not look happy.

"Richard doesn't think too much of himself either. Neither of my children do. Perhaps this is my fault."

Next we see a slide of Ellen and then one of Joshua.

Rebecca piped up and said, "Remind me to show my baby pictures for dessert."

Katie has been watching the slides suspiciously and has by now ceased to enjoy her Cornish hen and not because of its high calorie count.

Next slide.

"And this is Fred."

Katie interrupted, "And this is ridiculous! We did not come here to watch you show slides, Mother." As she spoke she got up and turned on the lights.

"Maybe the next one would have been of me," Rebecca said.

"That's alright, Katie, dear," Trace said. "Feel free to turn the lights back on. . . . You never did like the dark," she added.

"We were just a few slides short of Intermission. You see I was just re-introducing my family to each other since it's been quite some time since we all assembled and I thought a few slides from the early days might put some historical perspective on our lives today and on my will. After all, that is why I have gathered you all here. You are to be the recipients of my will.

"I would also like to take this opportunity to thank Baveral Flower. Without Baveral I could not have accomplished many things in my life, including one of the reasons for this dinner. He is an indefatigable worker who at the age of seventy-six . . ."

"Seventy-seven," Baveral corrected her.

" . . . went to four foreign countries this year on my behalf. He has helped me to set up a modest but ongoing fund in third world nations on behalf of children's hunger and it is because of him that I can stand here and say with confidence my affairs are now, as of today, all in order.

"And now everyone, let us have dessert."

Lady Landamere opened her jeweled Cartier box and lit a cigarette. She couldn't have been more delighted. The evening was going along perfectly. It was nine-thirty. As planned the dining room doors opened and Mr. James announced the arrival of Mrs. Pierce.

Lady Landamere arose. She looked at her guests. She was in total control. She knew what it felt like to be the cat that ate the canary. She smiled a wealthy smile. If this were theater she thought, and there were an act one curtain, she thought, I would say, Mr. James, please show them in, and the curtain would fall.

Katie looked at her mother with the knowledge that the ball was now in her mother's court and she was not pleased.

Trace was beaming. Looking at her guests she said, "I would like it if all of my family can have dessert together. Therefore Mrs. Pierce, if you please."

All that was missing was a drum roll. The dining room doors were flung open and first a young man aiding Mrs. Pierce entered with two devices that resembled high chairs. He proceeded to placed them so that they fit perfectly into the two empty chairs on either side of Joshua. He left.

A drum roll. There stood Mrs. Pierce.

Trace said, "Dear friends and family, may I introduce my grand-children. Most of you know Fred." Spotlight on Fred. All that was missing was some sort of anthem. Fred appeared aware of the drama of the moment and marched into the room. He was wearing a black formal bow tie around his neck. His walk was dignified and proud. His tail wagged in a fast marching tempo. First he greeted Lady Landamere with an abundance of kisses and then, with a little assistance from one of the waitresses, he took his rightful seat next to Joshua.

"And my other grandchild . . . Wan Ling," said Trace. Spotlight on Wan Ling.

Oh, my God. Wan Ling wasn't another Lhasa apso.

"Jesus Christ! She's a geek!" said Richard.

Wan Ling was definitely not a Lhasa apso. Though she did have a little red bow in her shiny black oriental hair.

Trace said proudly, "Wan Ling was a Cambodian orphan who at five months old was found in an abandoned village. She was close to death. Today she is a beautiful healthy fifty-three-pound little girl and . . . she is my daughter. And after this evening I would like to make plans for Wan Ling to be my granddaughter for it is my wish that Wan Ling be raised by Katie."

"I can't believe it!" Katie said. "It's the most insane thing she has ever done."

"And if for any reason Katie can not raise Wan Ling then I would like you, Rebecca, to adopt Wan Ling."

"I'm the one who can't believe it!" Rebecca said. "An entire evening of second billing."

"Unbelievable," everyone thought.

Wan Ling, all of eighteen months and dressed like she just ran over from the cast of *The King and I,* was helped into her high chair by the nice waitress from *Ain't Misbehavin'.*

Joshua looked to the right of him and saw Fred. He looked to the left of him and saw Wan Ling. Who was this stupid funny looking little girl everyone was making a fuss over? He started to cry. He reached toward his mother. His tears dropped freely onto Fred's head. Fred looked up and saw Joshua's tuxedoed hand. . . . Water. . . . Tuxedo. . . . Hand! He bit it. Joshua got equally hysterical and bit Fred's ear.

Trace suggested that Joshua and Fred not sit next to each other at future parties. She reminded Richard that this wasn't the first time the two of them had problems. Joshua who usually hung close to his mother switched seats with Ellen so that he could sit next to his father. He seemed to sense that his father had more power in this particular group than his mother.

Mr. James came in just at the proper moment with a big beautiful chocolate mousse cake that said "Welcome to the Family Wan Ling." Trace suggested that everyone eat dessert, be merry, and watch the remainder of her slides.

Peter couldn't believe what he was witnessing. It was, in its own way, beyond anything all of his psych textbooks or his practice ever explained.

Richard was hurt and angry. He was also keenly aware that whoever got Wan Ling was good for at least another ten million. He asked his mother, "Why haven't you asked me and Ellen to raise Wan Ling?"

Trace suggested he look to his right.

Joshua was making his eyes slant by pulling the skin around them very tightly across his face, and at the same time making monster faces at Wan Ling, who had yet to say a word.


It was impossible to get everyone to calm down enough to begin the second half of Trace's slide presentation.

Katie thought her mother had just pulled one of the most outrageously controlling acts of her illustrious career. Richard was still in a state of shock. Baveral, in an attempt to remain cheerful, was dangling his key chain trying to amuse Wan Ling, and Dr. Chase was attending to Ellen, who was having one of her infrequent but nevertheless severe asthma attacks.

Trace was trying to get everyone to settle down. The second half of her slides was beginning. None of her guests cared in the least about her low budget slides. The emphasis had shifted to what was happening live, and Peter suggested to Lady Landamere that whatever else was on her slides be dealt with in person since everyone was gathered at the table.

Lady Landamere asked him if he would have the audacity to make that suggestion to Ansel Adams, Federico Fellini, or Richard Avedon.

Rebecca was not exactly upset. She was bored. Her span of attention for dramas other than her own was remarkably short. She suggested that whoever didn't want to watch the slides could, like her, go inside and look out the window. It was suggestions such as the above that contributed to making her such an illustrious and inventive hostess.

Katie said she thought it was imperative that a family discussion take place, now. She was outvoted by one and only one powerful vote as the slides began again. Peter urged her to let her mother's slides finish and then they would all talk, and Katie accused him of being the Great Appeaser and then called him the worse thing she could think of. "Mother Lover!" she said in the tone usually reserved for Mother . . . something else.

He gave her a look that suggested she might have gone too far.

A series of slides of Wan Ling appeared on the screen. Undernourished and battered. Lady Landamere's narration followed Wan Ling's path from the war-torn Cambodian village that was once her home to Beverly Hills and her adoption just three months ago.

Like Rebecca, Joshua wasn't having any fun either. He had wanted *E.T.*, and he got a real life alien invader instead.

He took his piece of chocolate mousse cake and ran up to the screen. He proceeded to smear the mousse cake all over Wan Ling's beautiful little face.

Joshua was now happy.

The next slide seemed to have been Baveral Flower. It was

impossible to be certain because he now had brown dessert smudged all over his face, too.

Of course the projector had to be stopped.

One of the waitresses tried to wash the chocolate off the screen which only further smudged it. And so it came to be, through a twist of fate and ten little chocolate fingers, that a few of the guests were to get their wish after all. The rest of the evening would have to conclude without the use of visual aids. Trace told everyone how disappointed she was because they would be missing some excellent pictures.

"Baveral," Trace said, "let us skip around now that our program has been disrupted and let's get to this ridiculous business of my will."

Dr. Chase, who had consumed more wine this particular evening than in all of the last year, was feeling his feelings a little more than he was used to. He had nothing but admiration for this gutsy woman. He'd never spent an evening even barely resembling this one. The infighting, the energy. An adopted infant. The flamboyance. He wondered what it would have been like to have been married to Trace. It was hard for him to even imagine. He found her enormously attractive although quite clearly her looks alone were no longer her drawing card. But women who were once very sought after retain their ability to dazzle long after their physical appearance begins to fade. With Trace, she enchanted the good doctor with her charm, wit, and free spirit. They were close to the same age and yet he felt as though he could be her student in life, and here she was dealing with dignity and humor with what was the toughest part of it. The ending.

Ellen, just about recovered from her asthma attack, wasn't thinking anything remotely close to what Dr. Chase was thinking. Like Richard, she was thinking, Money. Money for Joshua. Money for

Richard. Money for herself. She was nervous. She was nervous about Katie and she was nervous about Wan Ling. A daughter and a grandchild suddenly materializing out of thin air. Why she'd known her mother-in-law for nearly five and a half years now, and she'd only met Katie once. She thought theirs was a relationship severed forever. The timing couldn't be worse to discover additional members of the immediate family.

Everyone had rearranged themselves comfortably in the living room. Everyone but one that was. Joshua was missing but Ellen hadn't noticed his absence yet. She could only be nervous about one thing at a time.

"About the will," Trace continued, "I've always abhorred the idea of families gathering soon after the funeral for the reading of the will. There's something carnivorous about it. It's also unfair because no one gets to tell the deceased how they feel about the way they've been dealt with in the end. So I would like to tell you all now what provisions I've made for the future; and you can all deal with your feelings about it and me while I'm still here to be of whatever assistance I can. So, Baveral, let's go through the basics."

Baveral began. "Lady Landamere," he said matter of factly, "through the years has amassed a personal fortune estimated at thirty-five million dollars."

A bolt of surprise went through the room. Rebecca was genuinely impressed. "Congratulations, Trace. That's terrific," she said. "You must have been keeping it under the floorboards."

"I don't know why you all look so surprised," Trace said. "Certainly you all saw me live rich. Why in the world would you expect me to die poor?"

Even Katie put aside her anger long enough to be stunned. She knew her mother had money but had she guessed at the amount it would have been a much more conservative estimate.

Baveral continued. Lady Landamere's wishes were as follows.

Ten million dollars was for the aforementioned Third World Children's Hunger Fund.

It was a fact that nothing touched Lady Landamere more than the sight of a poor starving child. Whenever she would flip though the dials watching television, she would be overcome with emotion when she would stumble across some B-rated Hollywood star making an overly dramatic appeal to the viewer to send a contribution to help feed these ravaged children. The celebrity moved her not at all. But the sight of these poor children broke her heart.

How bizarre, Katie thought. All of those years growing up with Trace telling her she was fat. All these years with Trace telling her to stop eating. It was all about starving. But it was never about food. It was about the emptiness. Sometimes there wasn't food enough in the world for the feeling of emptiness. And now she leaves her money to third world hunger. Amazing! Katie thought.

Baveral continued. The twenty-five percent of Fields Gelato, which Lady Landamere retained after giving the rest of the company to Richard, was, upon Lady Landamere's death to be given to Katie with the stipulation that she see to it that Fields produce and merchandise a Dietetic Gelato Dessert and that she oversee its initial presentation.

Now Richard was pissed. "Mother," he whined, "I don't want to have to work with Katie. We really don't even like each other."

"You really don't know each other," Trace corrected him. "Now it is altogether possible that once you were to know each other you still might not like each other."

She took a long look at Richard, then she looked at Katie and said, "In fact it is more than likely that you won't. But since you are from the same mother, it is only sensible that you investigate each other."

Katie looked at Richard and for one of the only times in their relationship agreed that he was right. The odds on their working well together were not very good.

"She doesn't know shit about gelato," Richard continued. "I don't want to work with Katie." He was still whining. "I'm the one who knows about making money. All she ever did was spend it. I bet she still doesn't have any money saved even with her dumb book."

This was the first time Katie heard Richard voice his feelings about her writing. "I guess you didn't enjoy my book, Richard," she said sarcastically.

"From the little I read I didn't. From the little I read it would be impossible to tell we had the same mother. My experiences with my mother were very satisfying. Yours, as you have so indiscriminately told the world, were 'shitty'! "

Trace looked at him skeptically. "What we all can agree Katie does know about," Trace said, "is dieting. She knows more about what dieters want than Jane Fonda."

"Boy, oh, boy!" said Richard getting in touch with his anger, "I see it pays to be estranged from your mother in this family. So far Katie's hitting the jackpot while poor Richard, Ellen, and Joshua Fields, the only family who's supported you and the only family you've known for the past three and a half years, are coming up empty, man, absolutely empty."

Ellen sat up proud. She wanted to say, Thataboy, Richard. You tell 'em! But she didn't, which was just as well.

Dr. Chase, feeling a little out of place, suggested that maybe the "members of the immediate family" wanted to be by themselves for a while.

Trace told him that his choice of the words "immediate family" made it sound like she had already died.

Katie was fast approaching the boiling point.

Back to the will. A trust fund of five million dollars set up for Wan Ling to be administered by Katie if she adopted Wan Ling. Baveral would co-administer the trust. She did not stipulate that Katie marry Peter, but she did suggest it would be an idea worth entertaining. If Katie declined to adopt Wan Ling, Rebecca was next in line.

A trust fund of two million dollars was set aside for Joshua, to be administered by Richard and Baveral with one major condition. Ellen and Richard must agree Joshua consult with a child psychiatrist.

Richard and Ellen were appalled. Not only at the suggestion that their son was anything less than perfect but in the three million dollar difference in trust funds for the two grandchildren. Lady Landamere explained that Joshua was her grandson, but until she found out about her present illness, Wan Ling was not to be her grandchild but her adopted daughter. She also reminded Richard of the wealth he currently enjoyed from the gelato windfall which she sent flying in his direction just a few years ago.

"That was no windfall. That was nothing until I made it into Fields Gelato. That was nothing!"

Richard considered storming out, but his avarice demanded he hear the rest of the will. So far this was the biggest outrage he had ever endured. When he told Trace his feeling, she said she was sorry.

For a moment Richard took slight consolation in the fact that his mother apologized, but then she said she was sorry that nothing more outrageous had ever happened to him. She said, "Soft lives make for soft backbones."

To Katie Trace left two million dollars, and to Richard Trace left two million dollars.

At last! Richard thought. At least it was something. At least it was enough to cover the trip. There were no conditions. She did add that she hoped it wouldn't stop Katie from continuing to write, because she thought someday Katie would be a great writer. (As soon as she finished with all those mother books!) To this end she was leaving Katie her unfinished, but nonetheless "Magical Memoirs" in the hope that Katie would organize and eventually publish them. She said she thought Katie might see both their lives from a new perspective after sifting through her forty or so assorted diaries. She was also leaving her all of her slides.

To Rebecca Trace left all her jewelry and furs. Including a floor-length sable coat. Rebecca was stunned. First, she knew that Lady Landamere's jewels were extraordinarily beautiful, and they were real. They must be worth well over a million dollars, Rebecca thought. What she said was "Why? I mean . . . I thank you and I'm . . . speechless . . . but why?"

Trace answered simply. "Because I care about you like a second daughter and because Katie loves you. And because I know you love her and me. And I don't know who else in this world you honestly feel that way about." As she was speaking she looked at Mark and her eyes offered her apologies to him.

Katie was tired of hearing herself referred to in the third person and she was tired of Peter restraining her from voicing what she was feeling. All of her hopes for the evening ending in reconciliation had long since faded away.

She looked at her brother and said, "You have every right to be angry, Richard, and so do I. But not for the reasons you think. You're angry because you think you haven't been left enough money. You should be angry because 'she' has been living your life for you. We have both been raised as nothing but puppets of a controlling and manipulative mother who now 'claims' to be dying. Every controlling mother I know of past the age of fifty is always claiming or threatening to be dying. Well, guess what! We're all going to die one day. And maybe she's going to die sooner than us and maybe she's not. The natural order of life says she will. But in the meantime, she's going to die having lived her life the way she wanted to live it and she . . ."

"She! She! Can you not speak to me. I am not dead yet. I am here," Trace said very firmly.

"You!" Katie turned and faced her. ". . . You are going to die having lived your life the way you saw fit and you want me to live my life the way you think I ought to. You have tried to manipulate my life from the day I was born. You have told me how to look and how to be and what was acceptable and what was not. You withheld your love until I pleased you . . ."

Her voice was charged with emotion.

". . . And now you tell me I'm to raise a baby that you have adopted 'for' me. Well, I don't want 'your' baby. If I want to have a baby, I'll have one myself. And I don't want to write your goddamn memoirs, and I don't want your money, if it means being controlled by you."

And then as she tried unsuccessfully to keep the tears from welling up in her eyes she looked at Trace and screamed, "Why can't you just let go! Can't you understand that. Just let go."

Standing now, she turned, quickly pulled her fur coat from the closet and ran out of the front door.

The room was silent.

Rebecca thought it was quite the soliloquy.

Peter wasn't sure what he was feeling. He knew he felt compassion and admiration for the way Katie stood up and held her own against her powerhouse of a mother, but Trace was her mother, and she was dying, and God knows mothers did really die. . . . But there was only one thing he could do because he loved Katie.

"I'm sorry, Trace, I really am," he said. "I'm sorry everyone." And he grabbed his coat and ran out after Katie.

"Let them go," Trace said. "I have not finished. Baveral, please continue, won't you, dear."

Trace was like iron. It would be impossible to know how she really felt about what had just happened, but she was not going to let Katie's outburst ruin her dinner party.

Richard couldn't believe that Katie, who was dealt with in the will like the heir apparent to the throne of England, had stormed out, and he was still sitting there to suffer the further indignities of this . . . will. But greed kept him in his seat while Baveral continued.

There were other bequeaths. A scholarship fund at Carnegie Mellon (Jack Harris's alma mater) for film education and restoration. She wanted Richard's father's films to live as long as there were filmgoers. A bequeath to the Heart Fund. But it was the final two bequeaths that put Richard right over the edge.

It seemed that the estate that Trace and her family lived in until she and Jack Fields were divorced was never sold and still belonged to Trace. It was learned she'd been renting and receiving income from it for the past seventeen years. Today it was valued at well over six million dollars.

She left it to Fred for the remainder of his life. Two and one-half premium acres in Bel Air for Fred to romp and urinate upon. You could almost hear each person in the room thinking out loud . . . Let's see, Lady Landamere bought Fred three months after she and Katie stopped speaking so that would mean . . .

Richard, the mathematician, figured it out first. Fred was only four and a half.

At the end of Fred's lifetime the home was to be donated to Actors for Animals, or some less than impressive sounding organization, which would use it to house unwanted pets the A.S.P.C.A. no longer provided shelter for.

And the remaining millions were given to Dr. Chase for further research in whatever area of medicine at Massachusetts General could best be served with her donation.

Richard couldn't believe it. His mother trusted a perfect stranger more than she did her own son. Who was this Chase guy anyway? Until two months ago he didn't even exist.

Richard was wondering how this whole thing had gotten this far away from him. A month ago there was no Katie, no Dr. Chase, and no Wan Ling. And Rebecca! Where in the hell did she come from! She could buy and sell the whole goddamn table. What did she need with Trace's jewelry. The rich get richer, Richard thought, feeling poorer by the second.

"Ellen, I want to go home," he said like an angry thirteen-year-old. "Where's Joshua? Go get Joshua!" If he stayed much longer he would have regressed to the same age as his son.

He looked at his mother and said, "I don't know what to say to you. You have offended me and my family beyond words. I have been a good son to you. It is my belief that you are finally getting even with me because my father left you for Susan."

Susan was, of course, the Susan that Jack made into one of the greatest sex goddesses on celluloid. He also made her his third wife and mother of his youngest and favorite child, Lucianna. When Jack died just two years ago, Richard was left next to nothing in his will because Susan was and is still very much alive and Jack was still very much in love with her at the time of his death.

Trace liked to say that even if he had left Susan millions of dollars, which is doubtful considering the disaster of his final films (which he cofinanced), she would still need every penny of it for plastic surgery. Trace said Susan was better preserved than any one of Jack's fifty-seven films. She also said she was older.

Trace assured Richard his assumption was false. No one would leave anyone for Susan.

"Why would I want Jack's films restored if I hated him? I loved your father deeply. As much as I loved my darling Austin. Fortunately I was not in my fertile years when I married Lord Edwin so I never had to deal with the experience of a child from a loveless union."

Again the voice of Ellen could be heard with the now almost expected chant. "Rich—ard, I can't find Joshua."

"How can you misplace your child?" Rebecca asked. "You'd think he was an umbrella."

"You really wouldn't know what it's like, Rebecca, because you've never been a mother."

"Well, I've played one in two films and in one I received an Academy Award nomination," Rebecca answered her, putting her in her place.

"Joshua! Where are you?" Ellen almost sang the words. Kind of like, "Ready or not, here I come."

Nothing.

Wan Ling was of no help. She spoke no English. Like a little porcelain doll she sat almost motionless watching the chaos around her.

"Look how calm Wan Ling remains," Rebecca said to Mark.

"It's part of the Eastern oriental culture thing. I think they're born with it," he answered.

Once again no one knew where Joshua was. Mr. James said the last time he saw him he was collecting all the soiled pink linen napkins from the dinner table.

Luckily, Lady Landamere thought to ask Fred where Joshua was and that was when she discovered Fred, too, was missing.

"Fred! Fred, come here this instant!"

Nothing.

"Fred, you answer me or there'll be no midnight snack tonight."
Lady Landamere meant business.

"Why don't you threaten to cut him out of the will," Richard
suggested. "I was born in that house in Bel Air. I loved that house.
Fred's never even seen it."

A sound was heard in the distance. It was muffled but it sounded
like it could be a bark. Everyone tried to hear where it was coming
from. The bedroom. No. The living room. No. The dining room.
No.

The kitchen! Fred was in the kitchen. With pink napkins tied
around his mouth so that he could hardly breathe, no less bark. He
was tied to the broom in the kitchen utility closet.

"He's my prisoner!" said Joshua, who was sitting on the floor of
the closet guarding the door, like a giant police dog making sure
Fred didn't get away.

One could almost imagine Fred saying, Thank you, God! Thank
you for hearing a little dog's prayers.

Joshua obviously had not forgiven Fred for the tuxedoed hand
incident earlier in the evening.

Trace told Richard both he and his father were somewhat unfor-
giving and that Joshua obviously took after them both.

Richard was glad to be leaving. He had suffered too long the
indignities of this evening, and there was no Jacqueline Bisset for
compensation. And Rebecca didn't even wear a dress that showed
her tits.

"By the way," he said to Trace, "I hope you don't take this the
wrong way, but when are you supposed to die? I mean when is all
of this will business supposed to take effect?"

"So that's where Joshua gets it from," Trace replied. "Ask my doctor, dear," she said with a hint of annoyance.

Dr. Chase took Richard aside and told him that his mother had entered the final stage of left ventricle something or other and according to past cases of record hadn't more than a few months left to live. Richard thought for a minute and then asked his mother if the will might still undergo changes. Trace answered him that as long as there was life there was change.

Richard thought of asking Trace if he could take Fred for the weekend. He thought of saying that it would give Joshua and Fred a chance to become friends, to make amends, and then he could let Fred loose on the West Side Highway. He rationalized that anyone in his position would have similar thoughts.

"Maybe they're all wrong," Rebecca said. "Maybe you'll prove all those bastards wrong. I've heard of real miracles, Trace. I have a nutritionist in California who . . ."

Trace stopped Rebecca. "I've lived an enormously full life, my lovely superstar. I wanted another chance to try and raise Wan Ling because of all the mistakes I made with Katie, but maybe this way is better. It's entirely possible that I might pop in and see your nutritionist when I get back to L.A., but you see, whatever the outcome, for the first time in my life, I'm prepared."

There was really nothing more to say. Dinner was officially over. All that remained was the gathering of coats, the goodbyes and the question of Wan Ling.

Trace said something about being sure that in a little time Katie would come to her senses. Richard wondered aloud how anyone could need a little time to inherit an extra "fifteen mil."

Rebecca asked Mark if he wanted to stay a while and hardly waited for his answer because she knew he would. Baveral was destined to drive back to the big house on Long Island alone, while Mrs. Pierce temporarily stayed the night with Wan Ling until her cousin could come and fill in. Richard and Ellen and Joshua were more than happy to be leaving as a threesome united in their outrage. It was Trace who asked Dr. Chase if he might want to spend the night in her suite since he seemed a little overly wined. He liked that idea fine.

"Just like a California dinner party," Rebecca remarked, glancing at her all-diamond watch. "Even with the added drama of Katie's hysterics the night is still young and it's all over."

"That's not only true of California dinner parties. The same holds true for most Hollywood careers as well," Mark said.

As far as dinner parties go, all's well that ends well and this one was ending if not well, at least early enough to watch the "Eleven O'clock News."

*Chapter*

17

*I*n truth, Rebecca was exhausted. Even for a mind like hers that worked overtime, the night's festivities were a lot to absorb. She was glad when Mr. James and his all-girl band packed up their last chafing dish and came in to say their final goodnight. This was the goodnight where Mr. James held your hand for a few moments longer than necessary, in case you wished to put a little something extra in his palm. The expression used in catering circles for that particular act is "greasing it." Rebecca did. She gave him an eight by ten autographed picture of herself. He said something to her about this dinner party being, "Crazier than a party for two hundred." She thought to herself that he and his crew really did work hard, and she asked him to wait for a moment. She went in to the bedroom and came back with four more eight by ten glossies and gave one to each of the girls. They were signed, "Thank you for a delicious evening, Rebecca Holmes."

"It was the perfect way to say goodnight to Mr. James and Company." She and Mark were finally alone.

"Quite an evening," Mark said with an almost smile. (Pacino types don't smile fully even when their smiling.)

Rebecca agreed. It certainly was quite an evening.

She went to the phone and dialed Katie, but her machine answered. She hung up. She tried Peter and left an answer on his machine. She told Mark she was feeling kind of guilty that she didn't defend Katie at the climax of her drama, but she said she wasn't sure that Katie didn't overreact.

"I mean she wasn't sentenced to death in the electric chair. She was left over ten million dollars."

Mark told her she had no reason to feel guilty and that made her feel better. As long as she didn't have to worry any further about Katie, it was definitely time to change the subject.

"Can you believe Trace gave me that incredible jewelry. That jewelry is so unbelievably magnificent. I had no idea she loved me that much."

"We all love you that much. I love you that much, too," Mark said. "I just don't have any jewelry to leave you."

"You don't have to own it and you don't have to leave it to me. You could buy it for me now, while you're still here to watch me enjoy it."

That's what was so amazing about Rebecca's thinking process. "While you're still here to watch me enjoy it." It wasn't so much that she was the center of her own universe, Mark thought. It was that she thought she should be the center of everyone else's universe as well.

He walked by her pinching her ass. "If you do not raise your eyes you will think you are the highest point." This was what he told her as he went to the bar to make himself a drink. "Want a brandy?" he asked her already knowing what she would answer.

"Puffy," she said. "Makes me puffy in the morning. Under here." He didn't have to look. He knew she was pointing to her eyes.

"How come you're not afraid to love me?" she asked him. "Most men are afraid to love me."

"Why should I be afraid of someone I can beat up?" he answered. "I can beat you up. You're just a girl." He walked over to where she had flopped in the big living room chair and playfully shadow boxed with her.

He wasn't sure if he loved her or not. He just knew that all the other women he spent any time with wore real thin after only a few nights. But Rebecca, even with all her craziness, was always challenging. Maybe it was that so much of her love was already committed to herself that made it challenging, but there was nothing Mark loved more than winning. Not even Rebecca.

"Well, what would you like to do?" he asked her. "Would you like to make love?"

"Can't. Lips!" She smiled at him seductively.

"Can't. Lips?" he mimicked her. "What does that mean?"

"Tomorrow. Revlon. Print ad. You know 'Summer Lips.' My own Beach Colors."

"Oh, of course" he said smiling to himself. "Well, we don't have to kiss." He was sipping his brandy.

"But I love to kiss. Anyway, it's late. But you can sleep here if you want to. Unless of course you only want me for my lips and my body."

By way of an answer, Mark started to get undressed. He was tired, and he could just as soon take a cab back to his hotel in the morning.

"No, that's not why I want you," he answered her with a smile. "I want you because Rachel Ward was busy tonight."

There was something about the way he treated her that she liked. It might have been as simple as the fact that he wasn't afraid of her. What was depressing was that she was not choosing to be with Mark from a long list of prospective suitors. One of the drawbacks of being a superstar is the phone rings less than for a regular star. It's just hard to elicit sympathy from your listener when you're idolized by millions all over the world.

Rebecca went into the bathroom to begin the long nightly ritual of taking off the makeup. She had heard of this doctor in Beverly Hills who could permanently tattoo your eyeliner on, but it seemed far too risky for her to chance. Besides, he advertised in the *Hollwood Reporter,* which Rebecca did not view as a good sign.

Because she hadn't seen Mark in a while, she actually thought about skipping the full eye makeup removal in favor of half removal. (This would leave her natural brown lashes looking as black and full as they did on her eight by tens.) But knowing what kind of a day tomorrow promised to be she wisely decided against it. Besides, Mark loved her for what she was. Her concession to romance was in sharing her bed at all, on a night before a shooting. When she came out of the bathroom, she had slipped into something comfortable and expensive. An authentic satin robe from the thirties.

"Art Deco lives," Mark said on admiring Rebecca's choice of garment.

"I think Ginger Rogers wore this in *Top Hat,* nineteen thirty-four. Can you believe how well preserved it is?" She was modeling the robe for Mark, who also shared Rebecca's appreciation for details. "It's a shame someone's never found a way to preserve human beings the way the studios were able to preserve their films and wardrobes."

"You could always be stuffed," Mark remarked.

Under the robe was a beautiful peach satin nightgown. Getting into bed Rebecca looked every inch the superstar. Ordinarily she slept in the nude, but she didn't think it was fair to get Mark all turned on tonight considering her decision to forgo sex.

She reached into the drawer of the bedside table. She took out a small aluminum tube containing a fairly thick white ointment that smelled like menthol. She proceeded to smear gobs of it all over her mouth. If she had been tan she would have looked like Al Jolson, when he sang "Mammy." She also took a decongestant (a little trick she used for reducing puffiness on photographs). She offered some of her secret ointment to Mark, who knew this routine by heart. He put a little bit on his lips, which were, now that he bothered to notice, feeling a little dry. If he wasn't going to be making love tonight, he might as well be making himself look better too. Who better could he look to for inspiration than the lady lying next to him.

They lightly kissed goodnight. Their ointments merged together. Afterward, Rebecca checked once more to make sure she still had plenty of it left on. Mark leaned over and turned off the light. In many ways they were a perfect couple.


Katie was glad that Peter was sitting next to her in the taxi they had hailed to go less than seven blocks. She felt exhausted and drained. So did Peter. Everything was moving very fast in her head. The dinner party. Trace. Wan Ling. And what's more, she was still angry, and she didn't know how to get rid of the anger. Katie looked at her watch. It was only ten-thirty and yet she was totally exhausted. Trace had that effect on Katie for as long as she could remember. As Trace's momentum and energy increased with each hour, Katie's decreased in direct proportion to the amount of time she spent in her mother's company. A most interesting equation, Katie thought.

It was almost as though Trace was an engine that ran on other people's fuel. She kept chugging away gaining steam, while those around her felt depleted and plain out of gas by the end of an hour.

This wasn't at all the way she wanted the evening to end. Yet, she wondered if unconsciously she had scripted it this way, but decided she was just being hard on herself. This wasn't her script. This was Trace's movie, cast by her as well.

"I'm glad you were there tonight," Katie told Peter. She put her head on his shoulder and closed her eyes. "Oh, Peter," she said, sounding somewhat overwhelmed, "what am I going to do?"

Peter liked it when Katie needed his help. Sort of. It made her more vulnerable. He definitely liked the traditional image it represented. Man! Woman! Man take care of woman. There was something right about it. It was how his mother led him to believe it was supposed to be, although in truth it was nothing he saw at home, and in principle there were times it just didn't work. Like the times he needed to be taken care of. His mother always did that. The truth was he was used to strong women who could take care of themselves; that's what he really saw at home and that was one of the things that appeared so attractive about Katie. He was used to women who were in total control. His mother was.

There was nothing Evelyn Carriston couldn't handle. That's why he felt slightly uncomfortable when Katie would occasionally come apart. It made him feel like he was supposed to do something; that it was somehow his fault; and since he couldn't make her all better, it made him feel helpless. And feeling helpless made him angry. The few times in their relationship when she fell apart would frighten him.

He had signed on for that woman he met at the "David Susskind Forum" in San Francisco. That's the Katie he fell in love with.

"I'm glad I was there, too," he answered, "and you were right. You do have quite a family . . . but I think there are better ways of dealing with all of them."

The last thing Katie needed to hear at this moment was anything that even slightly resembled criticism.

"It's easy for you to say. They're not your family, and she's not your mother," Katie said defensively.

Their conversation continued as they entered her apartment.

"It just seems to me that you may have overreacted a little," Peter answered. "I mean you dealt with it all like you were still that powerless child living under her control."

"Because that's what she wants to make me into. I would think you could see that," Katie answered and then added sarcastically, "You must be a real support to your female patients who have trouble with their mothers. What do you do if they don't get along with Mother, shoot them, or make them watch reruns of 'The Donna Reed Show'?"

"I don't get it," Peter said shaking his head. "Can I tell you something?" he said. "You've got to stop blaming her for who she is, and more importantly for who you are. I have to tell you, it gets kind of boring, Katie."

Katie looked at him with a mixture of hurt and surprise and then said dramatically, "I can't believe you would say this to me on one of the most overwhelming evenings of my life."

The truth was that she knew very well it was possible she had overreacted, but she wasn't about to admit it to Peter. At times like these, in Katie's mind, Peter and Trace became comrades in the same army and Katie, odd man out.

"It would just be a whole lot better for you if you just had some other emotions at your disposal other than rage," Peter said as he hung up their coats in Katie's hall closet.

"You're definitely right, Peter," Katie continued sarcastically. "I guess you think that I should have walked up and kissed her . . ."

"Maybe," Peter answered without hesitation.

". . . And thanked her for attempting to control my life."

She walked into the kitchen and began mindlessly exploring the contents of the refrigerator.

"It all depends on whether or not you want to be a mother," he said. It was a deceptively simple answer. "If your mothering instinct is there, it doesn't matter whether Trace wants you to adopt Wan Ling or not. And it doesn't matter what color the baby is or where she came from. It's about what you want. It makes no sense not to do something you might want to do just because Trace wants you to do it, too." He knew he was right and Katie knew it, too.

"And stop eating my ice cream cookies. You can't keep using your long ago past as an excuse to gain weight."

"You needn't be so concerned about my weight, thank you very much."

"You're the one who asks me to remind you," he reminded her. He walked over and unburdened her by taking the ice cream for himself. "I would much prefer if you would stop making me into your keeper. I never wanted the responsibility of counting your calories."

"And what responsibilities do you want?" She glared at him. "I hate that you can eat any fucking thing you want and not get fat. I can't stay in here anymore and watch you eat." She made no move to leave the kitchen.

"I'm not going to allow you to lead me into a fight," he said, already halfway there. "If you want to be a mother," he continued between bites of the chocolate brown ice cream cookie that at the moment was commanding all of Katie's attention and was looking a lot more appealing than Peter, ". . . then you're going to have to feed your baby, in the kitchen, and babies eat five or six times a day." He finished his cookie, rinsed his plate, and put it in the sink and walked out of the kitchen.

"Aren't you a good little boy," Katie said mockingly, almost as though she was not going to stop until she had managed to destroy the remainder of the evening. "You're perfect. Your mother certainly trained you well."

Maybe it was said to assure that Peter begin to distance himself from her because she wasn't feeling very lovable. Because it worked. He walked inside and began undressing, all the while trying to figure out what was happening. It was almost as if there were two Katies. The one who wrote those extraordinary books, the one who could hold her own in any and all situations, the one he was proud to love. And the other one. And that was the one she was being now and that was the one who he still, after three years of on again off again living together, had yet to figure out.

While Peter was undressing, Katie was back in the kitchen. She did want to be a mother. At least she always said she did. She just assumed that when it happened it would be because she was married and pregnant. A baby would be the result of planned choices. Even if she blew it on the biological clock and one day chose to adopt a baby, that too would be the result of choice, hers.

She was now back in the refrigerator, but this time with paper cups in hand. She was starving. She wanted something sweet but she wanted to preserve at least a morsel of self-respect, so she didn't want to eat any sugar foods. What she wanted was milk and cookies. She settled instead for cashews, raisins, and granola with apple juice. All mixed together in a little Star Wars paper cup. Armed with plastic spoon and a second empty paper cup for the remains she would taste and discard, she brazenly began her strange eating ritual.

In the past Katie often wondered what Peter's response would be to her food problem. In her heart she believed he would find it nothing less than disgusting, despicable, and real crazy. Nothing more than the very things she thought about it herself.

And suddenly there he stood. In the door, watching. He hadn't planned to stand there and watch but he was so stunned at what he was witnessing that he just stayed there frozen, and he kept watching. He watched as she was chewing something from a paper cup at a furious pace. Chewing like someone who hadn't eaten a meal in days, maybe weeks. And then he watched as she spit out the food into the other cup and then he watched her do it again . . . and again.

At exactly the same time that he was about to turn around and walk away, Katie turned around just to make sure no one was watching her; just like she did as a kid when she'd sneak her cookies from Trace's sight in the big kitchen in Bel Air.

"Listen, Katie, I couldn't help but see what were you were doing." Those were his exact words. But what Katie heard was "Criminal! Psychopath!"

Her heart was beating so hard she thought she was going to die. She was caught. She tried to lie.

She said that she had thought that she'd eat some granola but that it must have gone bad because it didn't taste right and that's why she was spitting it out.

Peter didn't even answer. For three years now he had looked for the missing piece of the puzzle. The thing that didn't feel right about the two of them together. The thing that was off about all of Katie's togetherness. And at that moment he knew he had found it.

Suddenly he saw it all. All the empty paper cups in the trash cans. All the plastic spoons. (She used to say she just didn't like having to wash dishes.) All the food that would just disappear from the kitchen that she would swear she hadn't eaten. "Must have been Maria Rosa," she would say referring to her cleaning lady. Maria Rosa weighed in at one hundred pounds and Peter had never even seen her stop cleaning, even long enough to have lunch.

He walked over and put his arms around her and said, "We've got to work on this one, baby. We've got a real problem here." And he hugged her. Tight. And he told her he loved her.

Katie surprised herself. There was no quick answer. There was no snappy retort. She began to cry. Not tight angry tears. And not helpless or pathetic tears, but tears of relief. Tears from all the years of pretending there was no problem. Tears that were hidden away and kept secret just like the problem. Peter never saw so many tears but he understood. He really did. And this time Katie's tears didn't frighten him. Because they were real. And he could deal with real. It was unreal that he couldn't deal with and that he couldn't understand. And that's what he told her. And he also told her he loved her.

He loved her.

He gave her a tissue and she wiped her eyes.

"Look at me" she said, without asking for sympathy. "How can you love me? I'm a fake. I'm a mess."

"You're not a mess. Just this part is a mess," Peter answered. "And I happen to love all of you. But you don't." And then he shared with her the most important information she was going to hear all night. He told her that this was the way she stayed tied to her mother. He told that she stayed attached to Trace all the years they'd been apart through her anger; and through remaining a powerless helpless child who was starving behind the false front she had created as the mother expert. "And that," Peter said, "is the lie."

She just looked at him trying to believe the truth in his eyes.

"Do you really love me?" She hated the banality of her question, but it was all that could come out of her mouth and she hadn't the desire to edit herself in an attempt to be clever.

"Yeah," Peter answered. "I do. But you've got to get through this, Katie. This has nothing to do with Trace now. And it has nothing to do with me loving you. I've always loved you. It's your ass that's on the line now. It's your life."

To Katie all of this sounded like a bad soap opera except she knew it was her life and every bit of it was real.

"You've got to tell me about this stuff. Do you throw up? Do you take diuretics and laxatives?"

Katie shook her head no. "Just the paper cups," she said. She figured she didn't have to tell him that years ago she did all those other things. The paper cups were humiliating enough.

"You've got to throw out the goddamn paper cups and spoons," Peter said.

"It won't be the first time," Katie threatened, as if preparing him for her possible failure. "Don't you think I've thrown all of this stuff out before?" she asked, relieved to be throwing it out again.

"Not with me here, too. Next time you're looking to fill up one of those cups, why don't you find me and fill me up a little. I can always use a good hug and kiss."

She couldn't believe Peter was using his *Principles of Loving* on her. Was it possible that his book, which at times she unmercifully teased him about, just might be for real? And then what was hers? Was all her research and all her theories just a lot of intellectual garbage?

She tried to explain how overwhelmed she was feeling to Peter, who was taking a metaphysical view.

"Things appear only when we are ready to handle them," he told her. "Katie, I know it's a lot to take in all in the same night, but I think we ought to adopt Wan Ling, and I think we ought to get married. I think it's an opportunity for us all to grow."

Katie just listened.

Peter continued, "Wan Ling is an orphan whose first year of life was violent and traumatic. She already has the deck stacked against her, the least we can do is give her every shot to have a good life. She needs to be part of a solid family structure. She needs a mother and a father for that."

"I don't know what to say, Peter. You just saw that I don't have my life together, and we couldn't even get it together with the two of us living together." She was getting ready to get into bed. "I just don't know, and I don't know if I trust myself to take care of a little baby, and I don't even know if I trust you. I'd appreciate it if you'd hold your offer till I can look at it all with a little more clarity."

"Like when?" he asked.

"Like in a couple of years." She laughed.

Peter got into his side of the bed and put his arm around Katie. She took a deep breath trying to release whatever anxiety was left. He held her in his arms and kissed her forehead. She was very glad that he was staying over. And she told him so again. And she also told him that she did used to take diuretics; and she did used to take laxatives. She wanted to tell him everything because it didn't feel loving to withhold anything. And besides, it was time to come clean.

So lying together in each other's arms, they talked. No subject was off limits and nothing was taboo, and that was a relief. At one in the morning they were talking about how their expectations of what love was supposed to be were getting in the way of really loving each other.

For Katie she had to learn to give up her fantasies of romantic love. After three years of being with the same partner, Katie still expected explosions, and explosions were not what real life was about; at least not every day. Katie's mistake was always wanting and believing there was more. She had to learn, living on romance had all the nutritional equivalent of living on Twinkies. She told Peter how she was always looking for love straight from a romantic pulp novel. She wanted him to make her "heart throb and her pulse pound" and she wanted to "ache all over with desire." She wanted "passionate burning stares and trembling quivering bodies." Peter told her if she ever felt that way to call for a doctor immediately.

They lay in each other's arms, continuing to talk for longer than they ever had before.

"Hey, baby, wanna make love?" Peter asked. "I can fill you up with something very delicious and not at all fattening."

Katie smiled a genuine real smile and agreed that it sounded like a good idea.

"Without Marilyn?" she asked.

"Yeah. She's out of town this week. She's making a movie," he said.

And so they made love and it felt better than Katie ever remembered it feeling for a long, long time. Maybe ever.

And when it was over, Peter told her he loved her again. And she believed him. And as proof of his love he told her he was going to forgo his usual après-sex chocolate cookie. And for Katie that was all the proof she needed for one night.

## Chapter

18

*I*f Richard knew that his sister actually made love watching Marilyn Chambers doing all sorts of lewd acts, he would probably die. He figured all women were like Ellen, except for the other kind. It was your basic Madonna-Whore concept. God knows Ellen wasn't the other kind. Richard was still waiting for the day she was going to give him head. Actually he was waiting for the night she was going to give him head. He knew day was out of the question. Where fucking was concerned day meant light and light meant disgusting. For Richard and Ellen sex was something you had in the dark and when it was over, if you were Richard, you had an English muffin, and if you were Ellen, you had a shower. Richard once asked her why she always showered when she's only going to bed and going to shower again in the morning.

"Well, honey," she answered in her version of what sweet, sexy, and southern was supposed to be (Ellen only attempted to be sweet, sexy, and southern after having sex and when meeting new important people at the club). "I shower 'cause I just can't go to sleep with all the gook all over me." She tried to smile over her real expression which was pewey (rhymes with chopped suey).

Richard actually agreed. He didn't like the gook either. It was slimy. The thought of it made them both wrinkle up their noses.

Richard and Ellen were both real repressed on the subject of sex. It's been said the more suppressed or repressed you are on any trip, the more you're actually hiding a very big and powerful part of yourself.

They got back to their hotel suite just in time for the "Eleven O'clock News." Ellen didn't know any of the newscasters so she got homesick for Houston and her own Eyewitness News Team. Richard couldn't believe she could be homesick after being away from home all of two days. Plus, she was traveling with her whole family.

"Who is it that you miss?" he asked her. "Dolores?" (Dolores was the Spanish cleaning lady.)

He called to Joshua to see if he was in his "jammies" yet. It was way past his bedtime. Most children get cranky when they get overtired. But not Joshua. He got hateful.

He walked into their bedroom looking as though he'd just lost his best friend. (This would be impossible because Joshua had very few friends to begin with and certainly no best friend.) He refused to kiss Ellen or Richard goodnight. Richard knew once Ellen struck out it was useless for him to even try and go to bat. Joshua then refused to go back into his bedroom until Ellen gave him his stuffed panda bear with the torn left ear. When she said she didn't have it he started crying in his usual fashion, which happened to be hysterically.

Richard tried to explain to him that he didn't bring his panda bear with him from Houston. He said panda bear was home sleeping with Mr. Smurf. Joshua accused Richard of throwing it out the window.

"Why would I throw panda bear out the window, Joshie?"

Ellen tried to bribe him by saying they'd buy a new papa panda in the morning. More hysteria.

They both tried unsuccessfully to get him to transfer his affection over to the little Cabbage Patch Doll he did insist on bringing with him from home. He wouldn't hear of it. He threw the doll head first into the bathroom. So much for adopted dolls.

It was a miracle that he ever got back into his room at all that night. But he did and Richard and Ellen, now in their bedroom, were finally alone.

Richard watched as Ellen was undressing. It wasn't that the sight was anything close to erotic, but for some reason he found it interesting. He was careful not to let her know he was watching or else she would have gone into the closet. His eyes were peeping out from over the top of the *New York Post*.

Whenever Richard was in New York he had certain rules that he adhered to. One: He always bought the *New York Times* and the *New York Post* but he read only the business section of the

*Times* and all of the *Post.* Two: He stayed at the Plaza Hotel (no matter what the guys at the club said about how the Plaza was "out"). Three: He ate dinner at least once at Elaine's because A, He was treated nicely being Katie's brother and Trace's son; and B, He was looking for a certain Jacqueline B. or Linda E., who when in New York were known to frequent Elaine's. And four: He always saw one hit musical, preferably one with great-looking chorus girls. (Needless to say, *La Cage Aux Folles* threw him for some loop!)

Back to Ellen. Ellen did not have a bad figure. She was just one of millions of American women who didn't particularly like her body enough to carry it as though she had a great figure. She actually had very nice breasts and a pretty attractive athletic bottom half (all those tennis lessons in high school may not have helped her game but her legs profited). She was just uncomfortable with it. Maybe it would have all been different if some hot stud would have connected up with her somewhere along the way, but growing up outside of Houston there were no hot studs at Middleview High School. What there was, were thirty-seven middle class boys all wishing they could find Natalie Wood in *Rebel Without a Cause* for one night.

Ellen was one of the few women Richard had ever seen in a bra and panties who didn't look sexy; and looking at her now he couldn't figure out why. Maybe the underpants were too big or maybe they came up too high on her waist. It's not that he'd seen that many women in their underwear, but even Katie looked sexy to him when he used to walk in on her while she was getting dressed. He actually used to wait until his sister was getting dressed to "accidentally" enter her room because he was at that age where he was beginning to be interested in girl's underwear. Probably around twelve or thirteen. If a series of psychologicals were run on Richard today, he might still register about twelve or thirteen in this same area.

They talked about the evening. Well, Richard talked and Ellen agreed a lot. Yes, he certainly was treated unfairly. They decided to not think about it till the morning. Strategy could be planned more easily over a hot cup of coffee, orange juice, and scrambled eggs, than over Estée Lauder's Cellular Night Repair. Ellen bought it but Richard used it to prevent aging.

It felt good to get into the big king-size bed. This evening sure didn't turn out to be the fun Richard had hoped it would. No stars and no money (compared to what he expected) and no respect. He sure would have liked to have seen a great-looking piece of ass; though he had to admit Rebecca did have terrific tits. He was having trouble settling down. Maybe it would help him to come, he thought.

"Hey, Mollybeeb," he touched her cotton shoulder. "Wanna do it?"

"Now?" she asked a little surprised. It wasn't even Wednesday night. She rolled over and looked at him. And he looked at her. She was wearing a high-collared cotton nightgown that looked like something Whistler's Mother wore while sitting for her portrait. It was hard. Well "it" wasn't, but life was.

Somehow they managed to begin. He wasn't big on kissing, and she wasn't big on any of the other oralities so that didn't leave much. Though neither one held to any strict religious beliefs, they both unspokenly agreed that the missionary position had the most dignity and morality attached to it (both mortal enemies of good sex!).

There was no screaming. In fact there was no talking. But there was a ton of fantasy. Naturally, Richard's mind was populated with a bevy of beauties to choose from. But tonight there would be no

Jacqueline Bisset fantasy. He was still angry that she wasn't at dinner. He went with an old standby. 1982's May Playmates. They were twins. Cindy and Candy Wilson. Doublemint had nothing on these two. What a pair.

Richard never thought about what Ellen might be thinking. Why should he? But Ellen was the surprise. The Wilson girls paled in eroticism next to the pictures running through little Ol' Mollybeeb's mind. The Spanish gardener with the big black moustache and those enormous arms, who tended their grounds; the milkman who had to be a disciple of Arnold Schwarzenegger to carry that much milk up to their door every Monday and Thursday morning, and Clay Thomason (one of Richard's friends from the club) were all there. Wildly naked. One was fucking her and one was sucking her and one was being caressed by whatever opening she still had available. It was savage lovemaking at its most torrid. Unbelievable. All from the mind of Ellen Fields and all without a sound. Well, there was one little "oooh" at the end. That's how Richard always knew that she was satisfied. "Oooh!" Kind of like if you were bitten by a very gentle mosquito.

As for Richard he rubbed himself on the bed to get started and then inside Ellen. The truth was there was very little difference in feeling. It was just better to leave the gook in Ellen rather than on the bed because he had to sleep on the bed.

When it was over Ellen of course had her shower. Richard had to modify his usual English muffin because there was no twenty-four-hour room service, but he made due with two of Joshua's three Granola Bars. He knew he'd have hell to pay in the morning but he'd deal with it then. It would just be one more thing to add to what promised to be a terrible morning list. He finished his snack, got back in bed, and positioned himself for sleep. Ellen was just getting out of the shower. Perhaps if Richard had some idea of

Ellen's fantasies, he'd better understand why she always needed a shower.


"Oh, Willie!" Lady Landamere called from her bedroom. Her voice was as energetic and alive as before the evening began. Willie had sunk himself into one of the two big living room chairs facing the fireplace. His tie was opened. His shirt rumpled. He looked as though he had just run the New York Marathon. He was altogether exhausted. Lady Landamere came booming out of her bedroom in an emerald green dressing gown looking as if she was ready to begin the evening all over again.

"No stamina!" she said. "I don't know what is the matter with all of you. I would like you to tell me why it is my heart condition never affected my energy, my sweet doctor?"

"Sheer will power," he answered. "It wouldn't dare."

Lady Landamere liked his answer. She laughed. "That's right. It wouldn't dare!"

"William, dear," Trace was auditioning names to see which one she liked most. "William, if I hadn't invited you to stay the night, where were you planning on sleeping this evening?"

Dr. Chase told her that he had taken a room at the Waldorf-Astoria, assuming it would be too late to fly back to Boston. He added that it probably was the sensible thing for him to sleep in it. He said a cup of coffee would be just what he needed to get him into a taxi and over to the Waldorf. "I don't want the night manager to stay up all night worrying about me," he said with a smile.

"You have such a nice smile, Willie." She decided she liked calling him Willie better than William. "You really ought to smile more often."

"I need someone like you around me, then I'd smile more."

Trace was flattered and she told him so. She was about to go into the kitchenette to make some coffee when Yolanda walked in from the second bedroom to tell Lady Landamere Wan Ling was in bed and on her way to sleep. Yolanda was a cousin to Mrs. Pierce and she was helping Trace while she was in New York with Wan Ling. Trace asked Yolanda if she'd please make them both some coffee. She sat down in the living room chair facing Willie.

"I guess you think me slightly mad believing I was going to do it all again. . . . You know with Wan Ling." She seemed reflective for a second, but then she quickly lit a cigarette.

"Not mad," he answered. "Just adventuresome and unique."

"Have you any children, Dr. Chase?" she asked.

"Two boys," he answered. "Men now," he corrected himself. "They're both grown. Charlie is a doctor. He's married and he lives in Boston where he's in residency. Phillip is twenty-two, and living in California for the last year. He's still trying to find himself."

"I assure you that's not the place to find oneself. To the contrary, it's far easier to lose oneself in California." She laughed again.

"Boys are easier than girls. At least that's how I found it. Not that Richard is any shining example of superb motherhood; but at least I was able to see him as a separate person from me. I would look at Katie and see so much of myself. . . ." She paused and thought of her daughter's exit this evening. "My word, she's still so angry. . . ." She paused again. She smiled at Dr. Chase. ". . . But I like her fire, Willie. I used to have that kind of fire."

"Used to?" William answered. "Trace, you've got enough fire in you to launch a rocket."

Trace laughed. "You know, William, I like you. It's a shame we didn't meet sooner."

186

"I know," he said. "But I'm glad we did meet, for however long."

Yolanda came in with coffee and a few assorted cakes and cookies on a tray. Lady Landamere said something like, how could anyone think of eating after the giant meal they had just finished. Dr. Chase agreed.

Fred did not agree. Lady Landamere and Dr. Chase continued to talk. Their conversation was as warm as the fireplace setting suggested. While Lady Landamere had eyes only for Dr. Chase, Fred had eyes for something else. When the time was right, he made his move. Quietly like a thief in the night, he ever so gently helped himself to a small brownie and a vanilla wafer.

Lady Landamere was thinking to herself that William Chase was definitely the kind of man she could have fallen in love with if the timing had been different. She listened as he told her about his family and how lonely life has been for him since his wife has been gone. For a split second she thought she was falling in love.

And so did Fred. He was back for a second brownie. It was that second helping that caused the plate to fall off the table which succeeded in breaking not only the plate but the spell as well.

"I guess Fred's dinner wasn't quite as good as ours . . . either that or he's just jealous of you, Willie." Trace laughed again, looking at Fred whose leatherette nose and mouth were all covered with chocolate icing.

Dr. Chase laughed, too. He looked down at his watch and was surprised how quickly the time had gone. He said that he thought he had better let Trace get some sleep. Of course, Trace said she'd have plenty of time for that when she was dead and she reiterated her belief life was for the living and said they should stay up and talk some more.

"Tell me, William," she asked him coyly, "did you think I was going to seduce you tonight?"

He smiled his very warm smile and answered, "I was hoping you might. Though as your doctor I would never have permitted it."

"Well, maybe, I will visit that nutritionist friend of Rebecca's. Needless to say I'm not a big believer in Rebecca's and Katie's disciplined approach to living. I think they are of the opinion (along with their friend Jane Fonda) they are going to get out of this world alive as long as they jog, renounce meat, and drink enough parsley juice. But you never know, Doctor. I'm certainly not above non-conventional approaches to living. I still might prove all of you wrong just like Rebecca said."

"Nothing would make me happier, Trace. Absolutely nothing."

And that's the way their conversation continued well into the night. They talked a lot about life. It was three-fifteen in the morning when Dr. Chase finally put his coat on and kissed Trace goodnight at the door. It was a kiss with more heart than passion but it meant a great deal to both of them.

Dr. Chase thanked Lady Landamere for everything. The dinner. Her generosity. He also thanked her for helping him feel again.

Trace graciously accepted his kind words. She said she had absolutely no intention of telling anyone that he didn't sleep with her tonight and told him, "If anyone should ask, I shall say it was the best sex I ever had." And then she added, "You know, in its own way, Willie, it really was."

She waited until she heard the elevator arrive before she closed the door to her suite. She undressed quickly because she knew in the morning there was much that still had to be done. She hurried through her ablutions and once brushed and creamed, wearing a big comfortable nightgown and her big furry slippers, and with Fred practically tripping over her in order to stay close, she tiptoed into Wan Ling's room.

She was fast asleep in her bed, her black hair was shining in the dark. Trace stood beside her bed, looking at her quietly. She leaned down and kissed her on her tiny porcelain cheek. When she stood up and walked back to her bedroom a tear could be seen falling from her eye.

She and Fred got into bed. Lady Landamere got under the covers on her side and Fred finally settled down on top of the pillow that would have been William's side of the bed.

Trace was finally tired. She turned off the light. She didn't realize it, of course, but standing at the front door waiting for the elevator, she never said "Ta-ta" to Dr. Chase.

# Chapter

## 19

*I*t was raining like crazy when Katie woke up. She checked the clock radio. Nine-thirty. Nine-thirty! Shit! She reached over expecting to touch Peter's thick head of hair resting on the pillow but Peter was gone. Instead she found a piece of paper. After splashing some cold water on her face she brought the note to the kitchen with her and read it while waiting for the water to boil for her morning decaf.

Dear Katie,

Got up early. A lot on my mind. Mainly you. Decided to get out of your way for today. Thinking is better done alone. I'll see you later. I love you. Signed, XXX (with a big) P.

Katie wondered how many other couples had their own original little ways of signing their notes, which were identical to all the other original little couples who thought themselves unique.

She thought about last night and felt good. Her coffee now in cup, she dialed Rebecca at the photographer's. It turned out not to be the best time for Rebecca to talk, because they were just finishing her makeup which meant it was time for her to do her lips. But the two women agreed to have dinner together saying they'd speak later and pick a restaurant. Katie added that she was really trying to watch her weight and hoped they could eat someplace where she could just get a salad or something. Needless to say, she was preaching to the converted.

On a normal day Katie usually drank her coffee while reading the *Times*. But nothing about today was normal. Not after last night. So she would forgo reading the *Times* to better concentrate on her own story. Was it really possible that she could give up this whole paper-cup affair? Could she finally, for the first time in her life, just eat like a normal person?

Her mind fixed on last night's dinner. The sight of Wan Ling. She completely understood why her heart almost broke in two upon seeing the face of the little infant girl. That was the same starving infant that was inside of herself. The one she refused to even acknowledge until now. She sat quietly, thinking. She felt calmer than she had in a long time.

She took a deep breath and decided to do her yoga, something she'd been forgetting to do recently. She wondered why it was she would usually manage to eliminate those things from her life that she knew made her feel better. Yoga, once you got past the maharishi of it all, helped her stay in tune with herself. And all it required was twenty-five minutes (or fifteen minutes when she was rushing, which meant she was doing it incorrectly). It was all about breath and balance and she figured she could use all the balance she could get. Today she would take the full twenty-five minutes; and today she resolved she would do it again tomorrow. She told herself everything was about to change. The only part that was frightening was how many times before she'd sensed the very same thing only to watch herself fail. Today was different. She told herself she could do anything she set her mind to. Today she believed it. There was something else she believed. "Peter loves me . . ."

She wasn't used to that thought.

. . . And he really wants to marry me.

She'd been married once. For five years and the best that she could say about it was that she had been married once . . . for five years.

Howard Beanerling! Being married to Howard was like going to the desert for a drink of water. Whatever it was she was looking for in marriage was not going to be found with Howard. He didn't have it to give. In that way she indeed married her mother when she married Howard. The best she got out of the marriage was her writing name: Katie Fielding. Howard, who she actually coerced into marriage, wanted her to write under the name of Katie Beanerling, and she wanted to continue using her maiden name, Katie Fields. Since Katie Fields Beanerling just didn't have the proper alliteration, and since Howard was adamant that she wear his name like a diamond ring (which he wasn't as adamant about her wearing), she combined the two names and decided she would be Katie Fielding. Her concession to Howard was to wear his "ING" since he never gave her the "R" anyway. Not because he couldn't afford a diamond ring, but because he thought he couldn't afford a diamond ring; which in retrospect seems to be the same thing.

Poor Howard was obsessed with money and worried continuously that one day there wouldn't be enough. He said that Katie made his worries even more intense because she was so extravagant.

At the time of their marriage, Howard was an art director at BBD&O advertising agency and doing extremely well, but at least biweekly he reminded Katie that in advertising it could be "all over by the time you turn forty." So even though Howard was only thirty when he and Katie married, and even though Howard was already making well over a hundred thousand dollars a year, he was convinced that in ten years he would be penniless; and with Katie in his life it could be as soon as five years.

The more Howard reminded her that it could be all over for them at forty, the more Katie knew it could be all over for her at twenty-five if she didn't get away from Howard.

Howard, she learned, was determined to be a loser in life even during the times when he was winning.

Katie was determined to be a winner. That was one of her primary motivations in marrying Howard in the first place. An unmarried woman at twenty-six was not a winner. Not in Lady Landamere's eyes, and unknowingly, at the time, Katie saw everything through her mother's eyes. So she married Howard, who Trace seemed to adore until after the marriage.

"Why in the world would you have thought I wanted you to marry Howard?" she asked Katie exactly three days after the little reception for the immediate family at Twenty One. "I assure you, Jamie Wyeth he is not and never will be."

No, he was not Wyeth nor was he Warhol. Though, he did share something in common with Andy Warhol. Both made their reputation through reproducing cans of Campbell soup. When Andy painted them, they and he became part of America's Pop Art History. When Howard landed the Campbell's account the very same cans became part of his "Back to Soup" September advertising campaign.

What made Howard a good art director was his excellent critical eye; and so it was that same eye was no less critical in his unending criticism of Katie. Another similarity he shared with Trace. Katie agreed with her colleague Nancy Friday that most women, on their first marriage, invariably marry their mothers.

The veal was just a little overcooked. The skirt just a fraction too long. The lipstick just a hint too red. There was no getting it right with Howard. All Katie could do was "try to do better."

Howard was good-looking. Howard was a good dancer. Howard was City College senior class president. Howard was a lot of things, but primarily Howard was a very big mistake. Katie left Howard and the marriage with no further desire to cook veal or anything else, wearing pants instead of skirts, wearing no lipstick at all, and with a first book half written. She also took her favorite Carole King album, her favorite James Taylor album, and not a penny in alimony. How could she take money from someone who spent so much of his time worried about it? Just getting out was enough.

But that was then. Now she was a thirty-five-year-old divorced woman who still thought of herself, too much of the time, as a girl. And when she wasn't being the mother expert, she was hiding behind her other identity: the misunderstood psychologically abused daughter of a powerful and crazy mother. But now everything was different.

Peter loved her.

She said it again to herself. Why does he love me?

Because I am a good person and I deserve to be loved. Not because I'm smart or because I wrote two best-selling books. Not because I'm attractive but because I am lovable. It is my birthright to be lovable. It is everyone's right to be. Therefore (and this was the part where she still had trouble), Trace is lovable too. Trace deserves to be loved. Not because she's dying; and not because she was her mother. But just because it was her birthright.

This was Peter's whole theory. This was the philosophy behind *The Principles of Loving.* To paraphrase Peter, if you put enough love out there, it would come back many-fold. Not necessarily from the same place. But it would come back. "Love," he said, "more than any force on this earth was the Great Transformer." Even in the face of the most "toxic" person, Peter held that love could, at very least, neutralize the ill effects; and with enough love, they too could make contact with their loving side.

Katie wondered if there could really be some truth behind Peter's homespun philosophy that already had sold one million paperbacks. She decided she was going to give it a try. After all, if her man were a dentist, she'd let him clean her teeth. It's just that Trace defied all the rules. But, on this the first day of the rest of her life (did she think that?), all vacillation aside, it was worth the effort.

Katie decided to call her mother. She would see how she was feeling today and apologize for leaving her dinner party in such an eruptive manner. She felt good about her decision. She also knew that Peter would like it a lot. And she wanted to please Peter because he was her man and she loved him. And, he loved her. A concept that was obviously going to take some getting used to. But that, too, was definitely worth a try.

Trace answered the phone as though absolutely nothing out of the ordinary had happened last night. "Oh, Katie!" she said happily. "Wan Ling and I were just sitting here having our tea and wondering when you were going to call us."

This was the difficult part; her total denial of reality, and it certainly was coming right up at the front of the call. Katie told herself it was only difficult if she perceived it that way. She would attempt another view.

"Well, here I am," Katie said equally cheerfully. "You and Wan Ling must be psychic . . . or does Wan Ling know how to read tea leaves?"

Trace walked right over Katie's joke and said that she and Wan Ling were thinking of taking a stroll over to her place (a stroll! She had a critical heart condition and it was not more than fifteen degrees outside) but now, on reconsidering, she suggested Katie come over to the hotel so the three of them could spend some time together. Katie heard Fred barking in the background. Lady Landamere quickly amended the count to four.

Katie didn't say no. She said she'd be there by one o'clock. She asked her mother if she needed anything. Something she thought to be a caring gesture.

"Well, I don't need a thing, dear. But Wan Ling could use a package of Marlboros. I smoked her last one a half an hour ago." She laughed and asked Katie if they should set a place for her. No, she didn't want any lunch. She'd eat something before she came over.

So far so good. Remember Peter's book, she thought. Rule Number One: Stay loving. And Two: Get off the phone quickly. It was Rule Number Two that Peter had failed to include in his Steps to Unconditional Loving, but Peter didn't have Trace for a mother.

She was getting dressed to meet her living/dead mother and her . . . what? Her mother and her newly inherited sister whom she just met who might soon become her daughter.

She put on jeans and a sweater and fur-lined boots. She hoped this whole thing wasn't going to throw her back into therapy. It would be far too boring to hear her old craziness being told to a new therapist . . . again.

Chapter

20

*P*eter was right in the middle of his session with Nadine
Auerbacher, a neurotic, forty-six-year-old from Kings Point, Long
Island, who on turning forty-six also turned blonde and who every
Monday at three-fifteen threatened to leave her husband of twenty-
one years and her three grown daughters ("two of whom don't even
live at home anymore!") so that she might discover herself more
completely. Every week by four o'clock, having recontacted her

loving side, she would leave Peter's office and proceed to drive back to Kings Point, Henry, and the girls, Band-Aids in place for another week.

The phone continued to ring. Peter excused himself. It was Trace. She wanted Peter to drop everything and come over. Katie was there and she had to speak to him.

Peter said he was in the middle of a session and asked if he could call her back.

Trace said she didn't understand why he didn't just go ahead and let his patient talk while he spoke to her.

"I'm certain that whatever it is you're hearing is not new. That's what's wrong with this therapy business you're in."

Peter said he'd call her back in ten minutes.

Mrs. Auerbacher looked at her watch. Ten minutes! It felt like she had just gotten there. She felt jealous of the voice on the other end of the telephone.

"I hope that won't be too late, dear," Trace said threateningly while puffing smoke through the phone receiver.

Once off the phone the session finished up. (Nadine wanted the two extra minutes Trace had stolen from her.)

Peter smiled at her warmly and put his hand on her shoulder. His message was clear. Love thy neighbor as you would yourself. Although with Mrs. Auerbacher this would not be the correct choice of words since last year she followed those words verbatim and ended up having a hot affair with her best friend Leonora Fishman's business manager husband, who lives exactly across the street at 4327 Pine Lane Drive.

With Karen Hofsteader waiting in the vestibule to come in, set to continue her biweekly saga about her bisexual romances (Every man I could have a real relationship with is gay!), Peter took a moment to return Trace's call.

"Listen, Peter, Katie doesn't know I'm calling you but . . ."

Peter could hear Katie's voice as though she were actually standing over his shoulder saying Trace was being manipulative.

"Why doesn't Katie know you're calling me, Trace? It sounds as though something is terribly wrong."

"Well, there is. Katie is having a problem making a connection with Wan Ling, and I thought if you could come over here in a hurry, you could do some of your magic love stuff and then I wouldn't have to unpack Wan Ling's suitcases. . . . Not that she has much to unpack. She's only a poor little orphan."

No wonder Katie was having trouble. Peter found himself empathizing with Katie. This woman was rough. She was nothing like his mother, Evelyn.

Peter decided maybe he had better come over. He didn't want Trace to undo all their progress from last night. He suddenly felt like Bob Newhart as he was preparing to leave his patient in the hallway.

"I'm very sorry, Karen," Peter said while putting on his winter coat. "It's an emergency."

"Peter!" Karen said surprised. "I had no idea you made house calls."

Peter explained this was a personal emergency. Karen looked into his baby blues and wished with all her heart she could be his personal emergency. But if she was, she thought, he'd probably turn out to be gay.

They rescheduled for next week, and Peter hailed a cab to take him uptown to Trace. When he got there he found Wan Ling was having her lunch.

"Say Kay-tee," Lady Landamere said for the umpteenth time to Wan Ling, who was sitting in her high chair smiling. "Kay-tee," she repeated.

Nothing.

"Peter, when do you suppose she is going to say something?" Peter told her impatience was not the answer. Wan Ling was not your normal infant. Traumatized, she never heard a word of English until she was flown to America two months ago.

Trace tried again. "Say Kay-tee."

Wan Ling was much more interested in the big gold hoop hanging from Lady Landamere's right ear lobe. She pulled at it with her little baby hands.

"No! Not my earring," Trace said looking around to find something else she could give Wan Ling to explore instead. She couldn't find anything except Fred's rubber bone sitting on a nearby chair. She went into the kitchen, washed it off, brought it back, and gave it to Wan Ling.

That's when Katie walked in. She was equally surprised to see Peter as she was to see Wan Ling, sitting at the dining room table with a rubber bone in her mouth.

"My mother is completely crazy," she said to Peter kissing him hello.

"Oh, hello, dear," Lady Landamere said smiling. "Come sit down and join us. We'll try once more."

"Kay-tee. See! Here's Kay-tee." Lady Landamere tapped her daughter's head. "Say Kay-tee?"

Nothing.

Fred jumped on the dining room chair next to Wan Ling's, and letting his sibling rivalry get the better of him, snatched his bone back from his new little sister, then leaped down and left the room.

Wan Ling still said nothing. Now she pulled on Lady Landamere's left hoop earring.

"I can't believe you would let her put Fred's bone in her mouth," Katie said. "It's so unsanitary. When Richard was born we had to give away the dog because you said he carried too many germs."

"I never said that," Lady Landamere pointed out. "Mrs. McPhearson, the baby nurse, said English sheep dogs were unsanitary. I always believed it was because she was Irish."

She addressed herself to Peter. "Peter, if she could see the filth and squalor this poor little orphan was living in she'd understand . . . just as I'm certain you do, how harmless Fred's toys are. Besides," she added, "it's good for both of them to learn how to share."

Katie couldn't believe the whole scene. She also was trying to figure out how Peter was able to leave his office so early. She looked at her watch. "Don't you have patients all day? I thought I wasn't going to see you till Elaine's."

Peter looked over at Trace.

"I thought Peter should be here since the decisions you're going to make will effect him as well."

Trace began to feed Wan Ling. Wan Ling liked to play with her spoon in the cereal more than she liked to eat it. She still was having difficulty getting it to her mouth without spilling.

"Maybe she'd do better with chopsticks," Katie said.

Trace voiced concern over Katie's flippant manner.

Wan Ling did not intend to finish her lunch.

"At least she will be spared having to hear about how she should 'think of the poor children starving in China, etc.,' " Katie said.

"I can't stand it when she doesn't eat everything on her plate. Here," Trace said, handing Katie her food and baby spoon, "you try and feed her."

Katie took the spoon with nervousness. She sat down across from the Little Oriental Princess. At least that's what she looked like in her white pinafore with silver beads on the bib of her dress. Katie never remembered being with a baby so close up. She paused and studied Wan Ling. She began to spoon feed her the cereal. And Wan

Ling began to eat. The whole experience felt alien to Katie. But it felt good.

Wan Ling was enjoying her meal although the cooked string beans and carrots were still of no interest to her.

"I used to worry when you didn't eat everything, too," Lady Landamere reminisced. "That's probably where your food obsessiveness began. I used to have the nurse tell you story after story until your plate was clean."

"What do we do with her now?" Katie asked. "Does she nap or play or something?"

Lady Landamere asked Katie why it was she remembered so little of her early childhood. Didn't she remember Richard as an infant?

"It was too painful," Katie said.

Trace shook her head saying, "Well, I refuse to feel guilty over what's past because it is just that. But I do admit to certain feelings of sadness that it couldn't have been better for you. There seems so much joy you missed out on."

There was no joy, Katie thought. False joy maybe. But nothing that felt real.

Mrs. Pierce came in the room to take Wan Ling to "toity" and then inside for her afternoon nap. The toity at eighteen months of age was far from a foolproof routine, but Wan Ling seemed to like sitting on the baby seat and seemed to know when she did good. Katie went along to watch. Fred followed behind Katie.

One thing worth noting: Fred's relationship with Wan Ling took a definite turn for the worse ten days ago. Things began deteriorating when Wan Ling, who was beginning to feel a sense of shame when she "pee-peed" on the floor, was asked by Lady Landamere after one of her frequent accidents, "Who did this?" Wan Ling wanted Lady Landamere to love her very very much and knew she had done bad. So she pointed to the puddle and then she pointed to Fred.

Well, that just wasn't fair. It was bad enough that occasionally Fred goofed and got punished; but to be blamed for something he didn't do was unsportsmanlike. The little stuffed China doll wee-weed whenever she felt like and still got pampered, powdered, and changed. If Fred wee-weed just once he got locked up in the kitchen for hours. His better judgment advised him, however, not to make an issue about it. Perhaps Fred knew, if he didn't play his Yummies right he could wind up living with Richard, Ellen, and Joshua in Houston and Wan Ling will be wetting her diapers all over his two beautiful acres in Bel Air.

Katie watching Mrs. Pierce change Wan Ling's diapers reinforced how much she didn't know about babies. Katie smiled at the little rubber panties. Wan Ling, who was simply being the little doll she was, started burping. Some of her cereal was reappearing at the side of her mouth. Mrs. Pierce, who didn't like her infants growing up too quickly, said she just needed to be burped again and asked Katie if she wanted to do it. Katie said yes. She picked her up, holding her ever so gently and patted her back until she heard a tiny burp.

Katie put Wan Ling down and placed her gently in her crib for her two-hour nap.

Wan Ling's naps were the high point of Fred's days. In anticipation of what was to come he started jumping up and putting his front paws all over Katie's knees. He wanted her to pick him up. She did. She held him in her arms and told him, "Don't worry, Fred. Everything is going to be okay." She patted him on his back. He burped. And then he licked her face.

Katie looked at her watch. It was three o'clock. She had six hours before she was to meet Rebecca. There was still time to get to

WNEW, back to the apartment and take a bath. Time to try and relax. She enjoyed the time spent with Wan Ling and Peter. It was the other time spent with her mother while Wan Ling napped that seemed to throw her off balance.

She had tried to talk to Trace today. She had tried to tell her about her ambivalence about being a mother. About the difficulty she was experiencing responding to everything that was happening. Even Peter noticed that Trace never stayed still long enough to listen. It's not as though she cut Katie off with anger, or even that she cut her off at all. She just never fully heard her. She was too busy, doing things: checking on Wan Ling, lighting her cigarettes, finding her cigarettes, jumping up to get a piece of candy, jumping up to offer Katie a piece of candy, jumping inside to bring out some almonds for Peter. It was just the way she was. Trace didn't walk over you, she talked over you. And if you confronted her, she denied it, whatever "it" was.

Peter tried to help Katie explain her fears to her mother. Peter said Katie was frightened because she knew nothing about raising a baby. Trace said, "She'll learn." She said, "What makes you think I knew anymore when I gave birth?"

Katie said she just needed some time to think about all the ways her life would change if she were to adopt Wan Ling. Trace said something about not knowing what was so great about her life now that she wouldn't want to change it.

Katie asked her why it was they were never able to have a real conversation with each other; to really own their feelings; and Trace said that they were having a conversation and asked Katie why she insisted on holding to those kind of "crazy" beliefs.

Katie felt herself getting angry.

"I don't want to keep getting angry at you. All my life I've been getting angry at you and then turning the anger on myself. I want to be through with the anger. I want to be able to love you. Do you think that's possible, Mother? Do you think we could love each other?"

Peter looked proud and Trace looked surprised.

"Katie, what are you talking about? Of course, we love each other. You happen to be crazy about me. Don't you think I know that!"

"We never touch. We never hug," Katie said.

"You could start now," Peter said. He really was making a house call. Both woman seemed frozen in their positions in the room. After what seemed like too long a pause, Katie walked toward her mother and hugged her. She felt her mother's long red nails nervously fingering her back. She felt her smallness, which had always loomed so large. She felt her heart beating and thought that soon it would stop. She thought how few times she had ever hugged her mother. How many years of hugs they had missed. Eventually Trace's fingers stopped fingering Katie's sweater, and she hugged her daughter back.

And Katie began to cry and Trace pretended not to notice. This was more than enough emotion for one day. Peter said, "What about me? Don't I get a hug too?" And he walked over and hugged each woman.

"Does this mean you're going to adopt Wan Ling?" Trace asked. "May I consider the subject closed?"

"No," Katie answered. "This means that we hugged. This means that I love you. It does not mean that because I love you I obey your every wish."

"Who said anything about my every wish?" Trace said regaining her usual pace. "We are discussing a dying woman's last wish."

Katie said she had a little more thinking to do and that she and Peter had to talk and that they would call her tomorrow morning.

She said she'd better be going because she had to meet Rebecca in a couple of hours.

She and Peter parted company outside of the Sherry-Netherland. He kissed her goodbye and said he'd either see her at Elaine's or meet her at home after dinner.

In the taxi she was feeling glad that she had gone over to see Trace. And she wasn't feeling worn out like so many of her visits usually left her. It was good that Peter was there. Peter was a walking force of goodness. She was beginning to learn from him instead of making jokes about him.

Trace had made jokes about people and sometimes they hurt. Katie was now finding another kind of humor. She could laugh with Peter about life and feel better.

"Miss Fielding, I have a question." The voice on the other end of the phone sounded genuine. "I am a forty-one-year-old woman with a ten-year-old daughter and I can't believe it when I treat her the same way my mother did me."

"We often treat others the way we were treated." Katie answered. "That is why abused children often become abusive parents."

Stan Smith who's radio show she was doing found that a real interesting concept. He asked if she had any research to back up her statement.

"Life!" was her answer.

Stan went back to the phones. Three more were lit up.

Katie was glad to be sitting in his studio, On the Air, sipping a glass of water, doing what she did best. It put her back in touch with that part of herself she liked. It was a needed break. How much could she obsess on her life's problems.

Another call.

"I want to ask Katie about the 'passive father' she speaks of in her new book. What do you mean, the 'wilder' the mother the more 'passive' the father.

"Often the mother gets more and more out of control in an attempt to cause a response from the father; her action causes him to repress his rage, retreating even further, thereby appearing even more passive."

Another caller.

"I love your books Miss Fielding and wanted to know what your next book is going to be about?"

"Relationships!" Katie answered. "I've spent so much of my life trying to figure them out I feel I have something to share on the subject."

Next call.

"Hello, Katie dear, this is your mother! I just wanted to say 'Hi.' I happened to be listening and I think you're doing a super job. Just super. Ta-ta!"

Katie couldn't believe it.

"I guess you get your share of crank calls," Stan said.

"Here and there." Katie answered. She took a sip of her water, answered three more calls, and got out of the studio in time to beat the rush hour traffic heading north on Madison Avenue.

Back in her apartment, she glanced at the needlepoint pillow sitting on her living room sofa. "Angels fly because they take themselves lightly." I must try and remember that, she told herself. She told herself there were people on this earth who would consider themselves blessed to have her problems. She walked into the kitchen and looked at the clock on the wall. Six-thirty. She was hungry and she wasn't meeting Rebecca until nine. She looked in the refrigerator. This would be a perfect hour for a paper cup cocktail. Not today. Instead, she poured a large glass of water for herself and walked out, if not less hungry, more full of herself. Maybe that was the key.

*Chapter*

21

*R*ebecca's limousine pulled up in front of Elaine's at the same time as Katie's taxi. They were each fifteen minutes late, which, as it turned out, was perfect timing. Katie was glad to walk in with Rebecca. Walking into Elaine's alone and waiting for whomever to show up was not on her list of "Favorite Things to Do."

Elaine was happy to see them. She got up from where she was

sitting with two men to greet both women. Elaine asked if they were going to join Richard. "Richard? Richard who?" asked Rebecca. "Richard Gere? Richard Pryor?"

"No, Richard Fields. Your brother," Elaine said to Katie.

"Oh no! Richard's here!" They seemed to say it in unison. If Katie strained her eyes she could see him sitting with Ellen at a table in the good part of the back of the room.

"No, thank you, Elaine," Katie said, almost too quickly. "We need to talk privately tonight . . . and Peter will probably be joining us for dessert." Elaine gave them both equal size hugs and, as important, a good table.

Once seated Katie told Rebecca the wonderful line she'd read in Gael Greene's *New York* magazine restaurant guide referring to Elaine's. She quoted her as saying, "To find the ladies room you make a right at Woody Allen." Rebecca laughed. Looking around the room at a fast glance they counted between them eight celebrated faces. Not bad for a Monday night at nine-thirty. Rebecca noted that if the restaurant were to go up in flames she would, despite the other famous names, still receive top billing in the morning papers. Katie asked her who might, in her opinion, receive billing over her. Rebecca thought a long time. "Well, maybe Jackie O." And then she added, "If John Kennedy were alive certainly he would. . . ." She laughed. "Oh, I'm sure there are lots of people. They just don't eat dinner here. Like Katharine Hepburn . . . I wonder where she eats. Do you know where she eats, Katie?"

"She eats at home. Where we should have eaten had we known Richard and Ellen were going to be here tonight."

Katie wondered how long it would be before Ellen spotted them. Or actually, how long before Richard spotted them. The last time they had dinner at Elaine's together Richard kept one eye on the front door the entire evening. Katie told Rebecca that the last time Peter was at Elaine's it was a slow night, and he left rather disappointedly having seen only Phyllis Newman, Adolph Green, and Carl Bernstein (and the last two had to be identified for him). Not only that, the tissuelike paper that wrapped his Italian cookie (which when rolled properly and lit with a match is supposed to fly in the air and the wish you made before lighting it is supposed to come true) flew into his eye instead and scratched his cornea. He had to be taken to the Emergency Room of Manhattan Eye and Ear on a full stomach of linguine and clams. All and all it wasn't a great evening.

Once seated, both women ordered white wine spritzers. Rebecca said she was starving so they ordered dinner at the same time. Poor dear Mario went through reciting the whole menu to wind up with two endive and arugula salads (dressing on the side), two orders of spaghetti squash, and an order of steamed broccoli and steamed spinach. It was almost embarrassing to hand that in to the chef. He actually apologized when he brought the bread to the ladies' table. Katie laughed.

"Couldn't I interest you ladies in a little pasta?" he asked.

Both women looked at each other. Should they? "No, thank you." Rebecca said. They both smiled victoriously.

Katie told Rebecca she was looking great and asked her if she had found any new diet secrets.

"As a matter of fact," Rebecca said, "I think it's because of this nutritionist I see. She's the one I want Trace to see. She's psychic. She holds your wrist and tells you what foods you can and can't eat. She found that my body just won't tolerate starches. For me they're 'lethal' she said. But sometimes I cheat a little," biting into a piece of Italian garlic bread.

Katie the writer couldn't help but voice some skepticism. The other Katie said she'd like an appointment on her next trip to California.

"Oh," Rebecca added, "here's a secret. Lots of water. Lots and lots of water. Carry a quart bottle of Evian water with you all day and drink, drink, drink. . . . See!" She pulled out a big half-empty bottle of water from her Halston pouch.

Art Buchwald was leaving and stopped by the table and said hello to Katie. Katie introduced him to Rebecca. Rebecca feigned pleasure in meeting him. Katie asked him what the big news around Washington was and he said that the story of the day was that the secretary of the interior was about to resign. After he left Rebecca told Katie that she'd never read his column because politics held no interest for her; except for Watergate, which everyone knew would be a movie, and for two senators and one prime minister all of whom she had dated. She added that she thought the secretary of the interior was Angelo Donghia.

Katie moved to more familiar ground. She told Rebecca about last night. She told her friend the events that followed the dinner party and how she saw it all as a turning point in her relationship with Peter. She said she thought that this might really be it. The real thing.

Rebecca told her that they had offered her the Glen Close part in the planned movie but she had turned it down. This was her way of avoiding the feelings of jealousy she was feeling toward Katie's relationship with Peter, which sounded a whole lot better to her than the one she had with Mark. Then she looked at Katie and told her more seriously that she didn't think she and Mark shared that kind of intimacy.

They talked about Wan Ling. Rebecca asked Katie what she thought it might feel like being a mother and being very very rich and at the same time and also suggested she consider buying a house in L.A. and becoming "bicoastal."

Katie told Rebecca she should try to eliminate that word from her vocabulary at all costs. She said it was too trendy. This from the lips of the same woman who earlier today told Peter she thought she'd have to "bail" on attending the ballet next week.

Katie said she had never thought about the possibility of living in California again. She didn't like it as a child but doubted if she'd have liked any place else better. "I was an unhappy kid." As for being very rich, she told Rebecca she knew in her heart, very rich was not the answer to anything. Certainly not to happiness. It just meant more of everything, and she had already learned that "more" was never enough.

"I'm not sure what I want to do about Wan Ling. I think I have very little choice really. If I don't adopt her she'll be orphaned a second time in less than two years. What do you think, Rebecca?" she asked.

That might have been one of the reasons Rebecca loved Katie. No one but Katie ever looked to her for advice. No one ever asked her advice or help except for Katie.

Rebecca thought it was because people didn't think her smart enough. That wasn't it at all. It was that people assumed she'd have no interest or time for their problems, and for the most part, they were correct. But Katie was different. Katie was her best friend.

"Don't think too much about all this, Katie. You've really got to get that there is no right or wrong decision. There's only different choices and they're all valid."

That was pretty good advice, Katie thought. She told her so, and Rebecca was pleased. She liked giving advice. It was such a nice change from her usual role of asking for help.

Encouraged, she continued. "I can't tell you what to do. I can only tell you what I would do. I would definitely take the baby. I see life as a giant movie and if I didn't take her I'd be missing out on a role I might never get to play."

Rebecca was content with her advice. "Now let's talk about me."

Katie laughed. She told Rebecca that such good advice deserved a quote for her book and handed her a typewritten piece of paper. It read, "The butterfly emerges from its cocoon when the time is right. Rebecca Holmes is synonymous with beauty and calls us upward from our cocoons to take wing and enjoy our femininity."

"Have you gone crazy?" I didn't write a book about fucking butterflies. I wrote a beauty book."

"Well, say anything you want then," Katie said generously.

"Well, the Rebecca Holmes being synonymous with beauty part is alright. But then just say, 'Every woman who dreams of being more . . . can be, after they read this book . . .' and sign it 'Would These Lips Lie? Katie Fielding.' "

Katie told her that was genuinely quite good. She also said that Rebecca could sell ice to the Eskimos and Rebecca answered, "I plan to."

Rebecca's book aside Katie still wanted to talk to Rebecca about Wan Ling. Rebecca wanted to talk about Mark. Rebecca agreed to discuss Wan Ling until the spaghetti squash came, then she would talk about Mark.

Richard and Ellen unfortunately came before the squash.

Even if Katie hadn't invited them to sit down and join them, they would have anyway. Elaine had generously seated them at a table that usually sat four, so the two extra chairs were already there.

"Well, this is quite a surprise." That was Richard's opening line. Also an indication of the level of conversation to follow. Ellen was wearing a different dress from last night but she still had on that same hideously fake smile. Rebecca was staring at Ellen, trying to determine whether it was fear that prompted anyone to smile that way or simply some mild form of insanity.

Mario came over to ask if either the lady or the gentleman would care to join the ladies with their wine. Richard said he'd like a Perrier. Mario went to refill Rebecca's half-empty glass and was surprised to see that they had all but finished the bottle. He asked if they wanted to order another. Katie said she thought a half bottle would do it. Ellen whispered something in Richard's ear whereupon he promptly asked Mario to bring a Black Russian for his wife instead of wine. As soon as she stopped whispering she immediately returned to the business of smiling.

"You two girls must be celebrating tonight," Richard said with noticeable hostility. "Dinner must be on Katie tonight! Isn't that right, Katie? Huh?" he asked.

Rebecca contained herself no longer. Still staring at Ellen, she asked, "Do you smile like that all the time or just when you're terrified or what?"

"Why, I don't know what you mean, Rebecca," she said in that sweet, southern and sexy voice she reserved for special occasions at the country club.

"I mean the way you smile," Rebecca continued. "It doesn't look real. I just wonder what you're thinking about."

"Well," Ellen said, honestly, "well, I was thinking that I was a little nervous."

"Then why, if you are nervous, are you smiling that smile?" Rebecca was relentless in her line of questioning.

"Because, Re-becc-a, just because I'm nervous doesn't mean I'm not happy to see you." The smile did not move.

Katie asked her brother and sister-in-law if they'd enjoyed their dinner in an attempt to keep the dialogue at a level they were used to and to move off the subject of Ellen's smile. She even apologized for Rebecca's directness saying that ever since Rebecca studied Method Acting she's felt a need to know everyone's motivation.

Ellen wasn't ready to drop it just yet. She said she was interested in knowing if Rebecca was real. "After all," she said, "she's the movie actress here."

"Well, you don't see me smiling, do you?" Rebecca answered.

Richard, still angry for his share of last night's pie, decided to pipe in and join the party.

"I didn't know you two girls liked to go out alone and get drunk," he said in the spirit of the evening.

Earlier in the day Richard had called Katie and told her that he wanted to have lunch with her tomorrow and they had made a date for one o'clock at Mortimer's. The thought of having to go through this again tomorrow at lunch was making Katie crazy. "Richard," she said, "what is it you wanted to have lunch with me about tomorrow? Why don't we talk about it now."

Richard shot her a how-could-you look. He felt totally betrayed. Without thinking he said, "I told you on your answering machine, without Ellen."

Katie felt badly. She had honestly forgotten that part.

Ellen felt betrayed by Richard. "Without me? Why without me?" Her voice was taut ascending and her smile had finally disappeared.

"I would think just to get a little relief from each other," Rebecca said. "It must get so boring for both of you."

The wine was not to be blamed. Rebecca, like Lady Landamere, said pretty much whatever was on her mind.

"That's just 'cause we're not movie stars," Ellen said shooting Rebecca a look. No one bothered to tell her what she had just said made absolutely no sense.

Mario brought Richard his Perrier and Ellen her Black Russian.

He also brought a plate of those little Italian cookies wrapped in the magic tissue paper.

Richard's voice was loud, even for Elaine's. It could be heard clearly by the table of three movie moguls and one television producer to the left of them, who had stopped talking percentages of the gross for the past few minutes and taken to eavesdropping, knowing good melodrama when they heard it.

"I want to pay you off," he said, his voice getting louder still. "I want you out of Fields Gelato before you even get one little toe in the door." He was speaking like someone who had seen one too many of his father's gangster movies. "I was treated shabbily last night. I was demeaned in front of my wife and child."

Rebecca interrupted Richard to ask him to please ask Mario for the check next time he passed by.

He started again. "I was treated shabbily last night. I was demeaned . . ."

"There he is, Richard," Rebecca, spotting the waiter, spoke right over him. "And ask him for a glass of water too, please," she added.

"Listen, Richard," Katie said. "Get this straight. I don't particularly want to spend my time down in Houston figuring out how to package Dietetic Gelato. But Mother . . ."

"Mother!" Richard was shouting. "Mother!" He stood up and in an impassioned voice he yelled, "You dare to call her 'Mother' when it was you who . . ."

He stopped. Dead in his tracks. At his table he saw her. Standing right in front of him. Jacqueline Bisset. He was so excited to see her he could hardly even see her.

"Hello, Rebecca," she said, kissing her hello on both cheeks. "I didn't know you were in town."

"I didn't know you were in town" is said as much at Elaine's as, "I loved your latest—."

Rebecca introduced her friend to everyone at the table and asked her if she'd like to sit down and join them. The famous movie star said she would be happy to for a couple of minutes until Alexander came through. He was saying hello to some old friends of his. Richard, who was already standing, offered her his chair and then went to fetch a waiter to get another one for himself. When Mario arrived with the extra chair, he had him place it right next to his, between him and Ellen. This meant that Richard had to personally shove Ellen's chair over (with Ellen still sitting in it) to make room for her. He wanted to be sure Jacqueline was going to sit next to him.

She slowly removed her fur-lined raincoat.

Please let her be wearing what she wore in *The Deep,* Richard thought. There was no voice of sanity in his head to tell him that she filmed *The Deep* in tropical waters wearing a wet T-shirt, and this was the middle of winter.

What she was wearing was a beige cashmere V-necked sweater. Not as tight as he would have liked and the "V" could have come down a half an inch further, but pretty fuckin' great. No doubt about it. He was trying to trace the outline of her body as the sweater clung ever so gently to her skin. He didn't realize he was starting to lean in following his eyes.

Jacqueline wondered what this man was doing inches away from her breast, but he was with Rebecca so she didn't figure it was anything nearly as perverse as it appeared. She continued her conversation with Rebecca and Katie while Richard continued to stare.

Ellen, who could no longer handle the sight, had checked out, split off, and taken to rolling up the cookie tissue papers into cylinders looking for the perfect one to light. She had rolled five of them and finally took the one that looked the most likely to fly and set it in front of her plate. She made a wish and lit the tissue paper.

If her wish came true, Richard would go up in flames and she and Joshua would be home in their little Texas beds by tomorrow night.

The tissue paper began to rise in the air. Instead of disintegrating into black cinder ash that falls back to earth after rising to the ceiling and granting your wish, as it is supposed to, one piece went up and came down still lit right into the "V" of Jacqueline's sweater.

"Oh, my God, Ellen! How could you?" Richard screamed at her. "Look what you've done to Ms. Bisset." Oh, my God! I'm so sorry for my wife's stupid clumsiness," said Richard to his Fantasy Goddess.

He was enroute to hysteria. "Let me help you! Please!"

"Get away from me. Please," she managed to somehow scream politely. How like the English to remain mannered even in the face of disaster. She was wriggling about trying to find the lighted piece of tissue paper somewhere inside her sweater. The more she wriggled, the closer Richard came to losing it.

He wanted to help her extinguish her blaze. The thought of just what might be burning inside her cream colored sweater was making him cross right over that fine line traveled between sanity and whatever lay on the other side. He jumped up in an attempt to save his Sex Goddess's tits.

Ellen, who also walked her own fine line in the mental health department, could not bear to watch her husband make an ass of himself.

At the sight of his hand entering Jackie's "V", she took the plate that had been holding the little magic cookies and smashed it over Richard's head. A piece of the broken glass cut his eye.

That seemed to do the trick. Elaine then did the honors of escorting Richard out onto Second Avenue.

The next day the incident appeared on Page Six of the *Post,* but

Richard couldn't read it because his eye was all bandaged and he was busy applying ice.

Ellen and Joshua had moved into a suite at the Sherry-Netherland.

## Chapter

## 22

"The only role model I had for a mother," Katie told Peter, while perusing the pages of Dr. Spock's *Child Care,* "was the kind I didn't want to be."

Peter, ever optimistic, told her, "Sometimes that can be the best kind."

While Katie and Peter were in Doubleday buying up every other book from the shelves designated "Child Care," Ellen was sitting, hunched over, crying hysterically on Lady Landamere's sofa. She'd been in that position for the past half hour and her face was covered with tears.

It was nine in the morning when Ellen rang Lady Landamere's bell. Through the rhythm of her continuous sobbing Trace pieced together the Saga of the Italian Fire Cookies.

Trace told her it was alright to have a good cry and brought her a box of Kleenex and a cup of chamomile tea.

After leaving Ellen alone for what she deemed a fair amount of time, she said, "Alright! That will be enough crying now, Ellen." She looked at her watch.

"That constitutes twenty-six minutes of complete and total self-pity, which is more than enough for any one miserable situation, including yours."

She called to Mrs. Pierce to bring in some ice cubes wrapped in a hand towel. "Here," she said, handing the towel to Ellen. "This will take care of the puffiness. It's a little trick I taught Rebecca, which I noticed she has now shared with the world in her upcoming book. If you apply it in time, Richard will never know you were crying."

"Richard wouldn't know if I was crying, anyway. First of all, his eye is all bandaged and besides, he never notices me."

This admission was enough to make her start crying again, but Lady Landamere would have none of it.

"I'm glad you brought that up," Trace said. "Because you're absolutely right. He wouldn't notice you and 'we' are going to do something about that situation." (This apparently was the royal "we.") "It is high time you stopped perpetuating this myth about your plain and boring looks."

"I never said I thought my looks were plain and boring," Ellen answered. If she weren't feeling so totally sorry for herself, she might have felt insulted by Trace's remark.

Trace answered, "Unfortunately you don't have to say it. One picture is worth a thousand words. So we are about to change that picture. Namely, you! Now then . . ."

Trace was clearly enjoying her new role as the Fairy Godmother having found her newest Cinderella.

"I want you to call Richard at the Plaza and tell him . . ."

Ellen made a face that said she didn't want to call Richard.

"Do as I say," Trace continued. "Tell him we will meet him for tea at five o'clock . . . better make that six, at the Mayfair Regent."

"Richard doesn't like tea," Ellen said meekly.

"That's alright. He doesn't like us at this moment, either, but he'll meet us, anyway. Now get dressed. We're going out! And hurry."

"But what about Joshua? I can't leave Joshua alone."

"Unfortunately, that's true. I wish you could. If he were given a fair chance to breathe on his own he might turn his adversity into creativity. Now, please, Ellen, we must get going."

"But what about Joshua?" There was no denying her whiny voice.

Trace told her not to worry about Joshua. She said he would be with Mrs. Pierce and Wan Ling. She had told Mrs. Pierce to take Joshua to F. A. O. Schwarz and let him play with the toys. She said Wan Ling would stay inside with Mrs. Pierce's cousin, Yolanda, because she was sniffling. She also said Rebecca was coming up before Wan Ling's nap because she wanted to spend some time with Wan Ling again. Trace was clearly in charge of the situation.

"What should I wear?" Ellen wimpily asked her mother-in-law.

Trace told her it made no difference because they were going to be buying her something new.

At that moment Ellen's depression began to lift.

The first thing Trace did was to deposit her needy daughter-in-law at the famous Messrs. Maurice et Jean Claude. Maurice was the brilliant business mind behind their highly successful partnership, and Jean Claude the true creative talent. Fortunately not all of New York knew this fact because they both styled hair.

After participating in the perfunctory kissing of both sides of the cheek, Lady Landamere said, "So, my Genius Hairdresser, tell me, what are we going to do with her?"

These were the precise words that used to make Katie feel so humiliated as a youngster. Here they were again. But every case is different. The expression on Ellen's face suggested she was in agreement with her mother-in-law and grateful that her problem was being recognized and dealt with.

Ellen was seated in the chair in front of the mirror, her mousey brown hair hanging limply around her face. She was trying hard to make her country club smile and failing.

Jean Claude asked if he could change "zee col-ur" in his finest French/American accent.

"You may change anything you like," Trace answered for Ellen. "That is precisely why we are here. N'est pas, Ellen?"

Ellen smiled meekly.

Jean Claude said he was feeling, "Blond. Definitely blond. And very layered." Sexy! Like he cut Raquel's.

One of last year's big rumors was that Jean Claude was really born in Brooklyn, but it was later said to be started by an ex-lover, who he had promised the world and ended up "doing roots" at Vidal Sassoon.

Trace said she had some things to attend to and asked what time she could pick Ellen up. She added that she wanted Ellen's makeup totally redone by Janna. (Janna was by now almost as famous as her mentor Jean Claude.)

"Two-sirty," Jean Claude said.

Perfect. It was now eleven-fifteen. Considering the amount of work to be done on Ellen, Trace thought that three hours was a miraculously short time. She mentioned she had to pick Fred up from his haircut at one, so they'd have time to grab a quick bite to eat and do a little shopping before she came back for Ellen.

Her last words to Jean Claude were "Ta-ta."

But right before that she suggested, only suggested, that he consider getting rid of her thick dark eyebrows. "They don't even work for Brooke Shields anymore!"

Half out the door she turned around and merrily added, "Good luck!"

*Chapter*

23

**R**ebecca did come down, while Trace was out, to take another look at Wan Ling. This made one time more than she'd looked at any other baby she'd ever known. Wan Ling happened to be napping by the time Rebecca made it downstairs from her suite. Mr. Rivera, private security guard to the stars, waited outside. Just why Rebecca considered her safety in jeopardy between the sixteenth and the tenth floor of the Sherry-Netherland was not precisely known, but Mr. Rivera, had, in his line of work, been paid to do far less. He once was put on twenty-four-hour guard with Gina Lollobrigida for two weeks in eighty-two, and only three people recognized her during the entire time.

Rebecca had been given Wan Ling's schedule, but she was just running a little later than she realized. (As a general rule, superstars run late!)

"Do you think you could wake her up for a few minutes?" Rebecca asked as she checked her watch.

Rebecca didn't see this as selfishness on her part. She figured it's not like Wan Ling would have a problem falling back to sleep. She figured babies were like puppies. They slept whenever they weren't eating or playing.

Yolanda was hesitant about disturbing Wan Ling's nap; particularly with Mrs. Pierce out of the hotel. But it was, after all, Rebecca Holmes.

"Alright," she agreed. "Let me get her juice. She likes to have a bottle after her nap."

Rebecca said that was understandable and asked Yolanda what kind of juice Wan Ling would be having. When she heard it was apple, she asked if she could have some, too. She loved apple juice.

"I'll take mine in a glass, though, please." Rebecca never being one to like anything to go to waste thought it a shame her humor went unnoticed by Yolanda.

Rebecca watched as Wan Ling slept. She walked around her crib looking at her from every angle. Then she reached into her enormous Halston pouch and pulled out her Canon Sure Shot. She popped up the flash and circled the crib again deciding on the perfect angle. Then she took a picture of Wan Ling. Flash!

Wan Ling jumped up. She was about to start to cry, but Rebecca was bending over the crib with her face close to Wan Ling's, and the little baby was fascinated by all the shiny color on Rebecca's lips and the nice smell coming from the strange pretty lady.

"Hi!" Rebecca said. "Did you have a good nap?"

It was almost as though Rebecca expected Wan Ling to enter into a conversation. The fact that she didn't was disappointing.

"When will she start to talk?" Rebecca asked.

"Soon," Yolanda answered. She pointed out that until two months ago she never heard English. Rebecca asked Yolanda about fifty different questions about Wan Ling. What time does she eat? What time does she sleep? What does she do every hour of the day? What do you feed her? If Wan Ling were a car, you would be certain Rebecca was planning to purchase one. She then asked if she could hold her. Yolanda, of course, said yes. She picked up Wan Ling and handed her to the superstar. Rebecca wanted to be sure Wan Ling wasn't going to make on her. Once assured, she held her in her arms.

She liked the way it felt holding this precious little thing. She walked over to the mirror and studied their reflection. She adjusted Wan Ling's hands a little to make a more perfect picture. Then she asked Yolanda to please take a few pictures with the camera that was sitting on Wan Ling's crib. Yolanda said she didn't know how to work the camera, and Rebecca assured her there was nothing she need know.

"Just look through the little hole and press the black button on the top."

Yolanda did as instructed and it worked. Flash!

What was it about this shiny-lipped woman that made all these wild flashes of light, Wan Ling must have wondered.

"O.K. One more!" Rebecca was saying. "Everybody smile."

Flash! . . . Flash!

"I'll make pictures for everyone," Rebecca told Yolanda. "I'm sure you'll probably want one, too."

She was counting to herself. She'd make ten of them. That should be enough.

She told Wan Ling she hoped that on her next visit she would be talking, and they would have an even nicer time with each other.

And then, like a true star she summoned Mr. Rivera, who had been waiting dutifully outside the suite, and she went back upstairs.

Chapter

24

*K*atie and Peter arrived back from Doubleday loaded down with child care books. Katie couldn't believe how many books there were on the subject. There seemed to be even more than on Understanding Your Personal Computer. A category she thought to have overtaken Understanding Your Child.

While in the bookstore she noticed Victoria Principal was now up to her third beauty book and wondered why she hadn't put all her beauty into one big book. How beautiful could anyone be to need three beauty books. Even Dr. Spock had only written one definitive baby book. Erica Jong was now on her fourth Isadora book, *Fear of Sequels and Space Shuttles,* and Jackie Collins had exhausted all of the husbands and locations in Beverly Hills and was currently up to writing about her infamous sister who had by now killed off half the cast of "Dynasty" and was running dangerously low on lip gloss.

Of course, both Katie and Peter nonchalantly checked their own stock, and Katie was happy to see there were only two *Mother!* books left and one *More Mother.* Peter's *Principles of Loving* was sold out. Peter said they weren't stocking enough or they'd have more in. It was good how they both understood that like everything else they were in the book "business," and like salespeople the world over were forced to sell their product. They smiled to the saleshelp who recognized them and even signed a few autographs. Suffice to say, everybody loves romance, and when theirs was hot and new, they were the Ryan and Farrah of the book world.

They were barely home more than a minute when the phone began ringing. Peter picked it up. It was Trace. She wanted Katie and Peter to meet her at the Mayfair Regent Hotel at five o'clock for tea. Peter said they had just walked in, and they were pretty wiped out; but she urged, cajoled, and then all but demanded they come. She said to tell Katie Rebecca would be there as well.

Katie's response was, "Not the cast of the dinner party again." She added that "even the Queen Mother had fewer Command Performances."

She picked up the telephone.

Trace told her she had a surprise for her. Katie answered, "Mother, I don't know about you, but my heart can't take any more surprises. Peter and I are still recovering from your last one."

The phone call ended with Katie saying they'd see her at the Mayfair Regent at five. She said as long as she got to her seventhirty appointment on time she was alright. In truth, there were worse things in the world than hot scones, jam, and whipped cream at five o'clock; although for diet reasons alone, she should have left her phone machine on.

Lady Landamere was not there at five o'clock. Neither was Rebecca, but Katie and Peter ordered what was to be the first in a string of teas.

The lobby at the Mayfair Regent was elegant, and being alone gave Katie and Peter a chance to slow down and share, at least for a moment, a quiet time together. Peter said they should think of doing this more often without meeting anyone. It was fun. Katie agreed and reached over to hold his hand. It was as though they were discovering each other again, and it felt like the first time.

Rebecca arrived twenty minutes late, causing the expected stir throughout the overly crowded lobby. Traveling incognito with Mr. Rivera, she looked every inch the star in her white cashmere pants and white mink vest, leg warmers, and boots. All she was missing was her own mountain.

Rebecca said she had no idea why she was summoned but that she was glad to see them both because she wanted them to be the first to know. She said she was going to call them and tell them.

Be the first to know what? Immediately Katie thought that Rebecca and Mark were going to get married.

"Well, tell us," Peter said.

Rebecca, never one to miss a dramatic moment, milked the scene while she paused to order a Perrier and lime and a cup of English Twining tea. She also asked if they could make her a plate of the little tea sandwiches without the bread. For an ordinary mortal it might have been the beginning of what could have been construed as a problem, but for Rebecca Holmes it was just a special request.

Katie glanced at her watch.

"Here," Rebecca said, whereupon she handed Katie a large envelope. Upon opening it she found two photographs of Rebecca and Wan Ling in three different sizes. Wallet size, coffee table size, and a size that would come in handy if you were thinking of re-covering a wall.

Katie smiled. "These are terrific pictures, Rebecca. Thank you." She showed them to Peter.

"Don't we look wonderful together?" Rebecca asked.

"Yes, you do," Katie answered. She also added that Wan Ling was too young to make feature films and that Rebecca should think about looking for a slightly older co-star.

"What I want to know, Katie," Rebecca said, "is if you and Peter are going to adopt Wan Ling?"

"Why? Are you working for my mother or for the *Enquirer?*" Katie answered.

"Because if you don't then I will, and if you do then I will begin proceedings immediately to adopt a little baby exactly like her. That's why I took the pictures and had them developed immediately. So my lawyers can get a special visa to enter Cambodia and find a baby exactly like Wan Ling."

Katie was stunned. She knew Rebecca better than anyone and yet. . . . She looked at Peter to see his response, and he was smiling and shaking his head.

Rebecca told them that the events of the last few days had all come together causing her to reevaluate her own life.

She said it was unlikely that she would marry Mark. Without getting depressing, she said she may never marry or have a child. She said there just weren't that many men around who filled the requirements for superstars with seven-figure incomes.

"It's not that I won't have men in my life," she explained. "I just don't know if I'll find *the* man. And even if I do, I may be too old to have a child. And then who will I leave all my money to?"

They both just listened.

"I realized that the advice I gave you at Elaine's was the same advice I should have given myself."

That was Rebecca alright. She didn't even want to part with her advice before she used it first.

Peter said he didn't want to be judgmental, but the idea of adopting a child so that she'd have someone to leave her money to sounded like the wrong reasons to adopt a baby.

"Oh, Peter," Rebecca said dramatically. "It's more than that. I want to love someone. Unselfishly. You of all people, Peter, should understand that."

"Did I hear the word 'unselfishly' coming out of those famous lips?" Katie said.

After letting it sink in, Peter said, "I think it's just a great idea."

Rebecca was beaming. She was also perspiring. She took off her white mink vest. Certain outfits were only good for entrances and exits.

"And if Katie keeps Wan Ling, or you and Katie adopt Wan Ling," Rebecca said, "then our children can grow up together. We can wheel them in Central Park together, when I'm in New York, and when you and Katie come to California they can play in the Malibu colony together."

"And when they get a little older they can open a Chinese restaurant together," Katie remarked.

Peter said all the supportive things Rebecca wanted to hear.

Rebecca noticed a pretty blond woman racing toward their table. Oh, my! Another autograph, she thought.

The woman went right up to Peter. "Dr. Carriston," the woman said, "I can't believe it's you! I've been on your waiting list for over a year now."

"Well, you seem to be holding together quite well," Peter said approvingly. Katie watched him give the young woman the once over.

"I loved your book," she said. "Would you please sign this for me?" She handed him her napkin. He happily signed his name and the woman left.

Rebecca looked pissed. "I can't imagine why she'd ask you for an autograph with me right here at the table. I would term that a 'true missed opportunity.' "

"She has no idea what she's missing," Katie said sarcastically.

"Katie, I detect you're angry at me. I hate it when you get sarcastic. You turn into Trace, you know. . . . You even start to look like her." Rebecca smiled, knowing she'd landed a solid punch.

Katie told her she hoped her little orphan would be trained in guerrilla warfare because the child would need it with her as a mother.

"Why is she getting angry at me?" Rebecca asked Peter. "Doesn't she know I'm her best friend? I thought she would be thrilled that I want to adopt a baby. I didn't think she would think I was being competitive."

"*She* . . . happens to be right here," Katie said.

So was Richard. Totally surprised to see the three faces in front of him and thoroughly confused.

In an attempt not to call attention to his left eye, Richard was wearing a Peter Falk hat pulled low over the bandage. In case the hat failed to disguise his souvenir from last night, he was also wearing big black sunglasses.

"I'm supposed to meet Trace," Richard said defensively, even before he said hello.

"So are we," Katie said. "Pull up a chair."

"Why don't we just think of it as one big family therapy session," Peter suggested, adding, "After all, we all are kind of a family."

"I don't remember you and Katie having any kind of marriage ceremony," Richard said still angry from the events of last night. "This family seems to be expanding rapidly since the reading of my mother's will."

Peter told Richard he thought that he was being unfair. "I have nothing against you," Peter said.

"Well, Katie does and you're with her. Besides I can feel it," Richard answered.

Peter asked him what he could feel and Richard told him he could feel his mockery and lack of respect. Peter told Richard he was incorrect. He said many times he thought that it must have been really rough for Richard to grow up in a house with Trace as his mother, Katie as his sister, and an absentee mogul for a father.

Richard sat up a little taller. So did Peter. He always felt better when he helped someone else feel better, which is why he liked being a therapist.

"I want to give Katie money. Lots of it," Richard said. "But I want to adopt Wan Ling."

"Why?" Katie, Peter, and Rebecca all asked in unison.

"Because it would be good for Joshua!"

"Good for Joshua?" the chorus repeated.

"Joshua needs a baby brother or sister. I saw it the other night at dinner. And I think it would be better for Wan Ling too. The truth is we're the only family unit that exists for Wan Ling. All of you are single and much too self-involved."

"It's not about family units," Katie said. "It's about love and consistency. You and I were part of a family unit and look at us."

"Why don't you and Ellen just have another baby?" Rebecca asked matter of factly.

Richard made a face suggesting that was a terrible idea.

Not one to pull punches she said they shouldn't let the way Joshua turned out prevent them from trying again.

She began to tell this long story about how when she was first starting out in the business, she would go and audition for all these parts and how her agent said to her when she would complain that the parts weren't good enough, "Rebecca, You have to start somewhere." Then she got a little sidetracked, and instead of making the point she started to make, she told a long and boring story, filled with run-on sentences about her rise to stardom.

Peter, Katie, and Richard all noticed the good-looking blond who was walking past the maître d' toward the table. Peter figured she might be coming over for Rebecca's autograph but secretly hoped it was for his. Katie looked at her and thought hers were the kind of blond looks she always found threatening.

Rebecca was still telling her story when Katie let out an astonished, "Jesus Christ! It's Ellen!"

"Holy Moses!" echoed Richard.

"Oh, my God!" said Rebecca.

Basically, religious preference aside, the sentiments were all the same.

"Surprise!" said Lady Landamere popping out from behind the pillar that the tea cart was resting against.

Well, it was nothing short of a miracle. Ellen made Eliza Doolittle look like an opening act. It was beyond belief. It was the most remarkable transformation.

"Hello, everyone!" Ellen said.

"I see they didn't get around to changing your voice yet," Rebecca said.

Rebecca wasn't so thrilled with mousey brunettes turning into Jessica Langes overnight.

Ellen didn't look quite like Jessica Lange. But she did. She really did.

Just what the table needed was another look-alike.

"Where did that body come from?" Peter asked, checking out curves he never even imagined existed.

Actually everyone, including Richard, wanted to know the same thing. Ellen always wore such shapeless clothes, they just did nothing for her body. Trace went right for the sex appeal. "No man I ever knew ever got turned on by a designer label," she told Ellen. "But the right sweater and skirt and it's a different ballgame."

Richard got up to give his seat to his wife, something Ellen never remembered him doing before. Trace was right. It was a brand new ballgame.

Lady Landamere told the maître d' that they needed a larger table. It was now six-thirty and the tables were easier to come by. The Mayfair lobby was not on the top of anyone's dinner list, unless of course they were headed into Le Cirque. Tea sandwiches lost their lure past five-thirty, and the waiters were setting up for the cocktail crowd.

Trace voiced her pleasure at seeing everyone together. Katie filled her in on Rebecca's surprise announcement. Trace was thrilled at what she referred to as the sudden "Baby Boom." She offered her congratulations to Rebecca telling her that in her opinion children "were God's little messengers, each bringing us his love and his hope."

Throughout the conversation Richard held tight to Ellen's hand. When he noticed Peter staring at his wife, he actually started caressing her hand. (A hand whose only experience of being caressed up until today was every Tuesday at four-fifteen when she had her manicure. Margaret would massage two drops of pink cream into each hand before she polished Ellen's ten slightly shortened fingers with Love That Pink.)

Well, that was then. Now, Ellen's Raven Red fingernails wrapped around her second glass of white wine, and she was having the best time. She got up to go to the bathroom, and Richard promptly stood when she left her seat. When she came back she told everyone how two men had tried to pick her up in the lobby. Richard was proud. He smiled.

Trace smiled, too.

"Well, that's my surprise for today." And like Cinderella's Fairy Godmother she announced, "And now I must be on my way." Katie expected her to click her heels together as she bid everyone "Ta-ta" and disappeared out the door.

Ellen smiled, too. It was not that country club smile. It was a smile that said that from now on not only Joshua would be going "Bang! Bang!"

## Chapter

## 25

*R*ichard, bewitched, bandaged, and bewildered, waltzed Ellen straight ahead into Le Cirque for a romantic candlelit dinner. Trace assured them that Joshua was perfectly fine and not even missing them, so happy was he with his autotron robot (in spite of the fact that it would not follow his command to kill Fred). Rebecca headed home, pictures in pouch, to meet Mark. She was excited about telling him of her decision. Peter said he'd pick up some food tonight and meet Katie at home. He knew he'd have no luck trying to convince her to cancel her seven-thirty appointment. Anyway he had to admit to some curiosity about what the woman would say. They kissed goodbye on Sixty-fifth and Park, and Katie hopped into Rebecca's limo. After she dropped Rebecca off, it would take her downtown.

"The door is open. Come in. Just sit down and I'll be right with you." Katie wasn't even sure if she was in the right apartment but that the room was thick with the scent of sandalwood; so she took a seat and decided this must be the place.

A little black poodle sat in the corner of the room looking up at her and coughing. Maybe he was coughing from the smell of all the incense, Katie thought.

Rebecca had recommended this woman to Katie. She said she was the best there was in New York. Her name was Azaria, and when she entered the room she looked exactly the way Katie had pictured her.

"That's because you are psychic, too, my dear." And then she introduced herself and her dog, whose name was Shanti. She also had two cats. Big gray furry ones, but Katie was allergic to cat hair so she never asked their names hoping they might just disappear if she pretended they weren't there.

Azaria reentered the room and said she was ready now to begin. She asked Katie if she'd brought a tape with her.

Of course she had. Everyone knew the rules for visiting a psychic.

Azaria, on hearing Shanti's insistent cough, apologized for his poor health. She told Katie that Shanti was going on thirteen years old and suffering from chronic bronchitis that affected him more in the winter than in the warmer months. She said she had even entertained the notion of wintering in L.A. or Arizona in the hopes of prolonging Shanti's life; but L.A. was overcrowded with psychics and Tucson was still primarily into turquoise jewelry. This was more than Katie ever wanted to know on the subject. In fact, all she wanted to know from Azaria, or any one else who was passing out advice, was should she adopt Wan Ling. She was totally obsessive in her pursuit of an answer.

The session lasted an hour. Rebecca had loaned Katie her limo, and driving back uptown to her apartment she sat in the back seat and began to replay the tape. It was hard to hear Azaria because Shanti was coughing over every fourth word. It was a loud hacking cough.

The limousine driver asked Katie if she wanted him to stop for some cough drops.

Katie laughed. On the tape she heard herself asking the same questions over and over. Azaria said she had already told everything she could on the matter, but Katie heard herself being relentless. In fact, at one point on the tape, Katie excused herself to go to the bathroom and when she was out of the room Azaria had left the tape recorder on.

Katie heard Azaria let out the longest "o-o-o-o-h-h" she'd ever heard. It was a sigh of exasperation that said, "I give up. Please. Enough!"

At least she could laugh at her own craziness. The psychic told her she had to take responsibility for her own life. She said she had to claim her own power. She told her a lot of real psychic stuff about Trace and Peter. She was very accurate unless, of course, Rebecca had already filled her in unintentionally. No! Rebecca wouldn't waste her time talking about anyone else, Katie thought.

The psychic saw her with a baby. But she said she might have been seeing her in a past life (see Shirley MacLaine's book, *Out on a Limb!*).

As for Peter, she saw him married. But she couldn't say for sure if it was to Katie. Other than that she was a wealth of information.

Katie listened to the tape and witnessed her own ambivalence. Katie the cynic. Katie the believer. Sometimes she could see herself inflating her life in the hopes of giving it dramatic relevance of Greek proportions.

Azaria suggested she listen to her own inner voice. Then the little psychic poodle began coughing nonstop. It was awful. He was practically having a full-scale seizure. Katie thought Shanti was going to his final reward right in the middle of her reading. Riding uptown she could no longer hear anything Azaria was saying on the tape. All she could hear was Azaria's coughing dog so she turned off the tape recorder. Maybe the lesson was being given to her as simply as this. The tape was unlistenable. All she could do was to try and listen to her own inner voice.

Inner voices need silence to be heard.

There was never any silence, Katie thought. Trace always filled the silence.

Now it was silent and now Katie was afraid. She was afraid of the day, in the near future, when Trace would no longer be alive to fill the silence with her sound.

# Chapter

## 26

*K*atie and Peter had stayed up talking well into the night. Over cold pasta salad (Peter had waited for Katie to eat) they listened to whatever parts of Azaria's tape that were audible. Over cold chicken and ratatouille they discussed consolidating households and hiring a full-time cook/housekeeper. Zabar's had outgrown its usefulness or, more to the point, they had outgrown the life of the

"Syrups" (Single, Young, Rich, Urban Professionals; this year's answer to the Yuppies!).

But most importantly, by listening not to Azaria but to her own inner voice, and by trusting it and Peter, Katie knew, with all her heart, that she wanted to adopt Wan Ling. She welcomed the chance to take care of a real infant and to forever silence the needy child inside herself.

Katie and Peter had planned to call Trace at ten and tell her of her decision, but Peter suggested they pick up some bagels and smoked salmon as a final goodbye to Zabar's, and bring it over to Trace for a breakfast celebration.

So it came as a real shock, upon entering the suite, to see the open suitcases lying all over the room. Mrs. Pierce told Katie that Trace was in her bedroom. What she didn't tell her, and what Katie didn't know, was that she was on the phone with Dr. Chase and that she wasn't feeling well. She didn't know it last night at the Mayfair when the pain began, and she didn't know it now.

Trace had called Dr. Chase and through an associate in New York, he had prescribed some medicines to be taken by her. He was now calling to see if they had been effective. Trace told him that she thought they were beginning to work. She said the pain had gone away. He told her to continue taking all three medications through Friday. He said he would prefer if she would stay in New York, but knowing she was determined to return to California, he added one more pill to be taken the day of the flight.

Katie walked into the bedroom. Fred was sitting on Trace's lap looking uncomfortable because Wan Ling was trying to sit on top of him. Trace waved hello to Katie.

"William, darling. I'd love to chat, but Katie just walked in the door and so I think I . . . Well, of course, you can say hello to her."

She handed Katie the phone.

Yes, Dr. Chase did want to say hello, but it was everything else he said that Katie would have rather not heard, although Dr. Chase made it clear in no way was he God and the future was always open to miracles. Katie tried to act cheerful and after wishing Dr. Chase well, handed the phone back to Trace.

Peter was in the kitchen emptying his Zabar's bag for Mrs. Pierce to arrange when Katie came in to tell him the bad news.

Neither Katie nor Trace acknowledged to each other their conversations with Dr. Chase except for Katie's asking, "Why the suitcases?" once her mother was off the phone. "Why go back to California when you can stay here . . . with us?"

"Movement!" Trace answered. "They can't hit a moving target!" Then she changed the subject. Her energy seemed as high as ever but her breathing seemed just a bit labored.

"Do me a favor, Katie," Trace said. "Take these and do what you like with them." She was still smoking away, which was making Katie very uncomfortable. Trace pointed to a stack of notebooks piled high on the floor, in the corner of the bedroom. She told Katie these were her thirty-five journals, and she doubted she'd ever get around to organizing all the material. She said it seemed appropriate to leave them to Katie, and she could do with them as she pleased.

She said she wasn't certain it was a book, but it was a life . . . and it was lived. "And that's what I want you to do with yours."

She asked Peter if she could have a moment alone with her daughter. "I promise you it won't take long. . . ." Then she added, "Of course, I know she tells you everything anyway, and I even think that's alright . . . though slightly foolish. I just think it important we have that obligatory few last words together. . . ."

Of course, he understood. He said he'd be inside with Wan Ling.

"Katie," Trace began, "this is what I want to say to you. So far, for the most part you've been an observer of life. You've thought about it, analyzed it, and you've written about it, but you've yet to live it fully. It's time to dig in. That's the only way to grab a big bite of it . . ."

Trace continued. "So much of your life is locked up in the past; in holding onto your pain and in making sure you're not like me. Maybe you have a right to your wounds. Maybe everything you felt as a child was justifiable. Maybe I wasn't ready to give up my great romance with your father and be confronted with you. But that's all past history. The best legacy I can leave you is to urge you to let it go now."

Katie was silent. She couldn't find her voice to respond. So Trace continued.

"I've lived my life as I saw fit and you've watched me all these years and resented me for it. You've tried to make me feel guilty for what I didn't have to give you, but I don't feel guilty. Oh, occasionally you were able to get to me but I did the best I could. . . . Your anger never stopped me from living my life for one second, but it has stopped you from living yours. I want you to start breathing, Katie. Stop holding your breath!"

She paused, as if to take the applause. "Oh, and in case you didn't know it . . ."

And now she took her longest pause. "I love you, Katie."

"That's it. That's my eleven o'clock number." She laughed. "As your father used to say, no, excuse me, let me say that again. As your stepfather used to say, 'This isn't New Haven, this is Broadway, Baby. This is no dress rehearsal!' "

Trace reminded Katie, in case she had forgotten, they were always a very theatrical family. Then she patted Fred on his head, put her cigarette down, saying she felt pounds lighter having gotten her soliloquy off her chest. "Oh, is there anything you would like to say to me?"

Katie looked at her mother and said yes. "I want to tell you that I love you and that I'm proud to be your daughter. And that . . ." She wiped her eyes which were tearing up fast. . . .

"And . . ." She was going to tell her about the whole food thing. About carrying around Trace's hunger and thinking it was her own. She was going to tell her about Wan Ling representing that child that didn't get enough to eat and she stopped herself. On a level that Katie knew was deeper than any level they'd ever reached together in conversation, Katie knew that Trace already knew it all.

"That's all," she said. "Just I love you."

Fred came over and licked her cheek. To misconstrue this action as an expression of compassion would have been a mistake. Fred, whose blood pressure was known to be slightly high, loved salt, and was on a sodium restricted diet. Tears were salty so . . .

In the living room, holding Peter's hand, Katie said to Trace, "I was supposed to work all this stuff out with you by now. You're not supposed to die until I work all this out."

Trace told her everything would be worked out the day she declared it worked out. It was that simple.

"Well, Peter and I have decided that we want to raise Wan Ling . . . together," Katie said.

Trace was visibly pleased. "Good. I could never have taken her luggage and mine in one limousine."

Wan Ling, who was sitting on the floor of her playpen, didn't seem to be affected by Katie's decision. She was affected, however, by Fred's hopping into her playpen and taking her bottle. She began to cry.

Katie walked over to Fred and took the bottle away from him. She asked Mrs. Pierce to wash it off, and now Fred started to cry. Katie had her first sense of what raising two children might be like. Trace came to the rescue handing Katie a second bottle.

"This one is Fred's!" she said. "Sometimes we just have to allow him his regressions." Fred, happy at last, lay quietly at Trace's feet, his paws steadying the baby bottle which he was quickly emptying in his mouth.

Mrs. Pierce came back with the sterilized bottle and handed it to Katie to give to Wan Ling.

Katie looked in the playpen at Wan Ling and was struck with the thought of the awesome responsibility it was going to be raising a child. Then she looked at Trace and said, "Listen. You know, all the times I fought against you, well I really ought to thank you. You're the reason I've become who I am."

Trace didn't really respond, except to say, "Maybe you'll get it right with Wan Ling."

Fred jumped up and put his paws around her warm neck. Trace patted his back and hugged him. "You know, I've always been more comfortable hugging Fred than anyone."

Mrs. Pierce had set the food out on the dining table and room service had sent up whatever Peter and Katie forgot to buy. The coffee tasted good, and Katie sipped it slowly. She was trying to savor the time at the table, knowing there was little left. How different from all the meals she couldn't wolf down fast enough, just to be able to leave quickly.

It was hard for Katie to stay in the present because her eye kept looking at the half-packed suitcases. She kept hoping against hope for something magical to occur to give the whole crazy thing its meaning. "Where are the happy endings?" Katie asked her mother.

"I'm quite satisfied with mine. You'll have to write your own!" Trace answered.

And Katie had no idea if her mother was telling her the truth.

# Chapter
## 27

"Joshua! Let's go now. Pick a magazine that you want and let's
go or we're going to miss our plane."

They were at a newsstand on Third Avenue on their way to
Kennedy Airport.

Joshua, wearing his aviator outfit, was looking every bit as adorable as he did just six days ago on his historic arrival from Houston.
Richard was waiting to pay the man at the counter for the maga-

zines. Ellen, wearing a fire-engine red suede dress with a hot turquoise sash that accented every curve known to man, looked more than noticeable. She looked "hot."

Joshua still hadn't begun to recover from the surprise of his transformed mother. Neither had Richard.

Joshua chose five pieces of reading material for his upcoming plane ride: two Captain Marvel comic books, one comic book called *Dondi* (the adventures of a little oriental orphan because it reminded Joshua of Wan Ling) one Spiderman comic book, and *Penthouse* magazine.

"Look!" Joshua said as he excitedly pointed to the Blonde Bombshell on the cover of *Penthouse*, skimpily and strategically clad in red suede ribbons tied around her anything but skimpy body.

"Mommy! Mommy!" He said flinging the magazine at his father. "Look, it's Mommy!"

The man behind the counter put on his glasses and was scrutinizing Ellen to see if the kid knew what he was talking about. Hey! It was possible. With the right lighting and a little air brushing. Sure!

"Uh . . . would you sign a copy for the store?" the manager asked. "Once we had Suzanne Somers in here and she autographed her *Playboy* spread for us. I was just recently offered fifty bucks for that issue," he said, pointing proudly to Suzanne's photograph, sandwiched between an eight by ten of David Brenner and Ruth Gordon, scotch taped on the wall behind him.

Murray took a copy of *Penthouse* from behind the counter and opened to the centerfold where the red ribbons had all but disappeared, save for one little ribbon around Melissa Malcom's neck (January's Pet of the Month).

Ellen, who had lived the first thirty years of her life asking celebrities to sign her menus and napkins, was more than happy to oblige.

"What's your name?" she asked the proprietor.

"Murray," he answered.

"To Murray, Nice meeting you!" Ellen wrote in her best penmanship right over Missy's braless bosom. She made a slight error and signed her own name "Ellen Fields." Quickly realizing her mistake, she added "a.k.a. Missy Malcom" and Murray seemed satisfied.

On the way to the airport, Joshua refused to put the *Penthouse* magazine down. He'd look at the magazine then look at Ellen and then bury his head laughing in his mother's new-found chest. He was playing with what was not too long ago his very own milk machine.

Richard didn't like it. He didn't like it at all.

"Stop it, Joshie," he said. "You're too old for that!"

"You weren't too old for that last night!" Ellen said smugly. "You know, Rich—ard, your mother has completely changed my life!"

"Yeah, mine too!" Richard answered. He just wasn't sure what all of it was going to mean.

On the plane, Joshua showed all the passengers in first class the picture of his mommy in the big magazine.

One of the stewardesses told him, "That's not your mommy, Joshua!" and he dealt with her in the most effective way he knew how. He took out his gun and he shot her.

What a surprise! There was no loud Bang! It seems as though Ellen, at the suggestion of the American Airlines Passenger Relations Rep, had removed the caps from his toy gun.

He went running and crying to his mother.

"Sit down, Joshua, and cool it," she said. "Strap him in his seat, Richard. He's got to start learning he is not the center of the universe."

This was quite a change. It said that not only Ellen and Richard were in for major life changes. Little Joshua didn't know what had hit him.

He could deal with his mother's mousey brown hair turning yellow. He could deal with her blobby shape turning curvaceous. But no caps in his gun! If he wasn't the center of his universe, who was?

There was no one to answer that question for him because Ellen was busily looking into her pocket mirror, applying hot pink lip gloss to her newly discovered lips.

Richard smiled.

"Hey!" he tapped Ellen on her shoulder and whispered in her ear. "Want to go into the bathroom with me, Mollybeeb?"

No reply.

"How 'bout it, Hotstuff?"

The possibility existed that "Mollybeeb" was in for a change of nickname, too. "Hotstuff" seemed much more to the point now. Richard was remembering Jacqueline Bisset's airplane scene where she did it in the bathroom of a 747 in one of her movies. Well, Ellen was looking mighty good and life was to be lived.

Ellen smiled seductively and said, "Meet me in the bathroom in a minute . . . And leave 'him' (pointing to Joshua) strapped in his seat. We don't want any more trouble with him."

Joshua was drawing pictures with the crayons from the little airline kiddie bag they gave him when he boarded the plane. He took the yellow crayon and started coloring all the cartoon hair in his magazines yellow. Spiderman looked a little odd and so did Captain Marvel and the little black-haired Dondi looked ridiculous, but Joshua had figured it out! The power seemed to be connected to the hair. Perhaps this is how the legend of Sampson was born! He practically used up all of his yellow crayon strapped into his big seat waiting for Richard and Ellen to return from the Bathroom in the Sky.

"Are you alright, Joshua?" the nice red-haired stewardess asked him as she walked the aisle offering passengers dessert.

"Mommy and Daddy went to the bathroom," he said. He was pouting. "I want my mommy."

"How 'bout some vanilla ice cream and hot fudge sauce in the meantime?"

"I'm not allowed to eat ice cream," Joshua whined. "I have to eat my daddy's gelato." Joshua was now doubly deprived.

The young stewardess on returning to her station happened to notice that only one lavatory was registering as "Occupied." The other was "Vacant."

She wasn't surprised. She was used to it. L.A. to New York was her usual run but maybe what she heard about these Houstonites was true. Maybe they did even more cocaine than the Hollywood set!

*Chapter*

28

*R*ebecca was on the phone with her lawyer. Well, she was on the phone with his associate partner and younger brother, Norbert Zifler. Stanley Zifler (her lawyer) had already left the country. Norbert told her that Stanley had been in constant contact with Baveral Flower before he left for Cambodia and was completely briefed and prepared for the mission. It is a Hollywood fact that when you work for Rebecca Holmes you work quickly.

Otherwise you work for someone else.

Rebecca was glad to be going home. Two weeks at the Sherry-Netherland was enough. New York was good for a shot of adrenaline but collagen was much better when shot by her dermatologist in Beverly Hills, and she was due. She could see a small crease beginning to reappear on the bridge of her nose and creases were no more acceptable in her face than in her clothing (with the exception of Calvin's wrinkled linen!). Besides, she was homesick.

The bellman was taking all of her luggage out of the suite save for the famous makeup case, which no one carried but she. Some of the products were from Paris, some from Milan, and there was even a set of Koal shadows from Thailand. Hers was an internationally famous face and her kit was irreplaceable. Wanda would travel in the limo with her to the airport. The luggage would go ahead in a separate van. Wanda was allowed to carry the jewelry case, and the scripts, but not even on special occasions, could she carry the makeup case.

Rebecca and Mark said their goodbyes last night. He told her he planned to be back on the coast in two days. She told him, of course, about her plans to adopt an infant like Wan Ling, and he wasn't even the least surprised. He did suggest, however, that Rebecca consider starting the infant on therapy at the same time as she began solid foods. It could be like preventive medicine, he said. Rebecca asked if they really had baby shrinks. Mark said they did. They were little six-inch psychiatrists who dealt with teeny little egos. She laughed. He also told her he'd be around to toss the baby a ball if it turned out to be a boy and buy it a doll if it were a girl. She told him that it was his kind of thinking that contributed to the disgusting female and male stereotyping in society today, and they were off. A word here, a word there, and it was clear that they were into their usual means of communication, which in their case was often miscommunication.

Still, he told her he would miss her and if she wanted him to come back and direct the rest of her movie he would.

Rebecca was glad to hear that. So far she hadn't found another director who was willing to come in where Mark left off and finish the film. "Sloppy seconds," they all told her.

"What makes you think it will be any better this time?" Rebecca asked him.

"It may not be," Mark answered. "But at least with me you know what you've got and I'm really not all that bad."

Rebecca had to admit his logic made sense. The director she met with last night was a nightmare. He wanted to reshoot the entire film as though she was some aging Anna Magnani/Simone Signoret type. And . . . he wanted to reshoot without any makeup. Well, after that, Rebecca only pretended to listen. The meeting was officially over the moment she heard "without makeup!"

She told Mark she'd think about his offer and they could decide when he got back to the coast.

There was a certain arrogance to these Hollywooders. Why did they assume that the coast meant L.A? What about the coast of Maine or the coast of San Diego, for that matter?

When Mark left, Rebecca was glad to have her bedroom to herself. This did not bode well for the long-term future of their relationship. Mark said something about L.A. being easier for them what with the luxury of separate bathrooms. Rebecca said she thought the luxury to be separate bedrooms. So they parted company (something they were quite good at), and Rebecca packed a few more items in her makeup kit that she wouldn't be needing before she went to bed.

And so looking rested, after a good night's sleep, Rebecca checked herself one final time in the mirror.

What a wonderful concept the mirror was. Imagine how much joy would be lost if she could never see herself the way others did. Of course, the irony was that she could not and never would! That mirror had seen plenty of action in the past two weeks.

She was wearing the bracelet Trace had given her, and it looked great with her all-black thirties suit with a black lace high-necked Victorian camisole underneath. She added just a little extra gloss in anticipation of the paparazzi who would be loitering in front of the hotel.

Rebecca made it a point to wear white in New York and black in L.A. "Never give them what they expect!" She'd made a whole career out of it.

She deliberately didn't call Katie or Trace to say goodbye. She never did. It was just how she was. They were her family; or at least she had designated them as such when her own family turned out to be such a major disappointment. Her alcoholic father was dead, and her mother was so self-centered and boring that she never even acknowledged Rebecca's achievements.

No! She'd rather call Trace when she was back in L.A. There was something about goodbyes she hated and today's most certainly was one she would rather avoid.

She checked the bedroom drawers to make sure she hadn't left anything. You can't be too careful when you're a superstar. Once she left her vibrator in the night table, but when the Pierre Hotel called her home in Beverly Hills to arrange for its return, she denied that it was hers. That was seven years ago and the next time she came to New York, and every subsequent trip since, she stayed at the Sherry-Netherland.

Wanda reminded Rebecca what time it was. Their flight was four-thirty. Pan Am 747. Even Rebecca knew 747's don't wait.

She had almost flown home on Regent Air, a relatively new

airline that took luxury to new altitudes. Gourmet meals by Spago's Wolfgang Puck, full-size bed and hairdressers and Deco bars and private compartments and videos, but she decided against it. It was for the California *nouveau riche* and famous, and Rebecca thought the energy of all those egos on one plane could cause it to expand to the point of explosion over Kansas. Besides how much better to be the big fish in the big 747 pond than a big fish in a little 707 pond. Leave Regent Air to the TV stars, she thought. She was a first class movie star and besides, all this month they were showing her latest film on Pan Am, and what better way to spend five and a half hours in the air.

And so makeup kit in hand, she was off. She asked the elevator man not to stop on the way down. He obliged. She got into her limo, and in the spirit of good will, she even waved to a few familiar paparazzi.

Safe in her limo, she took a deep breath. She was trying to remove the sadness she felt. Her mind couldn't erase the picture of Trace she kept seeing. She told herself soon she'd be up in the air and reminded herself once again that these thoughts were only temporary clouds blocking the sun. All in all, this had been quite a trip.

*Chapter*

29

He was eating his turkey breast in front of the television, watching the Knicks get trampled, when the idea came to him. If Katie wanted grand gestures, thought Peter, that's what she was going to get.

And get it she did. The first package arrived at eleven-thirty A.M., and the doorbell rang every subsequent hour until five o'clock.

A huge basket of toys from F. A. O. Schwarz. A beautiful white crib, trimmed in white satin. A pink high chair with Wan Ling's name inscribed on the top. It was when the electric hobby horse arrived at the door that Katie felt like one of those sweepstake winners who lived modestly in a small suburb with no room in her little humble abode to store all her winnings.

Trace was unbelievable, Katie thought. What excess! At five-fifteen the doorbell rang for the sixth time.

"No more!" Katie actually said aloud as she walked to answer the door.

There stood Peter with a box in his hands. Katie knew it was from Tiffany's by the wrapping paper. Ever since she learned about the finer things of life, she learned to recognize that Tiffany blue glazed paper and white satin ribbon.

"Hi!" Peter said looking very Redfordish, crew neck sweater and all. "The other boxes were all from me to Wan Ling. This one is from me to you."

It was all very romantic and Katie didn't know how to handle this outpouring of affection. What was worse, she didn't completely trust it. Something she was always looking for now embarrassed her. She heard herself thinking what she was about to say and tried to suppress it, but it was too late. With a force all its own it popped out.

"I hope you've charged everything to Wan Ling," she said sarcastically. "She's the only one of us rich enough to afford all this."

Katie was right to wish she hadn't said it. Peter looked hurt and said, "You always wanted a great romantic gesture. Well, here it is. Don't miss the opportunity to enjoy it. Go ahead," he urged her. "Open it."

She opened the box and actually thought she'd die. It was a diamond ring. A big diamond ring. A big classic emerald shaped diamond engagement ring. From Tiffany's. Only Arabs buy big diamond rings from Tiffany's.

Peter helped her slip it on her finger. "Diamonds are forever you know," he said teasingly.

Finally after what seemed like forever, she said, "I'm stunned!"

Peter, ever the practicing psychologist, told her that hers was an appropriate response for the situation.

Katie couldn't stop staring at the ring. "Does this ring come as a part of the whole marriage package? Is this door number two?"

"It's your choice. You can have it all, or any of the sum of its parts. Personally I believe in going for it all. At least that's the psychologically healthy thing to do."

"Well, I believe we tried it once and it didn't work out so good. Certainly not good enough to celebrate with this."

She held out her hand pointing to the extraordinary ring on her fourth finger.

Katie took off the ring and handed it to Peter. "I can't. It makes me feel too obligated," Katie said.

Peter looked hard at Katie. "Don't miss this look," he said, "I'm sending you a lot of love. See!"

Katie smiled. He could still push her romance button.

She thought for what seemed a long time and said, "Why don't we try it again? But not etched in stone." She gave him back the ring.

Peter came over and put his arms around her. "Didn't you learn anything in Basic Feminine Training from Rebecca or your mother? Never, under no circumstances, give back the stone. The ring maybe. But never the stone."

"You have a point there," Katie said. "Let me work on it," she said and gave him a kiss. She took the ring back.

"By the way, Peter," she said, "this makes up for all of the extravagant gestures you never made in the time we were together."

The sad part was that it simply wasn't true. Nothing makes up for anything, and when you are addicted to extravagant gestures, it's just a matter of time before you anxiously await the next one. But for the moment it felt true and Peter had suddenly traded in the Redford art of understatement in exchange for Mike Todd's flamboyant style.

As for Katie, she felt like she imagined Mary Lou Langhorn felt when she was crowned Rose Bowl Queen of Mississippi U, or like Elizabeth Taylor must have felt every time she was gifted by another husband with another bauble. Probably more like Elizabeth Taylor than like Mary Lou. She and Elizabeth both shared a weight problem. And Mary Lou Langhorn, as you may have expected, was blond.

# Chapter

## 30

Katie wasn't sure she was doing the right thing, going out to the airport with Peter. But it felt right that Wan Ling should drive home with both of them. They were to meet her mother and Wan Ling in the Pan Am Clipper Club. The plan was for Wan Ling to kiss Trace and Fred goodbye and drive back to the city with Katie.

Katie wanted Peter to come along because there was nothing

more to be said with Trace. No. There's always more. She asked him to come to help her with some of the pain. Peter told her that analytically it was "the pain of separation"; mother and child. But it was the finality of that separation Katie was dealing with and it hurt deeply. Not talking for three years was just pretend. This was real life. And it hurt.

So much thinking! Katie told Peter that Trace had asked her once if they ever had any fun together or if they just analyzed the possibilities, and Peter smiled and told her that Trace was very smart.

Trace was having a cigarette in the Clipper Club, talking away to Wan Ling, who was sitting next to her sipping a Mai Tai without the liquor. (Trace had stolen one away from an IBM executive about to board a Hawaiian charter flight to Maui.) Fred, whose Valium had already begun to take effect, was lying peacefully in his traveling kennel, content to let Wan Ling bask in the spotlight of the Pan Am lounge.

Trace was explaining to Wan Ling how bad Katie has always been with being on time, and that she might have to return to Katie's apartment in the limousine alone. Wan Ling didn't care in the least. She had just discovered pretzel sticks and was happily eating and playing with them at the same time. "You can't take it personally, Wan Ling. She's just more used to being late than she is used to you."

Lady Landamere looked splendid and not in the least bit ill. At least that's what the Pan Am public relations representative was telling her when they both noticed a flurry of activity at the door to the club. In the center of the storm stood Rebecca, with her famous wood-framed gold-initialed R. H. luggage. The luggage was so distinctively 1930s one might have incorrectly assumed it belonged to Rita Hayworth or Rex Harrison.

Rebecca saw Trace immediately and was totally taken aback. She remembered her yoga teacher telling her, "The universe will always provide you with what you resist in order to grow." The lesson she realized was that she should have called to say goodbye. There'd be plenty of time now. Five and a half hours to be exact.

Rebecca was in seats 3A and B (she always bought the seat next to her so she wouldn't be bothered) and Trace was in 4A and B. (After her trip in with the television producer she decided to give Fred his own seat.)

Before Rebecca had a chance to walk over and kiss Trace hello, Katie and Peter arrived.

The flight was boarding in five minutes. So the goodbyes would have to be quick. Everyone was recovering from the surprise of seeing each other. Katie had planned on calling her friend when she got back from the airport. She got very sad that Rebecca was leaving, too. She really was her best friend, and suddenly it seemed like everybody was going away.

"People don't even see people off on ships anymore," Rebecca said. "Why the delegation?"

"We're taking Wan Ling home with us," Katie said.

Rebecca asked Katie if the "us" was a permanent decision.

"Very," Katie answered. Peter hugged Rebecca and told her not to think of it as losing a best friend but as gaining a therapist she could call at anytime.

Ever honest she answered, "I'd feel more secure if you were an internist. What will I do with a hug if I have an abscess?"

Over the P.A. system all passengers on Flight 7 were being asked to board at Gate 31.

Trace was giving Katie a big hug. In fact it was the best hug Katie ever remembered receiving from her mother. And again, it made her eyes begin to water up.

Katie picked up Fred from his kennel and gave him a big hug, too. She told him to take good care of Trace, but Fred was in no condition to take care of anyone. He was now ready for the Betty Ford Rehabilitation Center. Trace had foolishly given him a sip of her champagne and orange juice which potentiated his Valium.

Everyone except Fred walked to the gate together. Peter carried him in his little box.

At the gate Trace gave Wan Ling a big hug, too, and told her how happy she was that she was going to live with Katie, . . . just as she planned. She told her how lucky she was. Then Trace gave Peter a kiss, too, and told him she hoped everything worked out between them. "I think you're good for Katie," she said. "And this is one family that certainly could use its own psychiatrist!"

Wan Ling was holding Katie's hand. She looked to Katie as if she might start to cry, but Peter told her that she simply was projecting her feelings onto Wan Ling.

Trace was the last one to board the plane. Rebecca and her matched set of sixteen pieces of luggage were already on board. She walked out to the entrance of the plane and stood at the door to see where Trace was. She saw her standing on the walkway to the plane waving goodbye to Katie and Peter and Wan Ling.

"Ta-ta, Wan Ling! Ta-ta, Peter! Ta-ta, Katie! Ta-ta!"

It was at that precise moment that Wan Ling said her first words. She raised her little baby hand high up in the air and waved to Trace. She said, "Ta-ta!" And once more, "Ta-ta!"

And Katie cried and so did Peter. And Peter said, "Ta-ta, Trace!"

And Katie said nothing because she couldn't say goodbye.

It appeared in the *New York Times*. Seven weeks and one day following Flight 7's return to California, a memorial service was held in New York City for Lady Trace Landamere. She was referred to as "a major force in the shaping of The Arts in her illustrious lifetime; a member of the President's Committee on the Arts and Humanities, The American Film Preservation Society, and a board member of The Joffrey Ballet." Her age was reported as sixty-seven.

Those reported at the service included her son and daughter-in-law, Richard and Ellen Fields, her daughter, Katie Fielding, and son-in-law, Dr. Peter Carriston, her grandchildren Joshua Fields and Wan Ling Carriston. Film star Rebecca Holmes and many of the countries most influential individuals were in attendance. In lieu of flowers, Lady Landamere had asked that contributions be made to the Third World Children's Hunger Fund. It noted that the service was also attended by millionaire dog Sir Fred.

Lady Landamere had arranged to leave him her title.

In accordance with her wishes the service was held at one in the afternoon at Le Cirque. Ties and jackets were not required and smoking was permitted.